I0745889

CARSON'S CONFESSION

BY

BERNARD BANNERMAN

Copyright 2018 © Bernard Bannerman

All rights reserved. No part of this book may be reproduced in any form or by any electronic or mechanical means, including information storage and retrieval systems, without written permission from the author, except in the case of a reviewer, who may quote brief passages embodied in critical articles or in a review.

ISBN (Print): 978-1-911124-96-2
ISBN (Ebook): 978-1-911124-97-9

Dedicated to friends from the 60s -
Robert Ness, Pat Bender, Cornelius Medvei, Jamie Wolsey,
Vici Williams and Karen Smith;

also, for Ross Bender, who it feels like
I have known just as long!

AUTHOR'S NOTE

The reader who is familiar with The Programme, by Andrew Arden, will notice similarities between The Accord, the cult which features in this book, and The Programme, which is at the centre of that. Historically, I first crafted it in an early draft of this book before developing it for that. When I re-discovered this book, years after The Programme was published, I made some changes but found that the structure of this book would itself have to go if I was to make any more: it was and remains my view that the similarities between late 20th century middle class cults are vastly more than the differences; that's my excuse for using it twice over!

CHAPTER ONE

'Oh, shit.' Carson flung the last of the small number of Christmas cards she had received onto the floor in the general direction of Alton's Tomy train track. To be accurate, one of the five Christmas cards she had received.

It was four more than I. My solitary card was a concoction created by my four year old son and heir at a time when he was seriously smashed on booze, dope or both.

It was fortunate that Alton was not present: the card sliced the head off his favourite engine-driver, causing a pile-up of passenger carriages that was big enough to guarantee many members of the Bar a healthy income for months to come when hired by relatives, unions and public authorities to represent them at the public inquiry that invariably followed a major transport disaster. Alton took any interference with the train set as a personal affront and, fond as he was of Carson, might well have taken her head off in revenge.

As he had finally agreed - for want of energy to argue any longer - to retire for the night and await the morrow before opening his presents, however, we were safe this first Christmas Eve together in the house. Tomorrow would be another tale: he would, I hoped, be too busy extending the set into the few remaining, unoccupied areas of the living-room with the additional track I had bought him to notice the damage.

Carson had bought him a rocking rabbit. Well, actually, it was a rocking hare, but it was destined to be called a rocking rabbit. She had bought it at a sweater shop. Don't ask me why a sweater shop would be selling rocking rabbits - or even a rocking hare - let alone why Carson had bought it for him. I didn't try to fathom Carson any longer: I'd thrown my lot in with a dark and mysterious, troubled soul, and living with the unexplained was part of the price. But it was beautiful, hand-carved and sturdy enough for me to straddle, which was what I was doing when Carson said:

'Oh, shit.'

* * *

I reached across the railway station, re-capitated the driver and righted the carriages. Before resetting the engine, I attached an empty goods container, on which I placed the offending card. Engine and Christmas card commenced the long and winding chug which - if the batteries held out - would transport them behind the television, up onto Alton's plastic school-desk, through the bottom shelf of the music-unit and around the bar before they arrived back within my grasp. Unless I had miscalculated, there would be time enough first to fetch another couple of ice cubes from the kitchen, refresh my Southern

Comfort, open a new bottle of Frascati for the Kangaroo Kid and light a Camel. Carson watched vacantly as I pursued these preparations. She was genuinely upset.

'And who,' I asked at last, having read the card, 'is Aunt May, now that she's coming to visit?'

'Uncle Nate's wife,' she said dully. 'Widow,' she corrected, in case I didn't get the point.

'Oh, shit,' I said, needing no greater explanation.

When Carson was fifteen years old, she killed her uncle. She'd never even given me his name, but I now knew it was Nate. Nor had she told me that he had been married. I knew very little about him save what Sandy had told me, primarily that, in a drunken rage, he had attacked Carson's father, who had been wheelchair bound since an industrial accident, and who had been saved by his daughter's ready application of a meat cleaver.

At the time, her mother was long since gone. She had abandoned the family when Carson was a kid. Her father was to waste away within a few more months, before Carson's trial, in part, as I understood it, because the incident had brought home to him how helpless he had become, how little he had to offer and how unnecessary he was to the future of his daughter.

Carson was acquitted, complimented by the judge on her courage, and left Australia as soon as she was able to do so, wending her way to England, where she worked at a variety of unrelated jobs and other activities until she ended up at Nichol & Co, the North London law-firm Sandy and I had founded but which was, at that time, entirely owned and run by Sandy: I was out of it - and everything else - in more ways than I can count.

Sometime towards the latter part of this period in Carson's life, Sandy and I made up. First, as lovers; subsequently also as professional partners. Sandy engineered my re-entry into the ranks of the respectable by allowing me to blend my burgeoning practice as a private investigator - specialising then in the misdemeanours and mishaps of members of the legal profession itself - with the firm's more conventional legal work.

Sandy was Alton's mother. We were just moving into the house in Cloudesley Road, in Islington, when she died of a ruptured beri aneurism brought on by an ill-timed ride on a whirly-gig at the Easter fair on Hampstead Heath. For the next year, Alton was taken care of most of each week by Sheila Dowell, the wife of my sometime friend, sometime sparring partner, Detective Chief Inspector Tim D.

Part of Sandy's re-engagement incentive was the full-time assistance of Carson, just back from a paralegal course. Not without difficulty, the coupling finally took and, since then, she'd been with me on all my investigations. At one point, just after Alton was born, she went back to Australia to sort out her feelings about the past, but she returned to England to help on my next case and here she had remained, initially staying part of the time in the spare room at Cloudesley Road and part of the time down at the club I own on the Old Brompton Road, which is run by her friend Natalie until, one balmy eve in Baltimore, Maryland, she blandly informed me that we were to become lovers. That's not an accurate description of how we ended up married in all but law, but it's a fair one and it'll do for now.

With Alton down for the night, the magic midnight hour having passed, we declined to impose on ourselves the same discipline to which we had subjected him and descended without further delay on the packages and envelopes lying beneath the tree Carson had insisted we buy and had decorated, notwithstanding numerous attempts by my son to impede her. It was not only Alton's attention-grabbing antics we wanted to side-step, but also the presence of our many guests: Jada and Frankie from down the road; the Dowell menagerie; and, Natalie and her current lover - a freckle-faced American young enough to qualify as a toy-boy but mature enough to put up with the taunt in good humour. Our intention had been to enjoy just a few hours as if we were the only people in our world: the perpetual fantasy.

Aunt May's card scuppered the plan. The hell with Carson killing Uncle Nate: I could cheerfully have wacked off his widow. I had plans for the evening that did not stop at opening the presents we had bought one another, but were to extend - pun intended - to their use. Once Carson and I found each other as lovers, I had discovered a new side to her - sensuous, indulgent, softly feminine - that I has never dreamed of when I knew her only as my aggressive, action-oriented assistant. Carson is not slight and the wall she had constructed to protect herself from further incursions into her psyche - such as that inflicted by Uncle Nate - made her seem a lot larger. What I had found out was that she knew how to use all of her body, and to teach me how to use all of it too. Amongst my gifts to her was a set of silk underwear which she now opened in a desultory fashion and let fall to the floor with barely a second glance and the sole comment:

'That's a present for me?'

'Do you want to talk about it?'

She pursed her lips and shook her head.

'Cars, we're going to have to talk before she gets here,' I urged as gently as I could.

'I don't have to see her,' she sulked. 'What does she want to see me for?'

'What were, uh, relations between you like after, uh…'

'After I killed her husband?' She finished my sentence for me flatly. 'What do you think they were like?' she snorted. She leaned down and picked the underwear up off the floor, as if she was having second thoughts about it, but almost as soon she let it fall again.

'I thought you said he was living with you and your father… and your brothers?' She never mentioned her two younger brothers: like I say, a lot goes unsaid. 'I thought Sandy said he was Ukrainian? A mechanic?' I dredged my memory

'I might have said he was Ukrainian: he was some kind of Russian, I don't know what. He owned a Volkswagen franchise. He and May were constantly arguing, separating; he was staying with us then.'

'And your brothers?' I reminded her gently, suspecting the answer before it arrived.

'There aren't any.'

She didn't elaborate.

'What was your last contact with her?'

'I haven't heard from her since I came back.' She meant the second time, when she returned to work with me. 'Why now? Damnit.' For the first time I realised she was close to tears. 'Things were getting so good.'

I got off the rocking rabbit and knelt in front of her, pushing her legs apart so that I could put my arms around her to hug her. I lay my head against her breasts as she stroked my hair absently. The occasional tear fell from her eyes onto my forehead. I wanted to cry for her.

Despite myself, I felt myself growing hard. Though she couldn't've felt it directly, she sensed it. She pushed my head away, then placed my hands on her breasts, hissing:

'Squeeze them. Hard. Hurt me.'

* * *

Carson's capacity for suppression had prevailed by the morning: she even managed a smile as Alton elected to enter the bed from her side, en route to his ever-loving father, without regard to her body or hangover. I won't lay false claim to the same tolerance: when he woke me up by banging on my eyelids, I banged back on his. Thus affectionately did Christmas Day commence.

Jada and Frankie were not due until midday. Frankie, however, was only twelve and five past eleven was the hour when they completed the hundred yard trek from their house down the street. As Jada stood by apologetically, Frankie thrust all of our packages indiscriminately into my arms and lurched towards her own pile with unerring instinct. Guilt had caused me to splash out on the twice-orphaned youngster and I had bought her - in all our names - the most upmarket iPod to replace the one she had recently lost. Her strict sister had made her wait for a replacement, ostensibly to teach her to be more careful, though actually by arrangement with me. She would, I know, listen repeatedly to her half-sister's latest album and her favourite track thereon, unambiguously entitled *Frankie*.

Guilt? Twice-orphaned? It's a long story and this isn't the place for it. I had no hand in the death of her real parents, Mick and Eartha Mellor. Afterwards, pursuant to the Mellors' testamentary instructions, she became the ward of, and went to live with, Russel Orbach, then a Queen's Counsel, later a High

Court Judge. I could not assert equally unequivocally that I had no hand in his death.

Jada was Frankie's half-sister, Eartha's daughter by an earlier marriage. Though still in her early twenties, she was a successful pop singer, on her way to becoming a successful actress as well, and the author of an excellent autobiographical account entitled *Where I'm Coming From*. I had been hired by her libel-fearing publishers to provide the material with which to back up her thinly-veiled allegation that Orbach had been responsible for Mick's and Eartha's death. The way it worked out, libel was not a problem: the dead can't sue; the accusation nonetheless remained veiled for Frankie's sake.

At the last moment, I had promised Orbach that I would help Jada bring up her half-sister, a promise I took for granted Sandy would be around to discharge on my behalf. Someone - who shall remain Nameless - didn't like my attempts to play God and showed me He could do it for himself: Orbach and Sandy died the same day. We were left living on the same street, bereft, saddled with different slices of the same story, to keep each other occasional company and provide a sense of family. Somehow, we had survived as friends. Rare now the day that one or other of us did not see one or other of them. It made no rhyme nor reason, but it worked for all of us.

Carson had the wit to charge the battery before wrapping the gift. Of course, Frankie had to go home to load Jada's album. By the time she returned, Natalie and Colin had arrived and the bottle of champagne they had brought with them had already been opened.

'I suppose I paid for it,' I groused, meaning it was from club stock.

Natalie puckered her lips and thrust them at me with her eyes shut, by way of alternative gift. I met Natalie through Carson: they were sharing a squat in Finsbury Park at a time when it was expedient for me - and safer for a pregnant Sandy - not to be staying at her house, in which we had lived until we bought Cloudesley Road. At the time, Natalie was saving up to buy her own bistro. We got on well; we were both, like Sandy, Jewish and she had the most electric body I had ever encountered. Looking back on it, it seems like everything had happened all at once. My friend Lewis, who owned the drinking club on the Old Brompton Road, near to where I used to live, died. He had left me the club, on secret trust to hold until his ex-lover Malcolm's criminal convictions had expired and he could hold the licence in his own name. Instead, it was Malcolm who had expired.

Tim tore up the only copy of the letter that evidenced the trust, reasoning that Lewis would not want some unknown, distant Glaswegian relative of Malcolm's to inherit by default, under the rules on intestacy, especially as the only other significant beneficiary under Lewis' will was the then unborn Alton, whose godfather Lewis had been intended to become.

Soon afterwards, Carson departed for Australia and Natalie confronted eviction from their squat, still a long way from being able to afford her own restaurant or even somewhere else to live. There was a flat above the club where once Lewis had lived full-time and, until his declining years, had continued to use for the seduction of waiters, customers and the occasional environmental health inspector. Offered both job and a place to live, Natalie had been hard-pressed to refuse my invitation to run the club for me, under an agreement that she need make no profit but wasn't to make a loss. Being Natalie, she couldn't do less than her best and, in the time since she took over, the club had so improved that it had been mentioned in some of the London listings as a place worth visiting to eat. It produced an income for me not much less than I took out of Nichol & Co.

I had met Colin only once before, during my most recent routine visit to the club to go over the books with Natalie and see what kind of dent I could make in the profits. His name was Colin Wrighton. He looked in his late twenties, though I suspected he was older, and he was as fair and tall and thin as Natalie was dark and short and mammarial where it mattered. He told us he had come to England with Burger King. He met Natalie at a catering exhibition at the Olympia Exhibition Hall, within walking distance of the club, and - as she had drunkenly bragged to me when we talked privately at the club - she had dragged him home with her before he changed his mind.

Colin and Burger King had a parting of the ways almost as soon as he got together with Natalie: how many free hamburgers can one man eat? He was presently living with Natalie, though - she stressed - only as a temporary measure. I didn't doubt it. Her lovers never lasted long. He'd helped out at the club on a few nights for pocket money and, he now explained to me as we strolled aimlessly around the garden with our champagne glasses to hand to escape the hubbub for a few minutes, was going abroad to do what he half-mockingly described as 'good deeds' with a 'group'. It sounded odd, like he was still trying to find a description for what he was going to do. Before this modern Don Quixote could elaborate, the decibels from indoors increased to the point at which it was no longer worth braving the cold. The Dowells had arrived. It was useful: Tim could flash his warrant card at any neighbours who called in to complain.

* * *

Theoretically, my relationship with Tim Dowell complies with the well-established model whereby private eyes and their official opponents have always co-existed: a one-way flow of information under threat of dire, criminal consequences; periodic insults to bolster the appearance of mutual distaste veiling respect bordering on affection; all credit for a good result kept by the copper, responsibility for foul-ups my sole preserve.

In practice, so co-extensive have been our respective remits that on occasion even officialdom - in the person of the Metropolitan Police Commissioner, the much (and unfairly) reviled Sir Randolph Dunlop - has acknowledged we work not just well together, but best of all. This was put to the test when Tim, for once, went it alone on a case and I was sent in by Sir Randolph to recover him from his kidnappers, in preference to his own men. That was the Leahy case. I still didn't like to think about it: Leahy was at large; he had been silent for several months; I hoped he'd stay that way for several decades.

The professional relationship between Tim and I had, since Sandy's death, been overshadowed by Alton. Tim had come to the hospital where Sandy lay dying. He took me home with him. The next day, Carson and Natalie, who had looked after Alton overnight, brought him to Ealing, where the Dowells cohabited with their own pair of micro-villains. Sheila took one look at Alton, a longer look at me, and decided that one was not safe with the other. Until last summer, when Tim did his disappearing act, she kept Alton during the weeks, and I had him at weekends. After Tim had been recovered, Sheila gave Alton his eviction orders: she had forewarned me during the case that if I didn't begin to act like a parent, Alton would forget that's who I was. My protest was muted by the knowledge that Carson would be around to share the burden. Her protest didn't exist; maybe she only moved in with me to live with Alton; I'm the outsider in the family unit.

I don't think Tim wanted to come to us for Christmas. Nor did Sheila, for that matter. Tim wanted a private celebration on their own, something sentimental to do with a time when he didn't expect to see them again. Sheila wanted to have Christmas with her sister's family. From out of the confusion, their two children - Andrea and Stephen - emerged triumphant: what they wanted was Alton and, as Alton wasn't on offer anywhere else but Islington, Cloudesley Road was the focus for festivities.

If it sounds like I had little to do with these arrangements, I have described them accurately: they were made by the likes of Sheila and Carson - close friends before Tim disappeared, intimate since - and the children. The only line I drew concerned the cooking: I wouldn't and Carson couldn't. (As I once put it, she cooks like an angel: the angel of death). My choice would've been Jada, who's a superb cook, but - greatest surprise of all - it was Tim who took command of the turkey and, though I'm loath to admit it, he did a splendid job of it. At least, I think it was good: truth to tell, by the time we ate, I was too bombed to know the difference.

* * *

'I hate Christmas,' were my opening words on Boxing Day.

For an each-way treat, Alton had stayed overnight with Jada and Frankie. Natalie and Colin were down in the spare room and I doubted either of them was coming up to crawl into bed with us. The Dowells had driven home in a state that would test his authority as a senior police officer. We were alone and, with a little bit of luck, could remain so for a recuperative morning dozing in bed.

Carson whispered:

'Go brush your teeth.'

'You've got to be kidding,' I protested, thinking first about the electric tooth-brush and only secondly about what she had in mind.

She rolled a leg over mine, kissed my throat and started to lick my nipples. I groaned. It was intolerable and it ought to have been impossible. Her breasts brushed against me; she was doing it deliberately; it was unfair but it certainly wasn't impossible. I did as bid and returned to bed a cleaner and wiser man.

I lay on my back:

'You're doing all the work, though.'

'Don't I know it,' she enthused.

She reached over to her side of the bed to grab a bottle of Body Shop massage lotion. There was a battle ahead. How near could she bring me without missing her own chance; how near dare I go? She started at my feet. I'm ticklish. She knows I'm ticklish. I stress and strain not to kick out. Then, behind my knees, a similar problem. By the time she's mid-ship, I'm quivering and moaning; for the first few seconds after she mounts me, I think I can't hold back. Suddenly, I'm fully awake and in control of at least this much of the operation.

Forgive me, Sandy, the sex between Carson and I is like nothing I've ever experienced. When we come it is, as usual, simultaneous: I'm left drained, sated and deeply in love. I tell her I love her. She says:

'Fat git.'

* * *

Aunt May was due in London on the first of January. We spent New Year's Eve at the club. Colin had already departed. Natalie was in post-relationship, anti-man mode. Carson was anxious about the forthcoming visit and took it out on me. Tim dropped in to collect Alton, who was going to Ealing for a few days' visit, and agreed to a quick one for the road while Carson re-bundled the boy. The place was nearly empty. Joannie, the first waitress to have lasted longer than six months and, now, Natalie's assistant manager, brought over the bottle with a bucket of ice and two glasses. She asked Tim:

'How's Wally?'

The unfortunately named Detective Sergeant Walter Wadd was Tim's personal aide. After the Leahy debacle, he had been returned to normal duties, to see if he still knew how to perform as a proper police officer, sort of like an alcoholic drying out. At the beginning of December, however, the Commissioner had agreed to his request to be re-assigned to Dowell. Tim was now directly answerable to Sir Randolph on account of a difference of opinion with Commander Millward, his former supervisor, about how hard Millward had been trying to get him back when he was captured. That's not quite accurate. It was common ground that Millward had tried as hard as he could: the issue was his ability.

'He's okay,' he eyed her suspiciously: 'Why?'

She shrugged, bit her lower lip and walked away without answering.

It was news to me.

'I thought he was happily married?'

'He was,' he scowled. 'You wanna know the divorce rate amongst coppers?'

'I'm sorry.' And I was: I was fond of Wally, and had considerable respect for him. I have omitted to mention that during my quest for Tim, I had myself momentarily been detained, by a different bunch of villains, the sort with diplomatic immunity to abuse, and that Wally and Carson were jointly responsible for my release. 'Where's he living?'

'Back in the Section House,' he shuddered at the prospect of living in a hostel with a bunch of young, single, snot-picking policemen. 'But he's looking for a flat. I'm bucking for his promotion. The money would help.'

'Will you lose him again?'

'Well,' he smiled craftily: 'It's part of a plan to expand me into a unit.'

Tim's brief, for many years, had been to step in where no hobnailed boot should be seen to plod. He was sent in when the powers that be had an interest in the outcome of a case which would be affected by the way it was handled. That was how we first got to know one another, and why our work so commonly overlapped. My own specialisation within the legal profession of definition interested the establishment: barristers' chambers, a firm of masonic solicitors, a couple of High Court judges of whom one was Orbach, a series of mysterious deaths on the government side of the House of Commons. It's why my cases never get to court.

Tim had always been essentially a loner, at least professionally; Wally was the first of his assistants to stay with him for more than a year. I was surprised at his suggestion.

'I can't go on doing it for ever. Besides, what happens when Dunlop goes?'

'Maybe they'll make Millward the new Commissioner; you'll be directing traffic in the Channel Islands.'

'Sark?' Where they have no traffic. 'It'll be harder to disband a unit than just to re-assign me.'

'Don't you ever want to do something different?'

'All the time, Dave. But it's got to be done. I'd rather I was doing it than some champion arse-licker.'

I knew why. Though he could and did keep cases out of court, he also usually managed to contrive an uncomfortable outcome for the culprits. If that didn't work, he let me kill them, I added to myself morosely.

He was still brooding paternalistically about Wally.

'I can't see it; what've they got in common; he's twice her size.' They were complaints, not questions.

'Alcohol makes strange bedfellows,' I contributed unhelpfully.

'Yeah, look at you and Carson.' He switched gear again, just as suddenly: 'It's still alright, isn't it, Dave?'

'It's great,' I admitted. 'The only difficult thing is the background.' Sandy.

'Do you think about her much?' In the old days, he had more time for Sandy than for me.

I flushed. Not enough.

'Don't feel bad about it, Dave. It was bound to happen some day.'

'I know. I just feel guilty, well, that it happened so soon.'

'You did all your grieving in one go.' He reminded me that I had, until his disappearance, spent the best part of a year crying and drinking. 'Most people spread it out over a longer period. It doesn't mean you loved her less.'

I looked him as straight in the eyes as my state permitted.

'To be honest, Tim, I don't think I know what the hell love is. If I loved Sandy, what did I feel for Julie?' Julie was my sole intervening affair between Sandy and Carson, ignoring a couple of times with Natalie which we both agreed to treat as if they had never happened. 'And if I loved Julie, what do I feel for Carson? And what did I feel for Carson all those years beforehand, while Sandy was still alive?'

He glanced over his shoulder as if to see who was the fount of wisdom to whom I was addressing these questions. Coincidentally, Carson emerged from the office with an over-excited Alton. It was stupid, but I resented my son's eagerness to go with Tim; I was jealous. I hugged him fiercely and told him to behave. Tim rose and, unprecedentedly, kissed Carson on the cheek.

'Have a happy one,' he said.

I didn't expect it, but Carson flushed, then kissed him back, lightly but on his lips.

'You, too, Tim. Stick around.' Then she remembered herself and added: 'Pig.'

* * *

By midnight, the place was packed. I had to help out behind the bar. Taking the tip from Frederick's in Camden Passage, my favourite restaurant, I had hired a Scots piper to bring in the New Year. The drunken crowd stomped their feet and clapped their hands and sang along to Auld Lang Syne, not realising as he drew it to an end that he was already marching out of the club to his next engagement.

By three o'clock, we had turned the last of the revellers out and most of the staff had gone home in taxicabs we had paid for. Only Joannie stayed behind: she was sleeping over in Natalie's flat, as neither of them wanted to wake up with no one to talk to. None of us was ready for sleep. Unabashed by the notion that it might be none of my business, I asked about Wally.

If she'd been any less drunk, I dare say where she would have told me to stick my question: Joannie has never been impressed by authority - anyway, not mine. She smiled tiredly:

'Oh, it was nothing, I suppose. I shouldn't've expected more.'

Which she had.

'When did you last hear from him?'

'When he left his wife. Before he left his wife,' she qualified her answer, telling us all what none of us would have had the nerve to ask directly: whether the encounter was during or since the marriage. 'You know the score; you never stay with the one you break up for.'

'Is that what he said he was doing?'

'No. No, he was dead honest. That's his trouble. He's too straight by half. Once it had happened, he had to tell her, and tell her their marriage was over. Then he came and told me what he'd done, and that he wasn't going to go on with me, not until it was all in the past anyway, he said.'

'Men,' Natalie snarled.

I sighed:

'Here we go again.'

'If you don't like it,' Carson contributed: 'You don't have to hang around women so much of the time.'

'Hey,' I took her hand to remind her we were supposed to be a couple: 'What's that mean?'

She pulled her hand away.

'Just what it says. Nothing. Don't make an issue of it.'

'Where's Colin gone, Nat?'

'Val d'Isère,' she said.

'Val d'Isère? The ski resort? He told me he was going off to do good deeds: he didn't say he was doing them for himself.'

'It isn't like that, though as a matter of fact he says he's a good skier. No, he's into some sort of group - outfit - organisation, I don't know what to call it,' she admitted. 'It's called The Accord. Have you ever heard of it?'

I frowned: it rang a very vague bell.

'One of those weirdo cults? Bring me your nutters, bring me your losers, bring me your discontented - preferably the rich ones?'

'That's what I think, though he says it's not. He says it's basically an organisation of expats - mostly Americans, some Canadians, Australians, a few South Africans, quite a lot of English...' The white, English-speaking world.

'Doing what?' I studied the half-empty magnum bleary-eyed: I'd had champagne till it was coming out of my greying hair; I got up to fetch my personal bottle of Southern Comfort from behind the bar - what was left of it after Tim's quick one or two or five. 'There's no ice left,' I complained.

'In the kitchen,' Joannie called out.

By the time I returned, they had moved the conversation back to the perennial. I heard the famous words 'they're all the same'. I don't even know who spoke them: at times like this, they're all the same. Either my curiosity about The Accord was unsated, or I didn't want to spend what was left of the night as the subject of their abuse. At the first available interval, I interjected:

'What does this organisation of Colin's do, then? Why are they in Val d'Isère?'

'I don't really know that much about it. He made it sound like a sort of voluntary service overseas for youngish expatriates who haven't made up their minds what they want to do with themselves, until they go home and settle down to raise children in Rawhide.' Was there a place called Rawhide? If there wasn't, there ought to be. 'Apparently some of them have gone to Val d'Isère to raise funds: bestowing, he called it; lotta money there at this time of the year.' It was true: Val d'Isère is one of the most expensive ski resorts in Europe. I knew about it because Sandy used to ski there and talked about it, though I had never gone with her.

'Bit of a...' Carson looked for a way politely to sympathise with her friend's slap in the face. 'Well, a bit of a let down for you.'

'Not really,' Natalie admitted. 'He wasn't the last of the great intellectuals - for that matter, he wasn't the last of the great lovers either. He was fun and young and horny. I should say no? Once he started spending time with these people, I was losing interest anyway. Also, I think there's a lot more to them than he makes it sound and I didn't want it around me either.'

I'd made Natalie too comfortable, in the wrong sort of place to find a serious partner. People came to the club to get drunk, to meet existing lovers, or to find someone new to fuck - occasionally, of the opposite sex, more frequently so since Lewis' day, when it had been about ninety-ten gay-straight. The only offer I ever had in the club was from Lewis himself, and that was only so I didn't feel left out. Natalie worked all the social hours and then some, lived over the club and - given the cost of housing in London - she'd be over the hill by the time she had saved enough to buy a flat of her own near enough to keep the job with which to pay the mortgage. She was a grown-up, I reminded myself: I wasn't responsible.

'Are they in London, then?'

'They've got some sort of office here, but that's all. Recruitment, I guess: entrapment, more like.'

It wasn't personal: she liked organisations no more than I did.

'He said they were planning to open a proper place here. They usually have some sort of restaurant or meeting-house, to get more people onto their hook, I suppose. As a matter of fact, I think he met them at the same time he met me; at the exhibition.' My confusion must have showed, because she added: 'Well, if they were planning to open some sort of restaurant or coffee bar here...'

Carson yawned ostentatiously: boring. She was right. I started up the taxi app: we had taken one over, not because I'm a reformed character but because the police are out in such force on New Year's Eve: it's a good time to catch up on their quotas. We sat in the back of the cab, holding hands, grateful the driver too was taciturn. At one point though, she stroked my thigh discreetly, until she could feel me start to respond, and, squeezing once and gently, half-whispered:

'I do love you, Dave. You do know that, don't you? It's not about that.'

'I know,' I said, equally quietly. 'We're neither of us best at sharing moods.'

* * *

I suppose because I knew her only as a relative of Carson's, alternatively because I have an unequalled inclination to stereotype, I expected Aunt May to be a strapping Aussie dame, bowed only by age - which I equally unthinkingly assumed to be great - her language littered with unseemly oaths and scarred by the broad gash of an Antipodean accent.

I was right about one thing: she had a very faint accent. It was not, however, Australian - though her decades in that country had contributed - but the remnants of an Italian accent. Aunt May was her relative by marriage - to her mother's brother, the aforementioned Nate - which also helped explain how she could be so small and dark, swarthy even, so different from

Carson. Also, she was beginning to go deaf, which was another dissimilarity because Carson can pick up a whispered word - especially one she is not supposed to overhear - at a hundred yards. Carson took the car to fetch her from her West End hotel, rejecting my offer to accompany her so emphatically I wondered what she was still hiding from me. Sometimes I despair of ever understanding her: mostly, I don't try.

What she said was that May still didn't know about us living together - though she knew about me as Carson's boss, from her last trip to Australia - and she wanted to warn her, but that wasn't reason enough. There had been no real further discussion: the circumstances of May's husband's death were more than sufficient to account for Carson's tension.

We had reluctantly, at her own insistence, invited May to visit the house, from where we planned to take her out to dinner before sending her home in a cab. I greeted them at the door, on my best behaviour: Alton was still not back from the Dowells - wouldn't be for another couple days - so he couldn't make a nuisance of himself either. I was missing him. I didn't miss the noise or the mess or the stream of constant chatter and I certainly didn't miss being woken up in an unconscionable manner at all kinds of unconscionable hours, but I missed holding him and I missed him worst of all when I recollected how he would cling onto me, as if he'd never let go, not when he was crying, nor even because he wanted something he didn't need or deserve, but when he was making like he loved me best of all and knew who he and I were and what we meant to each other in Sandy's absence.

Aunt May refused a drink: we weren't going to get on. At the restaurant, she asked for plain water; not mineral water, but tap water. I tried explaining to her that it was more dangerous than drinking neat liquid nitrogen but she wasn't to be moved. For a moment, I thought she was going to say grace before dinner. But it wasn't religion:

'Drink,' she condemned me and Carson both. 'Look where it got your uncle.'

'Great,' I muttered, too quietly for her to hear me but loud enough for Carson. 'Great conversational opening.'

'Hush,' Carson snapped.

I don't know what they'd discussed in the car, but though still understandably nervous there was considerably less antagonism on my partner's part than I had anticipated. I guessed I'd have to wait for the old crone to take her broomstick back to her hotel before I was told why.

She might've been deaf, but she wasn't daft. She spoke directly to me:

'I don't hold it against Carson. She was just a child.' At fifteen? Small wonder she had left the country. 'There always was bad blood between Nathaniel and Carson's father.' She referred to Carson's father not like she didn't know his first name but like she didn't want to say it. 'Oh, I know it was wrong, I know he was crippled, but that didn't make him a good man; he provoked Nathaniel, he was always trying to provoke him.' She held the scales of blame firmly balanced in his direction. 'My children, that's different. I understand; they still blame her,' she added matter-of-factly.

'Your children? I didn't know you had children.'

Carson had cousins? Recalling the conversation on Christmas Eve, when she had disclaimed her invented siblings, I was finding it difficult to know just what was and wasn't true.

'Oh, yes,' Carson acted like she'd just woken up: 'Amy and Alan. They're quite a lot younger than me. Amy's twenty-three; Alan's - how old is Alan now, Aunt May?'

'Just nineteen,' she shook her head sorrowfully: 'He's too young; I knew he was too young; I shouldn't have let him. But they were always inseparable, ever since Nathaniel... Ever since their father died.'

I let her get to the end of her sentence before I asked:

'Too young for what? What shouldn't you have let him do?'

Carson said flatly:

'They came to Europe, Dave; they came here a few months ago.'

'And?'

'And then they went to France where they were going to meet up with some friend of Amy's from Facebook, and that's the last Aunt May heard from them.'

Neither I nor Carson was into Facebook; we were barely into emails, and then only for professional communications.

'Kids,' I said lightly: 'No consideration,' I added equally flippantly.

'No, Aunt May doesn't think so, Dave. She got someone to try and contact them through Facebook, but she told her their pages have been taken down and there's no way of telling who it was they were coming to see. She thinks something's happened to them; she wants to go and find them. They're missing and she wants to go to France to find them,' she repeated heavily. 'She wants me to go with,' she added in a tone that told me she had already agreed.

I was going to have to keep my own company for a while. I was going to have to look after Alton. I wasn't so sure about missing him anymore. I wondered if the Dowells would like to keep him a while longer.

CHAPTER TWO

It was true, what May said about Dad always winding up Uncle Nate - like he used to wind me up, but that isn't why I still felt so guilty about what happened. That's something I once admitted to Natalie: that I'd loved Nate more than I had loved my father. Yet it was Nate who I had killed.

It was strange, travelling with May, sleeping in the same room. Did she know? We took the Eurostar, but first class. May had done well since Nate's death, I knew that from my last visit home; she had taken what little he had left her and translated it into a healthy estate.

Riding first class reminded me of the time Dave and I had travelled back from New York after our visit to Baltimore, when we could only get business class tickets. It was strange, too, to be travelling without - and away from - him. He was the longest I'd spent with any man and I wasn't tired of it yet. Oh, once in a while I could kill him to shut up, or yearn to find a space to crawl into where no one - not Dave, not Alton, not Natalie or Sheila, nor least of all anyone from the office - would find me, to have time to think and to be, but I suppose that's true of everyone. Nor does Alton leave that sort of option open; he needs me when he needs me however hard I try to convince him otherwise, which isn't very.

May asked about him. I told her:

'I was very close to Sandy, Alton's mother. He's known me most of his life. It makes it easier for him and that makes it easier for me.'

She scowled. She's ambivalent towards me. Part of her wants to make up, wants us to be friends, at least to be family, so she expresses interest and concern. But she doesn't want to hear that things are good for me: she only wants to hear I've got problems. It's not a conscious meanness; she's trapped by her inability to put the past behind us both. I can't blame her. I haven't put it behind me either.

On the train, she showed me a recent photo of Amy and Alan. I didn't see them when I was last back in Oz. They hadn't wanted to see me. I couldn't blame them for that either. They didn't look so different from when they were kids. They'd taken after their mother: small and dark, but a good-looking couple, quite alike - obvious siblings - and smart.

I was sad. I'm an only child, and I wanted to be able to think of, and enjoy, them as family. Being part of a family - with Dave and Alton, and a bit with Jada and Frankie - has taught me to appreciate the benefits; I don't have to suffer even the small aggravations of life entirely on my own, like it was all a personal plot against me; maybe that was why I'd told fibs about having brothers - maybe I meant Amy and Alan, but as I knew I couldn't lay claim to them because of how they felt about me, the brothers were an idea to fill the same space.

We arrived at the *Gare du Nord* and took a cab to the hotel. I had picked a hotel out of the Michelin Guide to Main Cities in Europe. I'd never been to Paris before and Dave was useless: it was more than a decade since he'd been there and, as he put it, he was drunk at the time. He did tell me to stay on the Left Bank, though, in the fifth or sixth *arrondissements*, the Latin Quarter. Because it was still holiday season and we hadn't booked ahead, a lot of places were full, so I worked my way down the list until I reached the *Hotel Saint-Germain-des-Prés* on the *rue Bonaparte*. They only had a double available: luckily, with twin beds.

May didn't object to staying on the Left Bank because that was where Amy and Alan had last been heard from though once I knew more about Paris I realised she would have booked somewhere completely different, probably off the *Champs Elysée*.

It doesn't need saying that May didn't do email, Facebook or anything remotely technological. I can't criticise; I'm the same. I didn't have the first clue how to use it. Nor did she know anything about this friend they were supposed to meet up with. But she had brought their last letter with her, though because she had packed it deep in her suitcase and didn't want to get it out on the train, I didn't read it until we were in the hotel.

The letter was from Amy; it was always she who wrote, May said. She said little, and nothing about the person they were supposed to be meeting. She didn't even tell her the name of their hotel but from the price per night she mentioned, it wasn't hard to work out it was at the bottom end of the range. The Michelin Guide listed ten one-star jobs in the Quarter which I conscientiously ringed in red on the street map I had picked up at reception while May steamed up the bathroom until it was seeping beneath the bottom of the door. Expecting her to take a while yet, I rang Dave at the office - Nichol & Co.

'Is he there, Ven?' Ven is short for Venetia, our own receptionist, a black woman with bones and a body I'd kill for. It always surprised me that Dave didn't put a make on her but - to be fair behind his back in a way I'd never be to his face - he seemed genuinely more settled these days, as if he too was enjoying our life together sufficiently not to be straining for something more, the way - before their last year or so together - he always was around Sandy. That makes me sound conceited, like he loves me more than he loved her, which isn't what I mean; it's just that everyone has their time for different aspects of their life and it felt like Dave's time to settle down had finally arrived, and maybe mine had too - I hoped so.

'Hi,' he said, sounding pleased to hear from me.

I wouldn't normally tell him so, but it felt good to hear him too, even if it was less than half a day since we'd spoken. Distance makes a difference.

'It's good to speak to you.'

'Traitor,' he hissed affectionately: 'Deserter. How's Paris? What've you bought me? What've you bought yourself?'

When Sandy died, the mutual insurance policy paid off the mortgage on Cloudesley Road. Once Dave made peace with Ruth Binder and James Coatman, the two longest-serving salaried partners, and agreed to their elevation to the equity, the firm began to make money. The club, too, churns it out, thanks to Nat's inexhaustible energy and initiative. We were, relative to previous experience and prior expectations on both our parts, pretty well-heeled financially. We sometimes went on spending jags so outrageous we could hardly believe ourselves. It was like we thought we'd be more comfortable if we were broke again. You don't want to know what the Timberland deer-skin shirt I bought him for Christmas cost, or the Rado watch he bought me and hid right at the bottom of my gift-stocking. It's ironic, because till now I owned no more than I could stuff into a carry-on bag; it was another way of trying to put down roots.

I laughed. I couldn't help myself.

'I've only been in Paris half an hour, dufus.' I don't know where the word came from, but it was one of his favourites and it made a change from 'schmuck'. 'What was the name of that restaurant you mentioned?' It was the only place he could remember from his last visit, years before; he swore by their oysters. He'd been back to France since, but to Lyon, not Paris, on some case he can't have handled well because I wasn't working with him yet.

'*L'Alsace à Paris*,' he recited in an accent as atrocious as my own. 'It's somewhere on the *Boul 'Mich*.'

'The what?'

'*Boulevard Saint Michel*. It intersects with the *Boulevard Saint Germain*, which you must be near. Maybe it's not on it, but near it anyway,' he added reassuringly. 'Don't forget, it's only a small town.'

'Great. You want me to drag May around town looking for one restaurant? For oysters? I'm not even sure I want oysters. I'd rather have meat and two veg,' I added, grinning, wondering if he'd be pissed off by my vulgarity or turned on by my message.

'Better idea,' he leered. 'Send her home to look after Alton, I'll come over and you can drag me around instead - or whatever.'

'I miss you,' I blurted, feeling like a homesick child sent away to boarding school. 'Well, I might if you miss me back, okay?'

'Deal,' he said gently. 'Take it easy, Cars; if it looks even remotely heavy, call.'

'Nah. It's just a couple of kids. They're probably stoned out of their tinies.'

'Maybe. Call me tomorrow?'

'Yeah. Kiss Alton for me. Kiss yourself too if you like.'

'Hey, Cars?'

'Yeah?'

'How come you never talk like this when we're together?'

'Forget I said it,' I snapped. 'Talk to you tomorrow then.'

Damn him; he was chuckling as he hung up.

* * *

L'Alsace à Paris was sufficiently well-known for the hotel reception to provide directions. The night clerk was on duty by the time we went out, and he hardly spoke a word of English - though he thought he was next best to fluent - but May's Italian background appeared to give her an adequate command of French and, back in a friendly mood, she agreed to my - or, rather, Dave's - choice of restaurant.

I liked Paris. There were more people in the street than in England. Hovering, talking, notwithstanding the weather many of the bars and brasseries were open-fronted. It's one of the things I dislike about the English: they keep themselves to their houses, whereas most other races and cultures live a lot more out in the street. I suppose it's got to do with climate. I suppose Norwegians don't hang out on street corners in the dead of winter either.

We wove our way through a crowded street, past a couple of Russian restaurants, with many shops still open, especially bookshops and music stores, until we found what we were looking for. Because May didn't drink, I opted for beer instead of wine: a litre of Alsace lager. She remained silent. I hadn't forgotten she didn't want to make the trip alone; she hadn't forgotten it either. She asked:

'Where shall we start looking?'

I shrugged.

'I don't know. I don't know about you, either. I think maybe I'd better do some looking around on my own first. Age,' I explained. 'People will talk to me who won't if they think you're an angry or anxious parent - which is what you are.'

She sighed.

'I knew I shouldn't have let them go.'

She had told me their plans. Amy had finished uni, and Alan wanted a year off before he went himself, to study film and media. They had money; as I said, May had done well. I didn't doubt she'd spoiled them rotten, though probably interspersed with parental nagging and guilt-inducing tantrums.

They had first flown to Italy. They had promised to try to make contact with members of her family still living in the old country. Amy had written to say that they couldn't find them; people had moved, or addresses didn't exist anymore. They had met up with some other Aussies, longer out, and were travelling in their VW bus up into Switzerland and thence to Germany, where they expected to part company and go it alone into France. Paris was intended to be only a first stop to meet Amy's Facebook friend. Amy had taken French Lit amongst her courses, and there were a number of places she was keen to see. I wasn't sure Alan could read - most Aussie men can't - but he would be happy to follow where his older sister led.

After France, England was the next stop on the itinerary. May had offered them my address, which is why she knew they still weren't prepared to make their peace with me: they had rejected the idea of seeing me out of hand. I pretended I didn't care and concentrated on my oysters. Dave was right: they were good; I ordered more to have some for him. May no more approved than she had of my beer; she knew what oysters meant. Maybe she thought I'd maul her in bed that night. I giggled and shuddered at the thought. It gave rise to another thought I didn't want, so I started listening again, only to find that she'd stopped talking.

She was watching a young man wend his way through the tables, proffering copies of the next day's International Herald Tribune. As he approached, we could hear from his accent that he was a home-boy. Natch, we bought one. On impulse, I said:

'Why don't you take a break? Have a brew?'

He hesitated, smiled boyishly, then squeezed in beside me:

'The management won't like it, but, what can they do?'

'Right. *Garçon*,' I called to a waiter old enough to be my grandfather, ignoring May's horrified expression. 'Beer.'

'I think you're supposed to call him *monsieur*,' my new companion said.

I think he must have been right, because I was entirely ignored until May caught his eye apologetically and ordered for me. Automatically, I asked for another for myself.

'Dwayne,' he said, and offered his hand to me first, grinning like he had me tagged for frolics to follow, then to May. 'Nice to meet you. Thanks for the brew.' Which hadn't yet arrived.

'D'you make much doing that?' I tossed my head in the direction of the bundle of papers lying at his feet.

'Enough to get by. It's an expensive town, but you don't have to spend a lot to live here. Where're you from?'

'I am from Sydney,' May said firmly. 'But my niece lives in London.'

'I was there last year. Most of it. Couldn't take the weather.'

'How long have you been here?'

"Bout three months.' Our beers arrived and he swigged his as if it was the first he'd had since he came to France. He smacked his lips. 'Great.'

'Cheers,' I said dryly, reminding him of his manners. Youth today. 'Did you meet any other Aussies since you've been here?'

'A few. It's not the season, though there's more Aussies than Yanks. Why d'you ask? Anyone in particular?'

'May's kids are over here; she was hoping to run into them.'

'What're their names?'

'Amy and Alan. Yavitch.' I added the surname just in case, though it was less likely to mean anything to him. I gestured May to give me the photo which, reluctantly, she handed over by a corner, by way of a hint that I shouldn't allow him to get his newsprint-dyed mitts on it.

He shook his head again.

'No. I wouldn't forget her.'

'I'm sure,' I said archly, as if I might be jealous.

'Listen,' he said, rising. 'Ta for the brew, but I've got to get going or I won't sell my quota before the bars close. You, er, you want to meet later?'

He had nerve, I'll give him that.

'Sure. What time?'

'I'm usually done by midnight. Where're you staying?'

I told him the name of the hotel. He didn't know it in particular, but correctly guessed where it was. He said:

'You know the church? *Saint-Germain des Prés*?'

'We walked past it from the metro.'

'There's a bar opposite. *Les Deux Magots*. It's sort of famous. How about it?'

'Midnight,' I confirmed.

* * *

Though it had only been a short journey from London - four hours door-to-door - May was tired. It wasn't just age, but while I had only travelled from London, she was much further and longer away from home and it was beginning to tell. By ten thirty, she was tucked up in bed. I had an hour and a half to kill. I went back onto the streets, gloved hands dug deep into the pockets of my leather bomber, scarf wrapped around my neck against the cold. I was armed with a street map, on which I had marked the ten hotels from the Michelin Guide; though I knew there would be many more, I had to start somewhere. Dave was right: it was a small town; I had finished in time to return to *Les Deux Magots* just after eleven thirty.

Although the preliminary search had turned up nothing, I felt good. I felt sophisticated, cosmopolitan, sitting alone in a French bar in the middle of the night, sipping Pernod, wondering why they'd brought me a jug of water that I hadn't asked for.

Dwayne also arrived early, though only by a few minutes. He had changed and washed his hands. He ran his fingers through his curly blond hair, accentuating his boyishness, and sprawled in a chair at right angles to me with his legs spread wide for me to get a gander at what was on offer. He nodded to the waiter and pointed at my glass, holding up two fingers to order one for himself and another for me.

'So, what's it like travelling with the old Auntie, then?'

I knew precisely what he was probing. I said:

'It's okay. She doesn't snore.'

He wasn't put out.

'I went back to change. I've got a room on the *rue de Seine*. That's round the corner: between here and where I met you.'

I met his eyes and bit back my first set of sarcastic replies. The waiter, in apron, tuxedo, paper dickey and bow-tie, arrived with our drinks. He tucked the bill underneath my saucer, along with the first; he knew who was paying. There was a new jug of water. I was about to ask Dwayne why there weren't any glasses to go with it when he topped up his Pernod from the jug. I got the point. Well, it was a bit strong on its own. I imitated him and sipped.

'That's better.'

'I thought you were some tough boozer when I saw you drinking it neat.'

'Is it difficult to find rooms in Paris?'

'Not if you're not too choosy about running water, bogs, that sort of thing. Why? Thinking of staying a while?' I guessed he was about to offer to share his.

'No. I'm still thinking about Amy and Alan.'

'They're your cousins, right?'

'Right. But I, uh, haven't seen them for a few years.'

'She's worried about them?'

I nodded.

'I figured,' he added superfluously - or perhaps because it had been such a significant intellectual achievement. 'Happens all the time,' he continued. 'Americans especially. Out of sight, out of mind. For us, I mean,' he added, including me in his generation. I didn't disabuse him. 'Then the parents panic. Usually it's nothing: met up with some French girl, can't afford the stamp or can't get to the Post Office in time.'

'How about you? You in touch with your family?'

'I sent them a Christmas card.' He finished his drink. 'You alright for another?' he asked, ambiguous whether he meant was I alright to drink another, or pay for two more. I nodded consent either way without comment, though treating me like a fifty-year-old American divorcee ready to pay for it took some of the fun out of passing for his age.

'You sure you never saw them?'

'I don't think so. I think I'd remember. But I see a lot of people - including a lot of Aussies - on my rounds.'

'Any ideas where to look?'

'Around the uni? The Sorbonne, I mean.'

'They aren't here to study.'

'Doesn't matter. No one at the Sorbonne studies. I'm enrolled. It's a place to be, to meet people, to hang out. If he's met some girl, or she's been picked up by some bloke, could be worth a look. Or the Art Cinemas?' It was possible: Alan was a film fanatic; it was a lot easier than reading. 'They're not, you know, into anything weird are they?'

'Like what?'

'Heavy drugs? Sex? Witchcraft? That sort of thing.'

* * *

I spent the whole week in Paris. I went there with Aunt May to find Amy and Alan but went home without any of them.

During that time, I personally checked every one-star hotel in the Quarter - which felt like every other house. I sent May to the art galleries, the posh shops, the theatres - the right bank, where the money was - while I hung out in student haunts around the Sorbonne and elsewhere, smoky night-clubs fending off sleek, pint-sized Latin boys half my size and black North Africans and West Indians who made me feel small, and checked out the avant-garde expatriate establishments, where notice-boards offered everything from Zen massage to house-sitting in the suburbs.

I tended to drift each day into Shakespeare and Company, an English bookshop Dave used to go to. It was on the Left Bank almost directly opposite *Nôtre Dame*. The shop was owned by a grizzled and grumpy old American who coughed phlegm into a tin can, and was run for him by a group of youngsters I didn't think were his grandchildren but could have been.

Wandering into its cavern-like, book-lined rooms, I realised that many of them slept on the premises. It was an anachronism, smacking of Kerouac and the American Beat Generation in the fifties, only mildly updated to the sixties. Much of the literature on display was in the City Lights series and, from signed copies, the Great Om himself, the poet Allen Ginsberg, had paid tribute when he passed through Paris. I thought of Dave talking of those times and photos of him in red flares. Despite it, I would've liked to do Paris with him. Maybe yet.

There were many Dwaynes but fortunately I managed to avoid that one in particular. He hadn't taken it well when I declined his invitation to examine French accommodation first hand; he hadn't taken it well when I said that I had at least expected him to offer to share the Pernod account; he hadn't taken it well when I mentioned that sometimes little girlies picked up the boys and the little boys had to wait until they were ready to do so. His final, snarled observation as he fled the bar was:

'Your generation, you don't know how to enjoy yourselves.'

I was less upset to have been returned to the correct decadal drawer than I might have been. I called after him:

'Try again when your IQ is big enough to vote.'

I gathered from the encounter that Oz men hadn't changed. He was all the tired, old but accurate jokes I'd ever heard. What's the Australian for foreplay? 'Are you awake?' Or: 'Brace yourself, Sheila.'

Though she'd been tired, by the time I got back in to the hotel that first night May had awoken and was sitting up in bed reading the newspaper we had bought from him. I think she was pleased to see me, though perhaps she'd have preferred it if I had stayed out all night and she had gained both a brick to beat me with and the satisfaction of seeing for herself that my relationship with Dave was not all I had cracked it up to be. Again, an unwelcome thought association I had to banish before I could concentrate enough to recount to her what little I had gleaned from Dwayne.

That was when I laid out my plan of action - in effect, dividing the city into two, not geographically equal halves but with a fair balance of attractions and locations where they might be found. I'd drunk enough that I slept through her getting up the next morning to find that she had gone off as directed, leaving me a note telling me what time she'd meet me for dinner that evening. Grudgingly, I admitted she wasn't about to waste her time; she really did want to find the brats.

This was the pattern we established for the first three days. In the morning, she would rise early, wash and eat breakfast alone in the dining-room downstairs. She marked a chunk of the city where she would spend the day and on her own street-map ringed all of its interesting features. Before leaving the hotel, she would arrange for my breakfast to be taken up to me at the last moment. I could sit up in bed, slurp my coffee and sprinkle croissant crumbs on the sheets without worrying about who was watching, and could give Dave a call to make sure he hadn't overslept or sold Alton to Colonel Sanders instead of taking him to the kindergarten. I enjoyed it. There was no one to nag me; not her, not them.

* * *

At midday on the first Wednesday of every month, a siren is sounded in every town in France.

Like London, there are building works on every street in the city centre, which makes working one's way around much like waltzing in an unlit construction site at midnight.

I learned that the buses are green and white and go to romantic-sounding destinations like *Trocadéro*.

Also, I learned not to eat *andouilette detroyes grilée*, which means Andalusian sausage and is composed of bits of pig - trotter-nails and all - which look as if they had not been cooked and smell as if not washed.

* * *

She disappeared on the fourth day. I didn't start worrying until about nine o'clock in the evening. I was growing hungry waiting for her to return, and getting pissed drinking from the pay-fridge without any food in my tummy. I'd even eaten the squidgy little dry cakes they left in a basket on the coffee table that May had told me were called madeleines - and that some bloke called Proust was crazy about - and not to touch because they were charging a Euro apiece and were worth about ten pence. Actually, what she said, with financial precision, was one dollar - meaning Australian dollar - and eight cents, but I find it easier to think in English.

Periodically, I rang down to the desk to ask if she'd sent a message. By that time, the night clerk was on duty and thought I was hinting I was lonely. I declined the invite to descend while I waited. To begin with, I thought she might've struck gold - or Amy or Alan at any rate. Then it occurred to me she might've bumped into someone she knew; she was sufficiently well-off to have friends who travelled to Europe. I'd read about how complete strangers from the same country who wouldn't talk to each other on the street at home would become the best of pals within minutes in another country. For a brief while I wondered if she might have picked up a bloke, until I remembered it was Aunt May I was talking about. Finally, I realised I had lost her.

I called home but the answering machine was on, which meant either that Dave was out - in which case, what had he done with Alton, I wondered - or that he was bathing Alton, which was a full time engagement. I left a message, and he returned the call half an hour later.

'Hi, what's up?'

'Why should anything be up?'

'We only spoke this morning, Cars,' he reminded me patiently, like he was talking to a child.

'May's done a runner,' I explained. 'She's always at the hotel by the time I get back for supper.'

'What's the time there?'

I told him it was an hour ahead of England.

'How's Alton?' I asked.

'Watching Thomas.'

I groaned, recalling a long drive to Wales to see Thomas the Tank Engine and his fellow engines in person. I kept hoping he'd grow out of it yesterday.

'What do you think I should do?' I hated to have to ask.

'Give it a while longer. Call me back if she comes in, or later if she doesn't.'

We replaced our receivers without the usual endearments or insults.

By midnight, I was as panic-stricken as I was pissed. I'd eaten everything edible in the room and - as I knew - the hotel had no room service. I hadn't dared pop out to any of the shops that would have been open until mid-evening, and now they would all be shut. I could probably score some food in the *Deux Magots*, but I didn't trust the night-clerk to understand it was my aunt I was inviting to join me there if she came in, rather than himself. Accordingly, for want of anything else to do, I called Dave back as instructed.

I should have guessed.

'I've got a number for you to call tomorrow.'

'From Tim?'

'Right. He doesn't think much'll come of it, but at least it'll give you some cover if anyone gets nasty about you poking your nose around.'

'Most people,' I pointed out tartly, 'would be pleased to have me poke my nose at them.'

'Yeah, sweetie, me too. Look, it's difficult just now, or I'd offer to come over.'

'No, it's alright: it's premature. I'll call you during the day, okay?'

It wasn't until after I had hung up that I realised I hadn't asked what the difficulty was: someone to look after Alton, I presumed. I felt guilty about being selfish but not guilty enough to ring him back; besides, if he'd gone to sleep, he'd be even more annoyed. I sighed. Listen to me, worrying about what he thought.

* * *

The next day, I rang Tim's contact first thing, but either he hadn't arrived at the office or else they didn't understand who I was asking for. I gave up and, instead of returning to my usual haunts, set out to hit the hard, cobbled streets in the section she had marked out for herself the previous day.

I didn't know what I was supposed to be looking for. I was hardly likely to see her lolling up against a lamp-post, pissed on Pernod. My French wasn't up to intensive interrogation techniques. Nonetheless, I packed a spare pic of Amy and Alan, and another of May herself, and pounded the *Quartier Chaillot* and the *Avenue Montaigne* for four or five hours, crossing over at the *Pont de l'Alma* into the square of the same name, created, so the guide book told me, in the time of Napoleon III - whoever he may have been - to commemorate the first time the unnatural allies - England and France - had won a victory in the Crimean War. It was heady stuff; I was learning more history each day than I'd ever forgotten.

In the west wing of the *Palais de Tokyo*, I swished through the exhibitions on cinema and photography, stopping guards and visitors - particularly those I could overhear speaking English - to ask if they recognised any of the pictures. The rest of the Palace was taken up with the Museum of Modern Art, as I proudly translated *Musée d'Art Moderne* without any help, some of which I enjoyed despite myself but some of which was so gross I couldn't understand it, or why anyone would want to preserve it for posterity - unless *pour décourager les autres*.

The area was beautiful; the buildings were magnificent and tall and obviously housed a lot of France's wealthy, and it was riddled with expensive clothes shops and perfumiers. I was about to buy a tiny spray until I realised I had miscalculated by one nought the conversion back into English currency. Guilty because I still hadn't allowed Dave to explore the more intricate applications of the underwear he'd bought me for Christmas, I indulged myself in a bra and three pairs of matching knickers, my usual wear-out ratio. I didn't even flinch visibly when I signed it off onto the supplementary card that would automatically charge it to Dave's Amex.

I won't bore you with more of the tourist routine; another museum, the usual clutch of churches, the fashionable French women and men, the multi-national beggars and hustlers in the street. Around midday, I was approached by one of the members of The Accord, the group Natalie's Colin had run away from her arms to join up with. They sold magazines they printed themselves, with apocalyptic photo-montages on the cover and headlines about Valhalla that condemned me to an eternity in England if I didn't hand over my spare change at once.

I bought one, but even though it was written in English, I couldn't understand every other word and didn't much approve of the ones I could. I'd asked the vendors about Colin, only just remembering his last name as Wrighton. There were two of them: a balding, bearded American of indeterminate age, anywhere from twenty-five to forty, and a gaunt-looking upper class Englishwoman who ought to have been at the Chelsea Arts Ball with Hooray Henry, each of them swaddled in a dark green overcoat buttoned up to the neck that might've looked good on Maid Marion but on them just looked weird. Both disclaimed all knowledge and responsibility but thought it must mean something significant that I knew him and now had met them. Like, about ten Euros significant, maybe?

I knew that The Accord ran a coffee lounge, meeting house in Paris. The first pair had told me so, and pointed to the address on the back of the magazine, which I'd promptly forgotten but had presumed would be on the Left Bank. I now learned that it was in the *Quartier Chaillot*, parallel to the *rue François 1er*, into almost every shop on which I had peered, searching for May. Reluctantly, I agreed to drop in; at least they spoke English and I would be able to eat and drink something without mispronouncing the menu.

The café was housed in the back of a huge house - six storeys tall, at least. It was dark and mysterious, creepy. I would have left unseen if I hadn't been spotted by the couple I'd bought the magazine from.

'I thought you'd be in,' the man said in a tone that said he was unusually gifted with foresight, an assertion I could hardly now take issue with. 'Welcome to our house. I'm Mordecai.' Like I said: weird.

'Carson,' I said, and took his hand reluctantly, hoping he wasn't going to either put a spell on, or make a pass at, me.

'Is that your first name?' the woman asked, adding: 'I'm Eunice.'

'Ask him,' I said, and tossed my head at Mordecai.

She looked confused but he laughed.

'It's alright, Carson, most people feel nervous the first time they visit us.'

By now, I had been invisibly prodded into a booth and had automatically picked up the menu. I had to admit the food sounded good: well, it sounded familiar. Another member - in a dark green sweater - took my order for a BLT, diet Coke and coffee, politely asking my immediate hosts whether he could fetch them anything.

Eunice looked like she could kill for a hot drink, but Mordecai declined for both of them.

'It's not appropriate.'

'What's not appropriate?' I asked disingenuously, once the waiter had gone.

'It's not appropriate for us to eat with outsiders,' he said in the same hypnotically gentle voice he had used both out on the street and since I had come into the restaurant. 'Please don't take offence. We try to eat with each other, in the order, so as to share food as an experience.'

'Did you read our magazine?' Eunice asked, shiny eyed.

'I had a look at it. Did you find anything out about my friend - Colin Wrighton?'

'What did you think of it?' Mordecai ignored the question. 'Did it interest you?'

'I, uh, I'm not much of a one for joining... groups, or anything.' I hefted my shoulder bag from the floor and extracted the pics of my missing relatives. 'Have you seen any of these people on your, uh, travels?'

They were confused by the word travels, thinking I meant when they had been in England or elsewhere in Europe. I explained I was looking for them in Paris. Both expressed due appreciation of such familial fidelity but ignored the question, handing back the photo without comment.

'What do you, uh, actually do, uh, here?'

Mordecai explained:

'A lot of people are looking for something more than a conventional, ordinary life-style can offer; they want more fulfilment, but haven't got the confidence to find it for themselves.'

'Or the ability?' I was thinking of Dave's line: *bring me your nutters, your losers, your discontented.*

He wasn't fazed. He said:

'We all have ability. Perhaps, though, they haven't the confidence to find the ability in themselves; yes, that would be a good way to put it. We provide a home, a framework, a purpose. People join us; some leave to go on to that self-same lifestyle they thought they didn't want. That's appropriate, it has still been a positive and helpful experience, they carry something away with them, and onwards into their lives; perhaps they even carry it onwards into the lives of others who never made contact with us.'

'What's the name mean?' I asked, my mouth full of sandwich. At least they knew how to cook. Their coffee was excellent, too.

'It means a lot of things', Eunice answered excitedly. 'It means the accord you seek to achieve for yourself, the accord that we all want to achieve.'

'Um.' There was no other answer.

Mordecai smiled.

'Eunice has only been inside for a few months; there's a lot she has to come to terms with.'

Eunice didn't take offence: she took his hand instead.

'And you? How long have you been in this, uh, The Accord?'

'Twelve years,' he said proudly. 'Since it began, almost, though I didn't move inside for a couple of years after that.'

'Inside? Outside?'

'Oh, we have members who are outside. From what you said, I should think that your friend Colin is an outside member, attached to one of the local Segments.'

'Segment?' French wasn't the only foreign language I was learning.

'It's what we call our groups; each is a segment of a whole. Between us, there is accord.'

'You have a place like this in Val d'Isère?'

'No. Segment doesn't mean a particular place, a building, a home: it's just what we call the group. When a group - a Segment - goes to another town or country, we call it an exploration. So if Colin is in Val d'Isère, he'll be on an exploration tour with a Segment. See?' He was talking down to me the way Dave sometimes did when he thought I ought already to understand the subject-matter: I didn't like it when Dave did it either.

'You still haven't told me what you actually do?'

'Ah, well,' he said philosophically. 'What we do now is collect some more magazines and go back out onto the street to bestow them.'

'Bestow them?' I might've been drinking neat Pernod for the spinning of my head. 'I thought you sold them?'

'It depends on your point of view,' Eunice said archly. 'We like to think we give more than we receive.'

'Don't we all,' I muttered as I studied my bill. I'd missed the location of the comma that separated Euros from cents - again. Maybe they'd bring the rest of the loaf if I waited long enough.

* * *

I was getting nowhere fast. I rang Tim's contact at *Quay d'Orsay* again. He was expecting my call. He asked where I was ringing from, and before I could finish trying to explain a cop car pulled up outside the bar and waved me to join them. I was impressed. I said so to Inspector Malthus.

'I like to impress the ladies.'

I groaned, hung up and went to catch my ride to meet him wondering whether men are ever capable of relating to women without trying to score. I never met one. Not even gays. They still want to be wanted by you even when they don't want you back. Fortunately, my driver and his companion spoke barely a word of English and didn't do more than smile knowingly, wink at each other and reach around to brush their hands against my knee as often as we rounded a corner. I didn't mind about his sidekick but the driver doing the same thing made me somewhat nervous.

We parked at the back so I didn't get a good gander at Paris' answer to New Scotland Yard, though I'd passed by in front of it and knew that it was a markedly more magnificent monument to law enforcement than its London counterpart. I was led in through a lower ground floor door, along echoing corridors, up stairs, bumping into policemen - and being bumped into by policemen - some with only side-arms in holsters, others with sub-machine guns slung across their shoulders, in dark blue uniforms with red flashes on them and blancoed-belts.

Malthus was a round-faced man in his mid-fifties, with side-burns that in England would have been called Edwardian but I didn't have a clue what they'd call in France. Napoleonic? He was wearing a tweed-jacket with elbow patches, a bit like Nate used to wear and May used to complain about having to sew on for him. All he needed was a deerstalker hat and he'd complete the Sherlock Holmes act. But his slacks were baggy, and slightly stained below one knee, and I decided I could probably do better.

'Coffee.' It wasn't a question. 'And how is Timothy Dowell? Do you know him long?' Despite the apparent excellence of his English - Dave would probably say it was a lot better than mine - there was the occasional lapse and I quickly reminded myself he wasn't a native before I gave him a smart-arsed answer he might not understand. 'I speak with him often.'

'I know him quite well. My partner - the man I live with - they've worked together.'

'Ah, yes, the Woolf man.' It was one way of putting it; I've always said he needed psychoanalysis. 'The private detective. This we discourage.'

'So do the Brits. Believe it.'

'Yet they are working together?' He poured a lump of black sludge from a pot; I was grateful the cup was only thimble-sized, though it made it difficult for me to pick up without spilling.

'Tim'll get anyone to do his dirty work for him.'

He laughed.

'Yes, you are knowing him long.'

'He's a friend. His wife's a friend.'

He frowned. He said:

'Your Aunt. Yavitch. She is gone.'

'Exactly. That's...'

'No. I mean today, she is gone. This morning, someone comes to the hotel - *Saint-Germain-des-Prés* - and takes her belongings. The addition is made.'

'What?' I'd been out and about the streets earlier than I usually woke up. I'd been stuck in museums and shops, I'd even had to eat lunch with those weirdoes from The Accord, and all the time she was calmly having her suitcase packed and checking out of the hotel. It was the last favour I was doing her. I said: 'I don't understand. How do you know about this?'

'Timothy. He is telling me where you are staying, so, of course, it is the first place I am asking. She is leaving the message that you go home. And making the addition. More I do not know.'

He shrugged gallically.

Someone entered the office behind me. I turned as Malthus nodded to see that it was one of the policemen who had picked me up earlier, together with my own suitcase. I raised my eyebrows.

'Am I being run out of town?'

'Please, my dear, if you are wishing to stay you are welcome. I am making convenience.' I'll bet he was. 'This is all.'

'Yeah, that's all.'

We both looked confused; our conversation was about as accurate as Alton's efforts to lay train track.

'Look,' I admitted. 'I'm not really sure about all this. You're sure there wasn't any other message for me? A letter, maybe? It isn't like her.'

'Nothing. You are close with her?'

Uh, yeah, sure: ever since I killed her husband.

'I need to ring London before I decide what to do.' I would be lying if I said I wasn't relieved to be let off May's hook, but duty told.

'Of course.'

I stepped outside of his office to call and, a few moments later, was on the phone to my loved one at the office.

'Mysteriouser and mysteriouser, boy.'

He was irritable.

'Just tell me what's happened.'

'You got a client already? Wonders will never cease.' Why did I get the idea he didn't want to play? Maybe because he didn't answer. I briefed him quickly on the development.

'Come home, then, Cars. Just come home.'

He sounded tired.

'Are you okay, Dave? You sound tired?'

'I'm okay,' he said crossly, then added, no longer annoyed but still sounding tired: 'Just come home, Carson, please. I need you. There's things been happening.'

CHAPTER THREE

It started a couple of days after she went to Paris. Jada rang me at about eleven o'clock and told me to look out of the window. She told me to watch about halfway between our houses, at a car parked on the other side of the street.

'There's a bloke been sitting in it for about an hour.'

'So? You want me to go see him off for you?' I assumed it was an over-enthusiastic fan or erstwhile boyfriend. 'I'm not even dressed, Jade.'

'It isn't me he's watching.'

'How'd you know?'

'He was there this morning. He followed you when you left for work.'

'You sure? Why didn't you say?'

'I didn't think much about it at the time. Coincidence.'

'Could still be.'

'I've just got a feeling.'

'I'll watch a while.'

I sat in a chair in Alton's room at the front of the house, on the first floor, portable 'phone on the ground, ashtray, glass. My boy was sound asleep. I could've played Don Giovanni without awakening him.

There was someone in the car. He, too, was smoking. He didn't care if he was seen; correction, he wanted to be seen. He flipped butts out the window. Maybe the police would send someone to bust him for littering. I couldn't make out a face. I only had Jade's instinct to go on that he was watching my house. If she was correct, though, he would be watching me smoking watching him smoking. A slow suicide pact. After a while, I decided to take the initiative. I slipped into my jeans and a sweater and opened the front door. I stood just inside, where he could see me, but at an angle where he wouldn't be able to do worse without exposing himself. Once he was sure he had my attention, he started the car, driving towards my house slowly, pulling up alongside without quite stopping, making sure I got a good look at his face before he sped away.

I could be sure of three things. It was me he had been watching. He wouldn't return to Cloudesley Road. I'd be seeing him again.

*   *   *

I missed Carson almost as soon as she was gone. I found it hard to take seriously the quest for her cousins. Maybe because she wasn't being paid; maybe because I figured them for a couple of inconsiderate kids who could by now be anywhere in the world; maybe because I didn't really like the idea of her being disturbed by these familial memories. Driving to work without her, I'd think of her humorous asides: like the time she asked me why Jews worship two giant rolling pins; or her insistence on referring to a half bottle of house wine as a maisonette, to my own confusion as much as that of the Austrian waiter. Current favourite, her office-outing rendition of *Ol' Man River* which began 'There's an old man called the Lord Chief Justice...', and ended: 'He just keeps sending them down...'. 'You and me, we sweat and strain, paid on Legal Aid again.' Going to sleep without her, it wasn't her humour I missed, but her body beside mine, warm and firm and protective.

So I was glad to hear from her shortly after her arrival in Paris, ostensibly to remind her of the name of a restaurant I had told her to look out for. After I hung up, I went next door, where Ruth Binder, one of my partners, was buried deep in the Supreme Court Practice - the White Book, as it is universally known.

She looked up immediately.

'How is she?'

In the oldest tradition of the legal profession, we are good about keeping professional privilege but great about sharing irrelevant gossip.

'What'd Venetia do? Send round an email?'

'Something like that. How is she?'

'She's only been gone a few hours,' I reminded her irritably. I didn't want them to share her: I'd come in to chat about my missing her, not them doing so.

'You want company for lunch?'

I grunted.

We disembarked at the nearest hostelry, though Ruth never drank during the daytime and hardly ever otherwise. I asked:

'How's Robin?' Her husband.

'Disillusioned. He seems to think if he can earn a fortune one year he's got an automatic right to the same again the next.'

'Times is tough all round.'

Robin worked in public relations, if that's not a contradiction in terms. Public relations, advertising, market research, even the law, were all catching up with recession. I knew firms with a hundred salaried solicitors last year who had cut to half this. Even our wee outfit would have to consider canning a carcass or two if things didn't soon start to improve. It made no difference that we were sixty-seventy per cent public funded through legal aid: one of the easiest cuts for any government is simply to stop paying its bills. So sue already.

'I know, but it doesn't help I'm buying into last year's turnover with this year's profits.'

Sandy had left me her share in the firm. I was the only other profit-sharing partner. Ruth and James Coatman had to pay me for their equity, but neither had any capital, so it came out of their slice of current income. It was a standard buy-in operation.

'I could maybe let you postpone a percentage into next year, if we can come to an agreement about interest.'

'You're all heart, Dave. I remember a time when I could count your contribution to the firm's income in my head, and not because I'm good at maths.'

'It's easy, kid; I just discovered how the rich stay that way, is all.'

'You're even boozing less,' she said morosely: 'Next thing, you'll start taking law seriously. This Carson's influence or what?'

'Something like that. I did a lot of messing around, wasted a lot of time, before Sandy; I don't want to make the same mistakes again.'

'I know,' she squeezed my hand gently. 'Of course, Sandy would never have asked for interest.'

'Don't you believe it; she was the one who never let you become a partner.' Nor had she; Sandy had a heart of gold: 18-carat, for which she'd sweat her own blood and everyone else's.

'You think...' She hesitated, then plunged on: 'You think you and Carson'll, well, have a kid?'

'I don't know. We haven't talked about it, if that's what you mean. And, well, it isn't that easy for me.' I'm not that fertile: Alton was a shock; if I didn't see the likeness each day, I'd still occasionally doubt he was mine. 'Why? Has she said something?'

Ruth shook her head, her dark curls bouncing messily about her shoulders:

'I wouldn't tell you if she had. It's just something I wondered. Perhaps... It's been on my mind,' she admitted.

'You're not...?' I was stunned: the last thing I needed was Ruth absent on maternity pay.

'Well,' she said slyly. 'If I was, we wouldn't be able to afford full-time help.' To allow her to work for the firm full-time.

'Nice try, kid. Tell you what, I'll buy you another Perrier.'

We both knew we'd work something out. I didn't want to set a precedent to which James could lay claim. He's a good lawyer but I neither trust nor rely on him as I do Ruth and I wouldn't pay extra - out of my own pocket - to keep him.

* * *

Why didn't I tell Tim about Leahy's visit, even though I spoke to him on Carson's behalf the next day? I don't know. I should have, not only from my own point of view but also because if we had a Ten Most Wanted poster, Leahy would head it. I think, maybe, it was because I wanted to handle it myself; also, maybe, I didn't want Tim to have to relive the experience he had far from enjoyed at Leahy's hands. Perhaps it was also because I still wasn't one hundred percent certain why Leahy hadn't shot me when he had the chance the first time we met, or last night, which was the second.

I didn't ring Tim. Leahy rang me.

'You know who this is.'

'Sure.'

'I want to see you.'

'I'll bet you do,' I said dryly.

'I could've done it last night; I could've done it yesterday; I could do it anytime.'

'Gee, thanks, I ain't had an invite like that since I was summoned to the headmaster's study.'

'I want to see you,' he repeated.

Oddly enough, I believed him. On both counts: that he could've shot me before and could yet do so at will; and, that he genuinely wanted to meet with me.

After a prolonged silence, he said, between, as it sounded, gritted teeth:

'I want your help.'

'You want my help?' This was rich. 'You've got *chutzpah*. You sure you're Irish not Jewish? Why the hell should I help you? Look at...'

'Look at what? How many people I killed? Was that what you were going to say?'

'Something like that,' I answered lamely, taken aback by his sudden fervour.

'Who did I kill, Woolf? Siobhan Cunningham?' Well, no: that had been another class of villain altogether. 'Her husband? Work it out; I couldn't of.'

I decided not to correct his grammar. Instead, I worked it out and decided he was probably right, though:

'You had a hand in it.'

'I didn't know about it beforehand. I was abroad, remember?'

'Yeah. I bet Annette Mallalieu remembers, too.'

'In Hell, maybe, where she belongs, where you and I'll end up both.' He was making the point that Mallalieu had been a player, as also Steve Hilton, Neil Somers, Pat Hughes and Ted Farlowe. Nor could I debit Julie Somers directly to his account; nor, of course, had he been the prime force behind the other deaths, more distant yet central to that case.

I dragged up another name:

'Helen Thornton.'

'Ah, yes,' he said sadly. 'That was part of the cost.'

'And I could get a longer list if I asked a friend of mine, couldn't I?'

He knew I meant Tim. To my surprise, he chuckled.

'Now that's a name to mention. Alright, isn't he? Ha.'

'You're claiming credit for keeping him alive? Oh, come on, Leahy...' Like I said, the man had *chutzpah*.

The man also had a talent for switching tack.

'Thus far, let's say.' The way he put it pleased him, so he repeated the threat. 'Thus far.' He said: 'Name a place. As public as you like.' Then: 'It's my risk, isn't it?' Meaning that he stood to lose more than I did.

'Why take it, then? Tell you what, I'll forego my risk if you forego yours.'

He had intrigued me, and he knew it.

'That restaurant you like to go to: *Côte.*' I thought about telling him he was wrong, I didn't like to go there; Carson and I had been just the once and we had agreed it wasn't up to some of the other places in the area. Then I remembered how long it had been since we were there: he was telling me was how long he had been watching me.

'What's the matter? You don't think Minogue's is a good idea?' Minogue's was a strongly Irish pub without, so far as I was aware, any Republican connections, but with a largely Irish clientele, amongst whom the majority were Republican sympathisers who might well identify Leahy and report his whereabouts back to an IRA command who wanted him more dead than did the Prime Minister or the police.

'*Côte*,' he repeated flatly.

I thought about it. There was only one entrance I knew about. From his point of view, it was a dangerous choice: easy to be trapped, difficult to flee. From mine, it was quite a good choice, unless he proposed to shoot me in front of a hundred witnesses and then shoot himself. Most important, as I didn't want to continue to eat there, it wouldn't matter if we left any dead bodies behind.

'Tonight,' he said.

'Yeah. Maybe.' I hung up without arranging a time.

It was only minutes afterwards that Carson rang from the *Quay d'Orsay* in Paris. Her opening words fit:

'Mysteriouser and mysteriouser, boy.'

I sighed. For once, I needed her to be serious. I said:

'Just tell me what's happened.'

'You got a client already? Wonders will never cease.'

I couldn't be bothered to rise to it. She told me about her Aunt. I said:

'Come home, then, Cars. Just come home.'

'Are you okay, Dave? You sound tired?'

'I'm okay,' I said. 'Just come home, Carson, please. I need you. There's things been happening here too.'

* * *

I let Alton stay at the house until Carson blew in, but he was to sleep again down the road. They made an odd couple: he still so small, and scantily clad after his bath; she surrounding him, larger than usual in the heavy sweater and leather jacket she had worn to Paris because of the cold. She concealed her surprise and disappointment that he was being banished until after he had been delivered along with his Thomas videos, a basket of toys and train track and a box of his current favourite cereal (pieces shaped like a train engine). I was certain he was going to grow up to be a train driver. If Britain's railway system continued to deteriorate, it was likely to be a more dangerous occupation than mine.

'You're crazy,' she said as soon as I outlined the evening ahead. She headed for the portable phone, lying loosely at the other end of the living room. I knew exactly who she was planning to ring.

I shrugged philosophically and casually unjacked the connection at its home base.

'Listen to me, Cars.'

She sulked and tossed the dead instrument from hand to hand, toying briefly with flinging it at me before, sighing, she sank onto the sofa, awaiting my words of wisdom.

Now I had to come up with something to say.

'We know how dangerous he is: if he's threatening Tim, which he did by inference, he can deliver; and not just Tim, but Sheila, the kids; and not just them, either,' I added ominously.

'I seem to remember, boss, once upon a time, you felt you and yours were being threatened by an equally dangerous man. Seems to me, you knew what to do about it alright then.' Orbach.

'He was always going to be trouble; we were never going to be free of him. If Leahy wants my help, why shouldn't he leave us alone afterwards? We can buy the threat out.'

'It's logical,' she admitted. 'But so what?'

'So what is, Leahy never did anything for the sake of it. He is logical. Irish, maybe, but logical just the same.' If I said it often enough, I might come to believe it myself.

It was true. His distant political past and the terrorist engagements to which it had given rise might well be referred to by most people as crazy or irrational, but pressed hard enough the same people would grudgingly concede that the IRA and the splinter groups to which Leahy had belonged - and in one case had led - followed a sort of logic. And there was nothing illogical about his more recent past as a highly-paid contract killer, unless you're one of those liberal, vegetarian, environmental-friendly, plastic-sandaled wimps who thinks killing people for money is indicative of an unhinged mind.

'You didn't arrange a time?'

'Nope.'

'He could be there now?'

'Could be. More likely, he's watching already.'

'Why not let Tim have him, Dave?'

'I can see it now. Screeching police cars. Loud hailers. Flak-jackets. Yeah, he'll hang around for sure.'

'So surround the joint after you go in? Ring to say if he's there.'

'Right.' I humoured my love. 'He won't mind a bit if I ask him to wait while I make a call. Listen, Cars, there's no way to be absolutely certain of catching him; he's a past-master at evading capture. Remember Cramlington.' She hadn't been at the house where it all went down, and from which he had escaped despite a veritable battalion of putatively intelligent agents, but she knew the details. 'If he gets away, he isn't going to be grateful for all the attention I will've called down on him, you know?'

She mumbled something that rhymed with tit.

'Are you going to, uh, well, take anything with you?'

I still had the four-inch barrel, S. & W. Combat Masterpiece I had been supplied with during Tim's disappearance. Since I wasn't supposed to have it, no one had thought to ask for it back. Carson, too, had kept her own particular souvenir of that period. And people wonder why gun crime keeps increasing?

'Seems like a good idea. And, uh, someone?'

She nodded just the once. It was better to do it this way, above board, because sure as hell if I tried to leave her out she'd be only a few steps behind me.

She shivered.

'I got time for a bath?'

'You want me to soap your back?'

'The same way you did Alton's?'

'If that's what you want.'

She grinned like an idiot.

'It's not.'

* * *

It was nine o'clock and I was seated at a table right up at the end of the restaurant when they came in together. Correction: Carson came in looking pissed off, with Leahy a couple of feet behind her, his hand in his own leather-jacket pocket holding a pleased to see ya.

I said:

'I only booked for two.'

He was surprisingly courteous. He held out a chair for Carson where the second place was already set and sat himself at right angles to us both. He said:

'I took hers, but you can keep yours if you want.'

'What makes you think I got anything to keep?'

'It's no matter to me.'

The times I'd spoken to him on the phone, he had sounded strongly Irish; now, I noticed the strain of Geordie that reflected the years he had used Cramlington New Town, north of Newcastle, as his hideout.

Since I last saw him, he had grown a bushy moustache, and though his fair hair was as thin as I remembered, it was much, much longer at the back. He was a small man, in his early fifties, strong and wiry, but with huge wrists and hands: those were the features I had particularly recalled.

A waitress came to lay the extra place and took orders for drinks. He wanted beer. Carson wanted wine. I needed Southern Comfort. As if a group of old friends, we studied and ordered from the menu. Last time, Carson and I both had avocado and shrimp on what was described as a light spicy sauce to start: it was curry; whoever put curry on the same plate as avocado had at least as much to answer for as Leahy. To follow, Carson had had chicken dipped in egg yolk, sautéed in what was called a 'delicate' spicy sauce but that turned out to be the same curry as the first course. She had complained that the restaurant was supposed to be French not Indian.

I warned Leahy and we all ordered simple and main courses only: minute steak and chips for me, shepherd's pie for him, sea bream for her. When our drinks came, and we had ordered our food, he held up his glass:

'Your health.'

'I'll drink to that,' I said, clinking glasses with Carson. 'You wanna tell me what this is all about?'

'I'd hardly be here otherwise, would I? Why did you trust me?' he asked suddenly, as if the question had only just occurred to him. 'This is all your army,' he added, meaning I had brought no other backup.

'Maybe. Probably. How can you be sure?'

'Maybe I can't. Then again, maybe I'm not alone.'

He opened his jacket wider to let me see the mobile phone clipped to his belt.

'I sort of had you figured for *persona non* with everyone who ever knew you.' If I traced a line between all the people he'd double crossed, I'd be able to sell it as an abstract masterpiece. If I wanted protection and a guaranteed supply of Guinness for life, I could use his phone to bell the IRA and finger Leahy for them.

He dug into his meal with gusto, like he hadn't eaten for a week, apologising when a large chunk of inadequately minced meat slipped down too fast and promoted an air-bubble into a burp.

'I have one friend. Someone I can trust who I don't have to pay. There ought to be two. The other one's gone missing.'

At last he was telling me why he needed my help.

'I don't do missing persons.' Or divorce work.

'You did before.' Dowell.

'That was different. He was a friend.'

'You never answered my question.' Why I had trusted him enough to show up. He knew the answer. 'He's still your friend.'

'If I have any.'

My uncharacteristically taciturn Carson kicked me beneath the table. Leahy missed nothing. He said:

'And a son, too. By the woman who died. Your law partner.'

'Fine, groovy, you know all there is to know about me. And you're threatening everyone I ever loved, right? What is this? A lesson in how to win friends and influence people?'

He shrugged.

'Habit, I should think.'

I shook my head in admiration.

'How've you survived so long, Leahy? I only ever knew one person who made enemies like you did, and he's dead. Deeply dead.'

'Orbach. The judge. Is he?'

I nearly fell off my seat. Not because he knew about Orbach: if he knew about my life as much as he'd already indicated, he'd've been a fool not to. The notion that Orbach might yet be alive freaked me beyond words.

Carson covered my hand with her own.

'That's the idea, Dave,' she said dryly.

Leahy chuckled.

'It worked, didn't it?'

It had never been possible to prove Orbach's death other than by - albeit powerful - circumstantial evidence. I had watched him enter the plane with one other man; I saw no one parachute from it; I watched as the plane came down. Bits of body were trawled from the sea before the fishes got to them, but the blast had flung many other bits too far to fetch. There'd been no unequivocal DNA result.

I stared at him the way I had done once before - the time we each had guns pointed at one another but neither of us had pulled a trigger. I hissed:

'Do you have any, any reason for believing he may still be alive?'

He smiled engagingly.

'Not a one.'

I got up.

'Go fuck around with someone else's head, Leahy. Mine's fucked up enough already.'

'Sit down. Please.' He gripped my wrist. 'I'm sorry.'

I sat, too puzzled to do anything else. The man was clearly in trouble and believed I would help him. I asked:

'Who's the missing body?'

'My son,' he said simply. 'It's his mother who waits.' Outside. 'I couldn't use anyone else for a job like this,' he added, almost to himself, as if still trying to justify her exposure, though incidentally reminding me that he had, notwithstanding his alienation from the IRA, no trouble hiring troopers when he needed them. 'I'm not threatening you, Woolf. You've got a son; you must know how she feels; you must know how I do.'

I think he honestly believed he was not threatening me by means of this reminder, or at least didn't intend to threaten me with it; not then. But there was more to the man than the moment, and virtually the same words five minutes beforehand had constituted just such a threat.

Because I still wasn't ready to do so, Carson said:

'Tell us about it.'

* * *

Leahy's son was also called Joe, but Donleavy, not Leahy. His parents were not married. The mother had named the boy after his father because neither of them - mother nor father - had ever expected Joe Senior to live long enough for it to cause confusion. Pre-emptive commemoration. Joe Donleavy was twenty-three years old. Until a couple of years ago, he had lived at home, in Cramlington, in the house where Tim had been held, with his mother and occasional visits from his father. He was - we were told - 'a gamer,' meaning he played games on his computer and even created some of them. He was very, very clever.

'Too clever by half, I sometimes think,' his father admitted. 'He takes the long way round because he thinks no one else will be able to follow. He likes to play around with situations, use whatever's around him to change its direction, for the hell of it, for the game of it.' He sounded like Orbach. 'I don't understand him,' he admitted. 'He may be a chip off the old block, but it's a computer chip and I can't be doing with it.' Another technophobe.

Junior had attended Newcastle University. He had read - irony of ironies - law and had got a First. Clever as he might be, he did not have a clue who his father really was, or what he did for a living. His head buried in a keyboard, he didn't follow news the way Joe - or I - understood it; news of new technology maybe. Donleavy was the name Leahy had used as his local cover and civil engineer the job to which he had laid claim, taking him from major construction to major construction all over the country and, on occasion, abroad, often for lengthy periods. Jeanette Donleavy's co-operation had secured the story sufficiently to keep it safe from their son's scrutiny, so they believed.

I was ahead of him.

'He found out?'

'Aye. That business, you see'. Big enough even for a gamer to notice. 'So you could say, you had a hand in it, Woolf; both of you.' He nodded at Carson.

I decided not to argue that toss, though I did argue with the evidence.

'But you'd moved them out beforehand, surely?'

'Her, anyway; a long way, too.'

'Where?' I asked idly.

He laughed.

'I think I won't be telling you that. And her name's not Donleavy anymore either.'

'I'm sure it isn't. So what happened?'

'He saw pictures of the house. He telephoned.'

'Where was he living then?'

'He rented a flat in the city, in Jesmond.'

'As I recall,' I said, as if I would forget: 'the line the news took was that the owner was absent, the house had been taken over?'

'Like I said, he read law. He's doing his training in Newcastle now. He'll be qualified soon.' I expected him to ask me to give him a partnership next. At least he'd be good for the money. 'He went out and asked around, amongst the neighbours. They confirmed the owners were away, but they meant me and Jeanette.'

Even though he had read law, he could add two and two. Should've been an accountant.

The waitress - sixteen years old maximum - cleared our plates and asked if we wanted dessert. None of us did, but we would all welcome another round of drinks.

I asked:

'What happened?'

'He rang and spoke to his mother.'

On cue, the Motorola trilled and Joe did the same. He listened then hung up without speaking.

'Problem?' Carson asked nervously.

There was plenty to be nervous about. We were eating, openly, with a wanted murderer and I most of all would be unable to claim I didn't know who he was. In addition, I was illegally armed. I wasn't sure which would be worse: to be taken alive or caught in the cross-fire.

'No. Time-call.' To make sure she was still on watch.

'Go on,' I instructed tersely. I didn't want to drag this out any longer than necessary.

'He was upset. Hysterical. Can't you imagine, man?'

'And?'

'And she contacted me. I went to see him. Within a day. We talked. We talked for a long time, the longest time. I thought he was going to be alright with it.'

'But?'

'Neither hair nor hide has been seen of him since.'

'Which is how long?'

'Since just after.'

Many months.

'You've been back to look for yourself?'

'Of course. The flat was empty. There was still his furniture in it, but few belongings. Just, like, well, abandoned.'

I caught the fleeting grimace cross his face. I guessed what he was thinking: all the places he had himself suddenly abandoned, homes to which there would never be a return; he wanted something different for his son.

'You've left it long enough,' before coming to see me.

He shrugged: it hadn't been easy to decide to ask for my help. 'What did you talk about?' I asked.

He thought for a while before answering tersely:

'Everything. I told him everything: everything I could think of; about my life, my childhood, the politics. How it all began.

How it went. How it came down at the end.' He smiled thinly: 'You. You and the man.' Tim. 'And her,' he graciously included Carson. 'Everything I knew,' he added, meaning about us.

'Why?' I was genuinely puzzled.

He frowned. He wasn't sure himself. He said:

'I think... I felt, if he knew it all, he would understand.'

'Why tell him about me?'

'You were all a part of it, weren't you?'

It was his way of admitting respect. It seemed his research into my background - from what he had said earlier, from what he was saying now - was not solely motivated by the prospect of revenge, or to put himself into a position to threaten me. There was a dash of real curiosity about the team that had - probably for the first time - bested him.

'Did you think...' I hesitated, not because I was afraid of making him angry, but because I was still formulating my thoughts. 'Did he have a girlfriend?'

'Aye.'

'And?'

'His mother rang her up. Lesley - that's her name - she said they'd broken up. She was upset; she knew something was wrong; not what; nor where he might be.'

'What about his job?'

'I rang them myself. Same thing: just gone. Not a word, no notice. His boss spoke well of his work. He wasn't very friendly to start out, but by the end of the call he was alright, worried more than angry. Said to keep him informed. Said...' This time he hesitated, then plunged on. 'Said it wasn't uncommon, in law, sometimes people couldn't take the pressure; he was worried he'd given him too much to do, not given him enough help.

Especially since so much of the work was defending criminals,' he concluded, the irony appearing to escape him.

I'll bet he was overworked. Trainee solicitors are essentially - and essential - slave labour. That's how Sandy and I had been treated; it was how we treated ours. One of my disputes with James Coatman resulted from the low productivity targets he had set for our current trainees. I'm a great believer in the notion that charity begins at home: it should stay there and go nowhere near the office.

'Is it possible... I'm not sure how to put this,' I confessed. 'But he was obviously in some sort of state of shock...'

'Who can blame him?' Carson interjected unhelpfully, leaving unspoken, but loud and clear, who she blamed for it.

'Get to it, man,' Leahy sounded again more Geordie than Irish.

'How Irish did he feel?'

He nodded his head energetically:

'I thought of that for myself. All I can find out says no.'

Carson asked:

'What?'

'IRA,' I explained. 'Might he have gone off to look for something to do, along those lines?'

'Bah,' she replied, scorning the idea. 'Though...' She remembered one of my earlier quips about Leahy's lack of popularity. 'Is there any chance...?' This time, though the words she left unsaid were still clear, she chose not to voice them out of tact.

He understood.

'No one - no one - ever made the link.'

'You were using the house,' I reminded him. 'You had people there.'

'No one who lived,' he reminded me in return.

'Even so,' I persisted. 'They could've made the link.'

'No,' he said flatly. 'I'm certain of it. If they had him took, it wouldn't've been to murder him.' He'd slipped back into Irish: it came out as 'murther'. Or else he didn't hold his beer as well as I had thought.

'What is it you want from me?'

'I told you: to find him.'

'Why me?'

'You're good at it; you - and her - you found your friend.'

It wasn't the whole reason. I waited. He shrugged.

'I think he might be interested in you too; he got the idea you're the reason everyone thinks I'm shite. I told him,' he added quickly, 'I told him it started long before you but you were, well, you were the anomaly.' Joe Leahy never wielded a sword that wasn't double-edged.

'What is he going to do if he gets to us? He's a lawyer: sue us?' Carson asked sarcastically.

'He's good at law because he doesn't believe in it; it's just another game.'

It rang true. The greatest lawyer I ever knew was a sometime anarchist who had been a chess genius as a youth, and some of the highest court judges had been mathematicians, which is another kind of game; it's all to do with how you put the numbers - or the values - together.

All the same:

'It still doesn't say what he wants to do with us. I mean, he's not, uh...'

'Not a killer, you mean?' I nodded. 'He was brought up in Newcastle; it's a rough town; he can take care of himself - I know his mother once found a knife in his things. He said all the kids carried knives, to defend themselves.' I'd have thought, with his money, Leahy would have put him in a private school.

He read my mind.

'I didn't have that much to begin with,' he explained, meaning when he first came over. 'And it would have led to too many questions. But you're right; he's not like me that way. I mean, I could hardly ask you, you know, if I thought...'

I wasn't so sure: we were not pals; the whole thing might be a trap - but I didn't think so.

'And what? If I track him down, you haven't even told me how to get in touch with you, remember.'

'All you have to do is find him,' Leahy said. 'Find him before... That's why I want you to find him. Find him before he finds you.' He didn't need to explain: before he did something that sent him down a path from which he could never come back; before he did anything to me or Carson, either. He said softly: 'Talk to him. Tell him to get in touch with his mother.' He hesitated, then added: 'Tell him it was me asked you to find him.'

The Motorola trilled again. He frowned and reached inside his jacket to switch off the sound but didn't extract it to answer the call. He said, extracting a folded sheet of paper from the wallet pocket:

'I can't do much looking for myself, now can I?' That was right enough. 'So I've written down all the details you'll need; there's a photo, too. You'll excuse me for a moment.' He got up and went into the back of the restaurant, where the kitchens and the toilets were.

And, when we realised he wasn't coming back, where we understood that there must also be a service entrance.

* * *

Carson was moody on the walk home. She wouldn't take my arm. I asked if it was because her gun had been liberated, but she muttered in reply that she was glad to see the back of it. I tried to joke her out of it.

'We didn't even discuss fees.'

'You know the fee,' she said tartly.

A good one, looked at that way: we would all be allowed to live.

Back home, she poured herself an unhealthy volume of vodka, a drink she only imbibed when a hell of a hangover was at the head of her next day's agenda.

'You thinking about working tomorrow?' I asked mildly.

She ignored the question, and the reprimand it implied, to ask one of her own:

'What is it with parents and their children?'

'You're asking me?' My relationship with my father was X-rated for the language I used to describe him. I got on better with my mother - she was dead. But my sisters and I didn't exchange more than the occasional Christmas card and rarely did they arrive at Christmas time. This year's came while Carson was in Paris.

'Look at me and mine; Amy and Alan with May; now this lad...'

'Leahy's hardly a conventional father,' I protested. 'Anyway, your real problems were with your uncle, weren't they?'

'Were they?'

She didn't elaborate.

I had not poured myself another drink when we returned: it's not automatic; I'm not an addict. Congratulating myself for a quarter of an hour on the wagon, I did so now, fetching ice for both of us. At least it might water down the effect of the vodka on her. I asked:

'Who were the problems with, Cars? It's hardly your fault if they fought.'

'Depends what they were fighting over, doesn't it?'

It was the first time she made the suggestion.

Another lengthy silence.

'My father thought Nate was getting too friendly with me. He thought I was getting too fond of Nate. Fonder of Nate than of him.'

'And that's true?'

'Yes, I was. At least, oh, I don't know, he had some sparkle. He could be a bastard, Nate, and by God could he drink; but in between times, he could be a real fun bloke. If you ask me, I was happier hanging around with Nate than Dad. Besides, you know, Dad was a crip. I wasn't all that good a girl; I didn't help him as much as I should've; I didn't stay in enough for him. That's why what they said in court, that I was a good girl, and all that crap...it made me feel guilty,' she concluded definitively.

'Tell me more about Paris,' I changed the subject. There still hadn't been time for a full report.

She recited the events of the week, leaving nothing out, not even her meeting with Dwayne, nor the surprising encounter with The Accord. I reached the same conclusion she did: it was weird. She said:

'Coincidental?'

It isn't supposed to exist: they teach you that in all the pocket detective manuals; especially in the pocket detective manuals.

All the same:

'It's hard to read it any other way. I know these organisations are exclusive and anti-parents and all that, but I can't see if they were hiding Alan and Amy why May would suddenly do a bunk. They aren't normally into kidnapping, and I don't suppose May would decide to join them herself, would she? No: my guess is

May got a hot tip and wasn't about to waste it waiting around till you showed up that night.'

'Then where did she spend the night before?'

I rolled my eyes, though I no more than Carson thought a one night stand was May's sort of scene.

'Maybe that's when she got the info she was after.'

'You're not making a lot of sense,' said my loved one.

Nor were my guesses that good.

The landline rang. I took the call.

'Is that Dave?' scowled an Australian accent.

'Yes.'

'I'm Alan. You tell my cunt cousin to keep her nose out of our affairs or I'll cut it off her the way she cut my father. That'd be appropriate. Okay?'

He didn't hang around for an answer, but hung up instead.

CHAPTER FOUR

Not so long ago, I had rashly assured Ruth Binder that I would either give up investigating or give up the firm. I had no intention of giving up the latter, but now I needed to find no less than four missing people: three Aussies and a Mick. Her cousin Alan's call had exacerbated Carson's concern about May, which I had only been able to calm by undertaking to find her relatives myself.

It was time to drag in Dowell. We met at the club during my weekly audit of the books, Natalie and the cooking while Carson stayed home with Alton.

I asked Tim about his contact in Paris, and whether he thought he'd be able to persuade him to put some real effort into tracking down May and her kids; we'd already ruled out the Facebook connection - it'd be easier to stay dry for a week than persuade Facebook to open up its pages, he said.

On the other matter, I asked if he could check out if someone had left this country by any of the identifiable routes, the sort where names get recorded in computers and sometimes come back out again. I gave him the only name I had. He, of course, knew the name because it had appeared on the deeds of the house in Cramlington where he had been held captive. He looked at me askance.

'Joseph Donleavy? From Newcastle, you say? Now isn't that a coincidence,' he said in a stage Irish accent.

'No,' I said honestly: 'It's not a coincidence. He'd like to hear from his son - as in, runaway kiddo.'

'Would he now? And did this loving daddy give you a phone number for his son to call when you find him?'

'Nope. No, he thinks he'll know what to do.'

'Phone home, right?' ET.

'Right.'

'But you don't happen to know where home is, right?'

'Right. I'm not lying, Tim. What do you think, I got a brief for this guy? Hey, remember, he nearly took out a friend of mine; hey, worse, he nearly took me out.'

'I'm the friend,' Tim snarled. 'You remember that.'

I snapped my fingers as if I had truly forgotten. I explained:

'Seems like sonny boy finally sussed out who Daddy was and took exception, did a big boo-hoo routine then a bunk. Mummy's upset.'

'Great, I hope they all get ulsters and die. Slowly and painfully.' I ignored the Irish pun so he concluded: 'So?'

'So, Daddy seems to think I can find the boy for him; seems to have faith in my powers of finding missing people.'

'Why're you helping him, Dave?'

I looked him in the eyes and shrugged:

'I'm a sucker for a sob-story. You know that, kid.'

'Just who'd he threaten, Dave? Alton? Carson?'

'Yeah, right, *inter alia.*'

It's okay to talk Latin with Tim: he did a law degree before he joined the police.

'As in your cousin Al?' As a matter of fact, though Tim didn't know it, I did have a cousin Al, living in Chicago, but I'd only met him once or twice when I was a student travelling in the States before we'd fallen into the family's usual friendship format - total silence; I didn't even know if he was still alive. 'As in your pal Al? As in Al di liddle Dowells, say?'

'You pissed, Tim? You're taking this pretty well,' even if playing excruciatingly bad word-games.

'I don't know anymore, Dave. Nothing shocks me. I never thought either of us had heard the last of Leahy: you've got to remember, I'm one of the few people who ever got a good look at him and who's alive to tell a tale to the judge and jury; you're one of the others. How do you want to play this?'

'If I could be certain he'd stay still long enough, I'd walk up behind him and pull the fucking trigger, what do you think? But if you're asking do I want to invest my faith in your lot, look at the job they did last time, for Christ's sake. How would you play it?'

'Pretty much the same as you. And talking pretty...'

'Sexist shit.' Natalie leaned down to give Tim a kiss and me an eyeful. 'You guys going to eat?'

* * *

I knew I wouldn't get any news from Tim for a while yet. Terrorism in the Middle East had almost completely replaced

Irish terrorism. Tim's particular brief - as always, completely out of kilter with everyone else - was to make sure that no one useful to the authorities was caught up in the melee.

I went to Newcastle for a couple of days, stayed at the County Hotel opposite the central station, talked to people who'd known Joe Donleavy, including his girl-friend Lesley.

'Were you shocked when he broke it off with you?'

'Not by the time it happened,' she said bitterly. Her eyes flashed with defiance. 'More like relieved, by then.'

'Because?' I prompted.

We were sitting in a pub in Jesmond, near Donleavy's flat, which she and Joe used to frequent. The flat had been re-let and neither the current occupiers nor the landlord's agents knew anything about the former tenant. We met early, while the pub was still almost empty. Later, as the pub filled up, a few people waved to her, or came over to say hello, but on my arrival she was sitting alone, a forlorn, waif-like figure in paisley shirt and plain skirt, pleasant, even perhaps attractive, but by no stretch pretty or beautiful, which slightly surprised me because, from his photograph, Donleavy himself was a strikingly handsome boy. She had lank, dark brown hair that cried out for serious styling, she could stand to lose a few pounds, and when I came in, she had been reading a hardback book, the title of which I didn't catch. Nonetheless, she was quick and intelligent and intermittently eager to help, anxious as much for Joe's mother as for herself.

'The last few weeks were awful. It was like watching something disintegrate, or someone. We had been together since university...'

'What did you study?'

'Why do you want to know that?'

'It's automatic, I guess; I keep filling in details until an answer emerges. Forget I asked, go on.'

'I studied history,' she said. 'I'm doing my Dip. Ed. now. I've been in teaching practice for the last few weeks.'

'You were telling me how long you'd been together; I shouldn't have distracted you; I'm sorry.'

'Would you like another drink?' she asked artlessly.

'I'll get it. What are you drinking?'

'Lager and lime.'

I bought her a half, not because I'm mean but because that was what she had been drinking before. I didn't bother to write it down; Leahy hadn't offered expenses. That was why I had taken the train; that was why I was staying at the County. For a change, I had the same myself.

'We were together since university. Most of the law students were brash, aggressive, ambitious. Joe was different. He was always gentle, easy-going.' It wasn't what his father had said; she didn't know him as well as she thought. 'I'm sort of quiet myself, happiest with a book. He had his games; he was always on his computer. That came from his childhood. I knew his father had spent a lot of time away from home. He was a civil engineer, did you know that?'

'Yeah. He specialises in demolition jobs,' I said wryly.

'Does he? I didn't know that. Joe never said.'

'Forget it. It was a bad joke is all.'

She looked confused. I didn't blame her.

'Some children might have reacted badly to that, but Joe didn't. He liked his parents. He was close to his mother, because of all that time they were alone at home, but he didn't resent his father. I got the impression it brought them all much closer together when his father was back.'

'Did you ever meet his father?'

'No. Is that who you're working for?'

'Yes. Well, I suppose for both of them. What about his mother?'

'Oh, I adored her. Jeanette. We used to see her every weekend until they moved. I suppose,' she was on the verge of tears, 'I really thought we'd be together, stay together, get married, have children. It all seemed so...what's the word? So perfect, anyway. We were planning to live together after I finished my diploma. He would earn a good living as a solicitor; I would teach for a while, then...you know. I never expected... I never thought... Then, he changed. It was all so sudden. I wasn't prepared for it.'

'Do you know where they moved to?'

'No.' She had won her battle for self-control.

'What happened?'

'He was terrifically moody. I'd known him to be moody before - who isn't sometimes - but his moods never lasted long. He'd be tired or angry about work, or worried he wasn't doing his job well, or surprised by a good victory in court. He got on well with his clients. Too well, I thought sometimes. Some of them were dangerous, professional crooks, gangsters almost. He enjoyed them, enjoyed going for a drink with them after court or a conference, enjoyed listening to their stories. Like a vicarious excitement. There was one he was particularly close to. It worried me.'

'It's common,' I said. 'I'm a solicitor, too. I think all lawyers who do criminal work feel something of the same. Otherwise, you couldn't carry on.' I didn't say that it seemed early in his career for Joe Donleavy to have developed the habit. 'Do you know the names of any of the clients he was close to?'

'No.' She was no longer interested in that line of conversation. 'Once, I couldn't reach him for several days.'

'You normally saw each other every day?'

'No. But we'd speak every day if we weren't seeing each other.'

'So where had he been?'

'I thought he was seeing someone else. I was so relieved when he promised me he wasn't - I believed him, I've never really thought it was about someone else - that I didn't press him on where he'd been. He did say it was about his family but that was all. I didn't want to nag him to tell me.'

'How long ago was that?'

'That was when it started. He was drinking a lot. Regularly. He took days off. He was hanging about some rough areas but he made me come with him. We drove out to Blyth. To the harbour. He left me in the car; I couldn't see where he went. Why would anyone want to go to Blyth? It's boring, there's nothing to do or see in Blyth. There's only the power station, and he wasn't interested in it.'

Personally, I hadn't found much to do or see in Newcastle either. If it was boring by that standard, I was surprised there was anyone alive in Blyth who needed the power.

'He became quite different. He was cold, distant, made me beg for comfort and affection. He dragged me around like... I don't know... The way you see some types, in a pub... Them, over there...' she whispered. 'That's what I mean. Like her.'

She gestured discreetly towards a small group of youths at the public bar. They were loud, working lads, several of them heavily tattooed. At one side of the group, wholly ignored, drinking when bought a drink, was a sullen, thin-lipped, overly made-up girl, maybe sixteen or seventeen, bored and pouting. Occasionally, the group's ring-leader would put an arm around her shoulder, absently, without turning to look at her, to squeeze her breast or pat her backside possessively.

'Was he trying to make you, well, I'm not sure how to put it: turn you off him, maybe?'

'I suppose so. He was showing me a side of himself... Except, it wasn't him, it wasn't the real Joe. What was he trying to do? Who was he trying to be like?'

I wanted to help ease her confusion. I wanted to tell her the truth, so that she would understand, cease to feel rejected, in time - when the reality sunk in - she would also come to realise that it could never have worked for her and Joe, that Joe was dead on his feet, stillborn. You don't ever shake loose from a father like his. It would all have been a fantasy; I wasn't going to do that to her.

I also couldn't do it. It was too dangerous for me. Not on account of Joe Leahy. If I found his son for him, I didn't think he'd mind who I'd told what, short of leading anyone to him. But I would be in trouble if it went beyond Tim that I had been in contact with - working for - Leahy, and had failed to involve the authorities.

* * *

I had an early evening appointment with Joe's principal, the solicitor with whom he was training, whose office was not far from Jesmond. I was not hopeful. I had to apply pressure to get an interview at all, point out that I was, after all, a visiting fellow solicitor, implying that professional courtesy required him to give me some of his time. I knew he wouldn't let me near his files. Even if, strictly, it was not privileged information what clients the firm - and young Joe - had represented, he wouldn't want to help make me a connection between a member of his staff - his own trainee - and a client.

Frank Morris was a plump, middle-aged, harassed-seeming man, a photograph of his wife and children prominently displayed above the disused fireplace in his office, a stack of files stretching from the ground almost level with the top of his desk. He said:

'Taxation. All overdue for taxation.' Bills of costs to be drawn up and submitted to the court and, where appropriate, the legal aid authorities. I knew how he felt. The stack in my own room was at least as high.

We talked around Donleavy for a while. As his father had said, Morris was sympathetic.

'It wasn't in character. I should have seen it coming; the way he was behaving the last few weeks should have warned me; it's my responsibility.'

I shrugged. I was not the person to offer guidance.

Notwithstanding the guilt, though, he was adamant.

'You know better than to ask. I can't let you look at the files, you know that.'

'His girlfriend said there was one client he had become too close to, but she didn't know his name.' I, like her, had assumed it was a man. 'She also said something about going out to Blyth. Would that mean anything to you?'

His eyes widened, his brow creased.

'No, no, nothing, nothing at all. I've told you. I can't help you. I'm sorry. I've got a lot of work to do. You need to go now.'

* * *

I flew to Lucerne. Then, a four-hour bus journey up high into the Alps, to Val d'Isère. It took me most of the journey to figure out why the route to such a popular resort should be so long and tortuous: I guess they couldn't find anywhere nearer to land the planes. The town was booked as solid as Baltimore during a convention but using Carson's newly acquired but already well-worn *Guide Michelin*, I'd found a hotel with a spare few nights if I didn't mind moving rooms every day.

It was late by the time I arrived. The bus dropped me at the Hotel Tsanteleina. I got out carrying my solitary bag: I could always pretend my ski-kit got lost on the flight. I did ski, as a child and teenager, but I wasn't there to recover my negligible skill at it.

Val d'Isère was little more than a one-street town, with a couple of supermarkets for the self-catering, a dozen shops selling fancy ski-wear and equipment, an excessive number of banks, a handful of boutiques, its very own Fauchon, the exclusive food store, and - mostly - more and more hotels.

The trail from Newcastle to Val d'Isère was more direct than it might at first have appeared. I had waited until the next day to drive to Blyth. It was on the coast, north along the A189 in the car I rented. I didn't know what I was looking for, or what I expected to find, except it wasn't a couple of men, in identical dark green overcoats, striding up the gang-plank onto the deck of a fifteen hundred ton tramp - the Geordie Queen - as if they owned it. You don't often see dark green overcoats. You don't ever see two people in identical dark green overcoats unless it's some sort of uniform.

I found Colin easily enough my first full day in Val, as I quickly learned was the socially correct abbreviation, intended to convey that, though France was riddled with valleys and towns called Val something or other, there was only one that mattered. I found him easily because Val is so small, because almost everyone is there to ski and during the daylight hours the town itself is all but deserted, and because, like I said, you don't often see dark green overcoats.

He was one of a pair of members of The Accord, stopping people on the icy streets, inviting them to buy one of the magazines he carried in a bundle in a shoulder bag. Apart from the uniform, his hair had grown, and he was now sporting a slight goatee beard. He was not at all relaxed about seeing me; initially, he was positively disturbed by it. Then he acted as if it was the most natural thing in the world for us to bump into one another, so much so that I asked him if someone had told him I was coming.

'No, not at all,' he hastened to reassure me. 'It's part of the teaching.'

'What? What's part of the teaching?' I had seen the magazine Carson had brought back from Paris - not the same edition as Colin was now selling - but had not bothered to read it, and it didn't have any kind of on line information which was odd, so I knew no more about The Accord than I did when Natalie first mentioned it, though from the picture on the cover I had automatically classified them - along with Scientology, Moonies, Hare Krishna, Royal Arch Freemasonry and any sort of outfit originating in California or Haiti - as vaguely occultist and committedly twisted.

He recited, more as if he was talking to himself than to me:

'Nothing is accidental, without meaning and intention. We learn not to be surprised by anything that happens, but instead to devote our attention to try to understand its purpose. Everything is part of the accord.' I assumed he meant The Accord.

Although the sky was clear and the sun bright, I was freezing.

'Can you take a break? Can I buy you a coffee?' I presumed he wouldn't be allowed to drink. All these nutter organisations are dry, aren't they?

He frowned. He wanted an excuse not to talk to me.

'I'm not supposed to leave my partner...' The other member of the group was a woman of, from where I was standing, indeterminate age or looks, on the other side of the street, directly outside the store with the Killy ski franchise opposite my hotel.

'I'll buy her a coffee too,' I offered. 'You must get a break, surely? It's too cold to stay out here for long.'

'I have to bestow my quota,' he explained. Fortunately, Carson had mentioned their proposition that whoever gave them money was considered to get much more in return, so I didn't have to ask him what he was talking about.

We compromised. I would return to my hotel and wait in the bar on the ground floor until they could afford a break, and I would then buy them both something to drink. While I waited, instead of coffee, I drank the local white spirit, which I had discovered the night before when I learned, to my horror, that Southern Comfort was not in stock: *Genépi Meunier*. It was thick and sharp and made from berries and I figured if I tried real hard I could learn to adjust. I was trying real hard.

* * *

The only hot food available during the day was toasted sandwiches, and Colin and Sarah, his companion, accepted my offer with alacrity.

Colin also took the opportunity to tell me:

'I'm not called Colin anymore; it's Saul.'

'Sarah? Saul?' What had Carson said were the names of their colleagues in Paris? Eunice and...yes, Mordecai. They were all biblical names, Old Testament at that. I asked about it.

'One of the teachings of The Accord is that for much of our life we are in a state of constant change. At certain points in your life, you have become so different from what and who you were that there is much to be gained from changing your name. I was Colin, but no longer.' It didn't sound to me as if he believed a word of it. I felt sorry for the sucker: what kind of personality deficiency had led him to hook up with these people? I stared gloomily into my nearly empty glass: if I had moved on from the man who drank Southern Comfort, would I have to change my name?

'How come the biblical input? I mean, is this thing a religion or what?'

Sarah, who was about Colin's age and almost as long and thin, with mud-brown hair that fell in waves behind her shoulders, said:

'Everything is a religion, and nothing. In The Accord, we recognise this and seek to absorb it as part of our training, before we move on beyond it. It's an important first step, to embrace the religious that is in each of us, which we do by taking biblical names in the early stages of our life in The Accord.'

'What happens if you, uh, get stuck in the embrace?'

She smiled pleasantly, ignoring my choice of words.

'If that is what is most appropriate for you, for a long time, perhaps for ever, if all your changes have been completed, then what's wrong with that? It gives you your place; it is a useful function.'

'Does everyone have to go through the religious stage? I mean, like, if I joined up, would I have to?'

'The only absolute rule is that there are no absolute rules.'

The other absolute rule was that they were absolutely ravenous and polished off their toasted sandwiches so fast I almost didn't register they'd arrived. I offered another round but they politely declined.

'We have to get back out onto the street,' Colin - whoops, Saul - said.

'I don't see how come a place like this. I mean, the streets are hardly crowded. How many of you are in town?' I asked idly.

'There are six members of the Segment.' Carson had also told me about segments.

They couldn't be making money from sales; especially not while staying somewhere as expensive as Val.

'Let me, uh, buy one of those magazines, would you? Can I see you later, talk some more?'

'Of course,' he said, as if he couldn't have meant it less, but extracting a note from the bundle I had withdrawn from my wallet, and sliding a magazine out of his bag onto the bench between us.

'Where are you staying?' I was still trying to work out how much money he had taken.

'We have a chalet, loaned to us by a friend, a friend of The Accord.'

In the absence of an invitation to meet him there, I asked if he would come back later. Sarah dragged him off before he replied but, half an hour later, she returned without him and invited me to dinner at the chalet. She sketched a map on a napkin and handed it to me.

'Half past seven,' she commanded.

* * *

I rang home before going out on my date. Alton bubbled like a cauldron but made less sense. I listened, occasionally responded, marvelled that this mind was made of my matter. At long last, I was permitted a few words with Carson.

'Tim's been trying to get hold of you.' I had spoken to him before I left, adding ingredients to the cake we were baking and asking him to follow up on Morris' clients with his pals on the Northumbria force. He had pals on the Northumbria force, not despite what had happened when we were last there, but because of it. They respected him as a rare species, a London copper who was neither bent nor namby-pamby about direct action and the hell with how many dead bodies and political careers get left behind.

'I don't think I've set the mobile phone properly.' I was useless at technology. 'Did you give him the hotel number?'

'Sure. But you don't have a room number, remember, and I don't think his French stretches far.'

'What does he want?'

'My body, your soul, I should think. Didn't say,' she added, in case I thought she was serious. 'How's it going?'

I told her about the invite.

'Maybe they're the ones after your soul. Be careful, Dave; I don't like those weirdos. I didn't like Colin beforehand.'

I had read the magazine I'd bought from him. I didn't like them either. Far as I could tell, they had love and hate notched up as two halves of the same coin and it wasn't altogether clear for which one The Accord was rooting: it was far from a novel notion, some would say bordering on the banal, but it was the first time I'd heard of an organisation built around it.

'It can't have been much beforehand. He must've been fairly well into it. And concealing what it was about.'

'Have you asked...' About her missing family. Me, I figured she'd be better off if they never showed their faces again, but until I convinced her of it, they were as high up the agenda as Joe Donleavy.

'No, not yet. It hasn't been appropriate,' I used The Accord's favourite word. When she didn't catch on, I realised how worried about them she still was. 'I'm not going to let it go, Cars, but I can't afford to lose ground because of it.' I still didn't have much of a reason to believe there was any tie-up; the use of a single word in Alan's call was all, and even if there was a connection between the clan Yavitch and the cult Accord, it didn't follow that it would link us to Donleavy, the sighting in Blyth notwithstanding. What I meant was, I couldn't jeopardise a clue in one case for the sake of another.

One other thing that had come out of the trip this far - *Genépi Meunier* aside - was that I had dramatically underestimated how cold I would be and, accordingly, was compelled to buy some new clobber to keep warm. There was no public transport, so I had to walk to the chalet. The sun had gone down, and there was nothing to remit the intensity of the temperature, not even the several shots of *Genépi* with which I had forearmed myself for what I presumed would be an abstemious evening ahead. Also, once I was outside of the town centre - all kilometre or so of it - there was no pavement and few lights.

It was - with the underlying concern about what I might be walking into - spooky, like being in the countryside after dark. I built up such a pace and rhythm I nearly marched straight past my destination and probably would have done so if my eye had not caught the colour green through the window into the ground floor store-room, used in most buildings to stack skis and related equipment. There were skis here too.

The storage room was level with the road. There were steps to a porch where the front door was located. The building was modern, but the outline traditional. Come to think of that, too, I supposed there wasn't a lot of scope for any kind of roof other than one that sloped sharply, to allow the snow to slide off and pile up at the sides of the house. It wasn't a large building: only two levels in addition to the ground floor, which meant that six of them would have to cosy up to keep each other warm at night. I mounted the steps slowly, carefully, anxious not to slip in the snow.

'I am Rupert de Villiers,' the man who opened the door said. He was a tall, golden-haired Englishman, older than I, with slightly pitted skin and a martyr's features for a face that was already familiar from a large picture of him in the magazine I had bought that afternoon. The skin notwithstanding, he was one of the most beautiful men I could recollect meeting. I was immediately drawn to him. He was dressed casually, and not in green. 'You are Dave Woolf, Saul's friend.' It wasn't a question but a personal welcome.

I was struggling to remember if there were any Ruperts in the Old Testament and, concluding that there were not, decided that Rupert was past his religious stage. Rupert was not just past his religious stage, but all of them: this was Mr Big himself; he didn't belong to The Accord, he was it.

For no particular reason, I had assumed there would be other outsiders present but it was only me, along with the six of them. Saul and Sarah were the two most junior. A stunning, self-assured redhead in a tight, *aprés-ski* outfit - of dark green - that wouldn't've looked out of place in a night-spot in this town or anywhere else rose languorously from the rug in front of the blazing fire to take both my hands in hers.

'I'm Mercury. Saul's told us so much about you. I've been dying to meet you.'

Oh, alright then, I'll die to meet you, I thought but, before I could say so, she had drawn me to meet yet another beautiful woman, like Rupert not in green, somewhat older than he - maybe in her fifties - and with one of the most striking, enticing expressions I had ever seen. She was dark, though not black: perhaps Middle Eastern, I thought. She remained seated on the sofa, a glass in one hand that I was hoping against hope contained alcohol, but extended the other in my direction. I wondered if I was supposed to kiss it. Mercury said:

'And this is Felice Hayat, Rupert's wife.' Right, the god-mother. Only, as she welcomed me, I gathered from her accent, a French godmother. Actually, I was later to learn, half-Algerian; what is more, a half-Algerian Jew.

Rupert had gone upstairs as soon as he had introduced me to Mercury. Now, he descended leading yet another woman by the hand. I was beginning to think this Accord thing wasn't all bad, as long, at least, as I could get to be number one: lots of hocum pocum, with emphasis on the latter. The newcomer was called, I was told, Dolly, another non-biblical name save to fans of Country and Western. She was the youngest of them all.

She was little miss fantasy, not much older than the age of consent, about the same age as the girl Lesley had pointed out in the pub in Jesmond but a million light years beyond in every other way. She had tight, curly, jet-black hair and was entirely without makeup, unlike Mercury who wore more than I was usually comfortable with, and Felice, who used a little for emphasis. She was wearing a thin robe, in the dark green I was now familiar with, the same robe that all of them save Rupert and Felice were wearing, but with, so far as I could tell, nothing beneath; despite the hardwood floor, she was barefoot.

I began to realise just how warm it was and removed the ski jacket I had bought that afternoon, with the twin slashes down the arms that were designed to look wonderful swooping across the slopes in the sunshine but I doubted were ever going to find out.

The chatter before we ate was idle, aimless, unfocused. Memories of Paris; favourite places to eat. I was offered a glass of sherry. I took it. Saul - as I was learning to think of him without stumbling or laughing - and Sarah served dinner. There was red wine on the table. Rupert sat me at his left - Dolly was on his right, Felice at the other end - and poured a glass for me, with a twinkle in his eye.

'Saul said you were fond of your drink.'

'I've loved women passionately but less,' I confessed.

I noticed that only he and Felice took wine with me. He neither offered it to any of the others nor did they ask. I knew little about wine but picked the bottle up to study it: it was extremely old, a vintage I guessed, and not cheap: nothing they did was. I wondered, not for the first time, where all the money came from.

Once we were settled with our drinks, he fixed me with a hypnotic gaze and asked:

'So, Dave, what are you doing in Val d'Isère?'

* * *

I awoke in the middle of the night. For several minutes after awakening, I could remember nothing, not even where I was or how I had got there. Then images started to come into my head, some of them so vivid I had a hard time convincing myself they had been but dreams.

Then I had such a hard time trying to convince myself they had been dreams that I began to wonder if they were. I used these internal dialogues like ropes to hang onto while crossing the open deck of a ship in the middle of a gale: a ship like a fifteen hundred ton North Sea tramp. That was how my head felt: tossed and turned, like these vivid images was what also had happened to my body.

I was naked and in bed. Automatically, I reached down and touched my penis: that's the first thing I usually do on awakening; I've always assumed it's what other men do too. It was tumescent but not hard. It was sore, like when I was an adolescent - say, until my late thirties - and I had masturbated too often. It was flaky, though, like after sex with a woman. The strongest image in my mind was of lying on my back on the carpet in the living-room, the logs in the fire high ablaze, my arms held down by Colin and Sarah, both my legs by Rupert, being ridden by Dolly, herself in a half-trance, naked, held upright by Mercury and Felice, one to each side of her, also naked, fondling her, licking her breasts, kissing her, stroking her, occasionally one or other of them would reach down behind her and stroke my taut scrotum, my naked feet were pressed against something strange, silken yet hard, my toes curled to try and hold onto it, Rupert's erect penis.

Groggily, I sat up in the bed. I was alone in the room. I switched on the lamp. There was an empty glass and a small bottle of mineral water on the table beside me. Thoughtfully, my ashtray and cigarettes were also there. None of my clothes, though, but a dark green bath-robe was hanging on the back of the door. I realised I was not alone. There was a curtain hanging the whole way across the room, from the other side of the door to the other side of the window. It, too, was dark green. I could hear gentle, rhythmic breathing. One rhythm or two?

Carefully, groggily, I stepped out of the bed and pattered to the curtain, not knowing at which side of the room would be the head of the bed behind it. I pulled it back an inch and peeked around. I was looking straight at Felice; she was looking straight back at me. It was a double bed, unlike the one in which I had awoken. There was a second body in the bed, entirely concealed by the duvet. She watched me wondering who it was, then smiled and pulled it back enough for me to see the tip of Dolly's black locks. She licked her lips sensuously, then held up the duvet on the side nearest to me in invitation, exposing her leg and the very edge of her pubic hair. I shook my head, as if she had asked me nothing more unconventional than whether I took sugar in my tea and let the curtain fall back to shut her out of my view more than to shut me out of hers.

I took the bathrobe off its hook and opened the door. I slipped into the bathrobe while I surveyed the landing. There were three more doors off it. The first one that I opened contained another double bed, but only the one occupier, Mercury. She was fast asleep, snoring lightly, contentedly, and did not stir as I watched her. The next door was to the bathroom. I went inside and pulled it shut. I badly wanted to pee, but I couldn't. I even tried turning on the water tap. I was aching but I couldn't relieve myself. I sat on the lavatory. I still couldn't work out how much had actually happened and how much was a dream; I wasn't a hundred percent sure I wasn't still dreaming. I dug my nails into my thigh, hard, until it felt as if I was bound to burst the skin. I wasn't dreaming, but that still didn't tell me what had gone before.

I still couldn't piss. I couldn't shit, either. My arse was sore. Another image. Rupert between my legs. He'd gone down on me. On my prick. Not just my prick. I could see his. Insanely, I struggled to see whether or not he was circumcised, which he was. At this point but, I believed, not earlier, Colin - Saul, I recollected - and Sarah, too, had taken off most of their clothes, but still wore underpants. Sarah had next to no tits. Had Rupert fucked me? I had no memory of coming with Dolly. I flashed on rolling around the floor with Felice and Mercury. I had no memory of being fucked by Rupert. I had come with someone. Though cold in the bathroom, sitting on the lavatory with the bathrobe hanging down at its side, my legs chilly and uncovered, I was sweating.

I stood up and, automatically, pressed the plunger. I stepped into the shower and stood directly beneath the water, soaping myself again and again. No one tried the door handle, to come into the bathroom to confront me or to see who was using it. I dried myself quickly on the bathrobe. I unlocked the door and stepped cautiously out onto the landing.

I peered down the stairs into the living area. The fire was still flickering. I took a few steps and knelt so as to be able to see fully. No one was there. My clothes were neatly piled on the sofa where Felice had been sitting when I arrived. I trod as quietly as I was able to pick them up and put them on. It felt like recovering myself. I wished I could recover more of the evening. I wished I could recover at least some of what had been said and done between

Rupert's question and those images of myself in front of the fire. I knew now what had happened. I had been drugged, drugged and raped. Raped at least by the women, maybe by Rupert. God knew who else. I had been trapped into an orgy. What in God's name was I going to tell Carson? She would never believe the truth. She would never forgive what she would believe.

*Fully dressed, not bothering to be quiet, I stomped angrily back up the stairs and burst into the last of the rooms, which was the one where Rupert had to be. If I'd thought I would get the advantage by shocking him awake, I was wrong. The room was divided much like mine, but the curtain was pushed back against the wall behind the door. Sarah sat - wearing a dark green nightdress, which I realised now was what Dolly had been wearing from the first moment I set eyes on her - cross-legged, in the classic lotus meditation position on the single bed that was the equivalent of the one I had woken up in, her eyes lightly shut, humming or chanting so quietly that I couldn't tell which. Colin/Saul was kneeling on the double bed, his eyes scrunched up in pain, trying to avoid my gaze, biting his tongue to stop himself crying out so hard I could swear I saw specks of blood on it, while a hooded man who must have been Rupert - putting me instantly in mind of a murderous freemason I had once caught somewhat differently **in flagrante** - pounded into him from behind, humming or chanting along with Sarah, his eyes wide open and glistening like oncoming headlights, beckoning, inviting me.*

* * *

I awoke in the middle of the night. For several minutes after awakening, I could remember nothing, not even where I was or how I had got there.

I was in the second of the rooms I had occupied at the Hotel Tsanteleina. I said the name over and over, until I realised that it meant Saint Helen. The thought comforted me. I sunk back against the solitary pillow with which I had been provided, lit a cigarette from my pack on the bedside table and struggled to remember what had happened the night before.

I felt confident that once I did so, all the images that were pressing into my mind would prove to be dreams and would accordingly dissolve. I struggled like I was hanging onto a rope while crossing the open deck of a ship in the middle of a gale.

After I finished my cigarette, I got up and went to take a shower.

CHAPTER FIVE

This is what I believe happened.

I had been drinking *Genépi* all day, with which I was unfamiliar. Then they gave me sherry. Then red wine, which always plays tricks on me. I had gone to see them with my head full of the graphic imagery of their magazine, multiplied by paranoia about cults and an unresolved, age-old anger about anything to do with religion. Finally, in place of the hoary, grizzled witches and wizards of my imagination, I had been immediately - unusually - attracted by Rupert and, less unusually, impressed and affected by the wealth of female talent he kept around him.

He asked:

'So, Dave, what are you doing in Val d'Isère?'

'I might ask you the same,' I said.

'True. You might. Are you?'

I chewed slowly on a piece of meat, relishing it. It was fine filet, expensive. I said so.

'Yes, we live well. Have you read the magazine?'

'Yup. More or less.'

'Then you will know that it is a major part of our purpose to reach an accord between our conflicting impulses: good and bad, generous and mean, altruistic and selfish...'

'Love and hate?'

'It makes a point. It obviously made an impression on you, didn't it?'

'Yes, but a negative impression. That can't be what you want?'

From the other end of the table, Felice said:

'Why not?'

'Excuse me?' I was confused.

'If our purpose is the reconciliation of opposites, would it matter whether your interest is positive or negative?' Her accent was strong, but her command of the language equally so.

'Only if you're right,' I said, and immediately wished I hadn't when she replied without hesitation:

'But we have to believe that we are right, don't we? There would be no point otherwise: it is a given.'

Only Rupert and Felice spoke and never to each other: they spoke past each other, avoiding each other, avoiding a crash was the analogy which came to mind: whatever else they were or weren't, they were not a couple. The others - even Mercury, who had been so expansive before dinner - kept their eyes modestly lowered and concentrated on their food. Rupert explained without my needing to ask:

'It is not just a question of living well - at times - but of appreciating it. You only have to compare this meal with that available this minute to an overwhelming majority of the world's population to realise how privileged we are. It enables us to undertake other, more onerous, less enjoyable tasks with much greater will.'

'Isn't there some sort of contradiction there? If you spent less on a meal - or on coming to Val d'Isère in the first place - your people wouldn't need to spend so much time earning money on the street.'

'You are ignoring the act itself. You are approaching the question as if the end was the point. Why should the means not be of equal importance? What else should they be doing?'

'Skiing?'

It went without saying that neither Rupert nor Felice spent time out on the street. I doubted either Mercury or Dolly did so. I also deduced that the skis I had observed in the store-room were for the leaders' use. The way I saw it was, they didn't go anywhere without an entourage, however small, to take care of their needs, both psychic and physical. Between the other four, a semblance of normal Accord activity - on the streets, 'bestowing' - would take place, the chalet would be looked after and, unless they were straighter than I would have the discipline to be, there were other requirements fulfilled by the disciples. The way Rupert had led Dolly downstairs told a tale in itself.

'Mercury was on the Northern States university ski-team for three years. I myself skied in the army. Felice came here constantly as a child.'

'You were in the army?'

'For several years. My family has a long military tradition.'

'How do you get from there to, well, this?'

He poured me some more wine, and for himself too, before he answered:

'There are similarities. Both are organisations designed to bring people together to do what cannot be done alone, to bring out the best in people in a way they can't do on their own. We have come, in the West in the last few decades, to despise and deride organisations, to forget how essential they are for many people. The decline of religion and the family, the rise of individualism, antagonism to the collectivism of the East and Eastern Europe, all play a part.'

Little he said was arrant nonsense: in itself, in isolation, I could agree with much of it. It didn't explain why love and hate were different names for the same thing, though, let alone why anyone would want to construct it into a lifestyle in its own right.

'Doesn't it? What is the purpose of an organisation - any organisation?'

I shrugged: debate isn't my strong point. He didn't want an answer from me anyway. He continued:

'The whole purpose is to bring together different character-istics, characteristics that are different in different people, so as to open up to all of them access to what they can make together, to reach an accord between them. That includes opposing char-acteristics. We define what is appropriate by whether or not it serves that end.'

'But, surely,' I protested, 'what you're talking about in that magazine is the reconciliation of opposites within individuals?'

'No, that's not the point. The point is to make of the organisation the product of that reconciliation, out of which fuller, rounder, more complete individuals can emerge. It's not an individual process in itself.'

'How come you haven't got any material about yourselves on line? Like, uh, a Facebook page or something.' As if I knew what I meant.

'For us it's all about bringing people together. You can't bring opposing characteristics together on the internet.' He didn't sound much more clued up than I. Nor was it difficult to imagine what sort of effect their material might create on the internet and the sort of people it might bring in.

'What's with the green outfit?'

'The green or the outfit?'

'Both.'

'The outfit serves the same purpose as any other uniform: identity, belonging, playing down individualistic differences. As for the green, it's the traditional colour of spiritual sickness.' I raised my eyebrows; I would have expected the opposite.

He said:

'That's the point.' Reaching an accord with opposites. 'It's important not to deny one's failings; we may be striving to overcome them, but we have a long way to go.'

'But you and Felice, you don't wear green?'

He laughed.

'No more we do.'

Felice interrupted, a sudden edge in her voice:

'We mustn't bore our guest. And the others are still at table. Why don't we move back around the fire, so we can all take part, and perhaps ask Dave a little bit about himself?'

'Join me on the sofa,' Rupert said, taking my arm in case I had any different ideas.

* * *

By this time, I was drunk well into the Bermuda Triangle. From here on in, there was nothing consecutive about the conversation as I recollected it. Did I ask about Alan and Amy, and by way of afterthought May too, to encounter bland and blank denials I had no basis to gainsay? Did I tell them I was looking for them, that this was my reason for coming to Val d'Isère? Did I ask them about Donleavy? If I did so, I could not recall how I linked any of them to The Accord. My usual vague mix of half-truths and outright lies probably didn't convince them any more than they convinced me. Colin was, I insisted, coincidence, even if they believed no such thing existed.

Once we had removed to the fire-side, the others had technically been allowed to re-join the conversation, and to drink again, although Dolly, who had barely spoken before dinner, hardly spoke afterwards either. Colin - Saul - and Sarah were also too junior to mutter more than occasional polite agreement, and all of them were markedly more temperate than I or their leaders. Kneeling beside the sofa, her arms resting casually on both Rupert's and my thighs, bringing the three of us into a physical chain, Mercury recited:

'Everything is of the one accord. Time is continuous. Space is contiguous. We have all come from the one, same place - history. If there is no accord, there is nothing that is whole. If nothing is whole, there is no purpose. If no purpose, no direction. If no direction, no journey, just a meaningless, meandering exercise in exiguous self-expression. If only self-expression then only self. If only self, then only one self. If only one self, only one accord.'

'What about war?' I protested.

'What better example?' Felice answered. 'A struggle for the soul of mankind, for its direction, for its reflection.'

It was way over my head.

Rupert said:

'We all come from one. It doesn't matter if you call it God, an atom, a unit of energy. It's what we're all trying to get back to, or to get back - that sense of oneness, of belonging.'

'Is it anything like man being a fallen angel?' I made my one attempt at engagement. 'The cast out son of God?'

'If you care to see it that way. It doesn't matter what terminology you use: that's what I was trying to say earlier. The more different ways you can see in which different people or people of different beliefs say the same thing, the stronger my point becomes: it's all an attempt to do the same thing, to reach an accord, to cease to feel so separate, so alone. To do that, we have to bring it all together, all the different strands, all our different emotions and sensations.'

I was listening to him but watching Felice, who wasn't. She was in an entirely different place or on an entirely different plane. I could not tell if her detachment was because she knew it all already or because she was uninterested in it. Whichever it was, it did not feel benign - towards me or towards Rupert. Though she occasionally took part, she was holding a lot back; I did not know what part of The Accord it represented.

While Rupert had been talking, he had stretched an arm out along the back of the sofa and, now, I realised that his hand was resting on my shoulder, bringing the line of contact that Mercury had initiated into a full circle. Mercury began to stroke the inside of my be-jeaned thigh with her fingernails. It would be a lie if I tried to deny I was aroused. That much had happened.

Was it then, or much later, that Dolly stood in front of me, unprompted, and reached behind her to grasp the material of her thin dress at the waist, pulling the dress so tightly to her body I could see every contour, every ridge, every ripple, every recess? She said, in a mid-Atlantic accent that could've been English spending too long with Americans or the other way around, her voice clear as a bell:

'I am beautiful. Whose is this beauty? Mine, because it is my body, or yours, whose eyes see it?'

She sat down again, cross-legged, on the floor, next to the armchair in which Felice Hayat sat, watching as they enveloped me in discourse and delight in equal portions, absent-mindedly running her fingers through Dolly's curly locks, urging the child to incline her head until it was lying against her knee. Dolly was young enough to be her daughter; she was dark-complexioned, too. but the gesture was as far from maternal as may be.

Mercury intoned, playing the part of the devil's handmaid:

'Beauty is to be debauched, to be spoiled, to be despised, not to be revered but treated at the level at which an animal is beautiful.'

I twitched uneasily, trying to pull away from her touch. She laughed merrily.

'It's a joke, Dave, don't you see?'

I wasn't laughing.

Rupert said softly:

'The point she is making, my friend, is to challenge your response to Dolly's beauty. Where did it come from? What was your response: an act of beauty, an act of recognising beauty that was itself therefore an act of beauty, or an animal response, sexual and selfish?'

'How the hell should I know?' I complained. Drunkenly, I recited a line once used to me by a civil servant, somewhere in the bowels of the Houses of Parliament:

'These things are for finer minds than mine.'

They caught the mood and laughed with, not at, me. All except Felice.

* * *

Later, Rupert insisted on walking me back to the hotel, even though a car was available to him and he would have to walk back alone through the now silent town and the dark streets and roads. Once, early on, I slipped and nearly fell. He took my arm and didn't let it go until we were outside the hotel. Then, he gripped both my arms and turned me to face him. I felt like a woman about to be kissed, but instead he said:

'Do you understand it all, Dave?'

I shook my head, numb with cold and dumb with confusion.

'I'm not even sure I can remember it all.'

He smiled, his eyes like lasers:

'You don't. You won't. You will have to decide for yourself exactly what happened. I will come for you again tomorrow. By then you will have decided.'

I don't even remember him turning away to leave, and within seconds I couldn't see him.

* * *

So it was, after all, a dream. A mixture of booze, fear, suspicion, unexpected sexual attention, a warm fire and a sense of someone else's family subtly supplanting my own.

This is what I decided to believe.

I hoped Carson would believe it too.

* * *

He had said he would come for me the next day. He kept his word, arriving early in company with Mercury. He found me in the dining-room, catching the last breakfast.

'Come skiing.'

'You gotta be kidding. No way.'

'Be adventurous, Dave; you came to see us last night - that was an adventure, you were afraid of that, too, weren't you?'

'Maybe,' I conceded. At breakfast, I'll agree to anything as long it shuts up and leaves me in peace.

'I thought you were pretty adventurous last night,' Mercury smirked, conveying exactly what it sounds like she was trying to convey.

'Don't confuse him. He has decided he was not adventurous after all,' Rupert rebuked. 'And if that is what he decided, that is what must be true.'

'I'll come skiing with you; I'll do anything with you, as long as the pair of you be quiet.'

They took me to a ski rental shop to kit me out in boots, skis and poles. I refused to wear *salopettes*, ignoring their advice that my jeans would soon be soaked through, but purchased a pair of ski gloves and some cheap goggles. I didn't plan to be using them for long. I wouldn't buy a cap, either, insisting on my Timberland baseball-style suede number instead. Then, laughing, they tested me out on the baby slopes to ensure I would stand a fifty-fifty chance of making it to the top of the nearest blue run without falling off the pulley. I did fall off the first couple of times but finally made it, arms waving for balance, stumbling and nearly falling again as I cast the anchor away from me.

If you're waiting to hear how much damage I did, how I slithered on my backside the wrong way down the mountain, how I broke a leg or twisted an ankle, you'll be disappointed. To my pleasant surprise, not to say astonishment, I found that, like riding a bicycle, the childhood training had not all been forgotten; it came flooding back and though I had not of course improved over the years since I had last stood upright on skis, I was able to follow Rupert and Mercury slowly, taking turns wide, crouching down to take some of the impact out of the bumps, letting my body follow instead of standing upright and rigid, sufficient to enjoy the sensation. Like tennis with a partner of equal inability, once you're playing it can feel like centre court at Wimbledon or, in this case, the hot run at the Winter Olympics.

They seemed wholly unconcerned about being held back from the red and black runs they usually swept down at great speed, devoting themselves to the task of teaching me enough to take me up, by the end of the day, to the top of the mountain most directly overlooking the tiny town beneath. We ate lunch out, splitting a bottle of wine between us; the soul of genial courtesy, Rupert permitted me to pay for it for the lesson and their lost day. The afternoon went better. Drunk skiing has a lot to commend it. Fear of falling and the accompanying, inhibiting tension have gone; the feeling of sun on face, snow below, wind hurtling past, is dramatically enhanced; there's a bit less damage to others possible than drunk driving, though not to oneself.

We were amongst the last of the day at the top. The ski-schools had finished, the lift operators - SNFC, the railway people - ready to pack up. We waited to let others go before us. Mercury said:

'See you at the bottom.'

I was alone with Rupert, and entirely dependent on him for any realistic chance of arriving back in the town alive.

He said:

'Now tell me what you want with us.'

* * *

My breathing was shallow. We were very high up, though how many feet above sea level I'm not sure: it was enough for me to realise that my ears badly needed to pop and that it was a struggle to persuade the thin air to fight its way into my nicotine encrusted lungs.

'What do you mean?'

We were standing directly facing each other, on skis, mine wide apart to help my balance, his precisely parallel between mine. He thrust one of his ski-poles into the hard-packed snow of the pathway at an angle, so that it was slightly beneath my boot-binding. He leaned lightly into it, until I could sense how easy it would be for me to topple. I couldn't move my ski; it was trapped by the pole, and besides, my feet were already too far apart. Above us, the vast steel wheel of the ski-lift was still, the chairs waving eerily in the wind, hanging empty, ghost-like.

'Tell me what you want with us,' he repeated.

'What makes you think I want anything with you?' My teeth were beginning to chatter, with cold I like to think.

'Perhaps something you said last night.'

'Like what?' I couldn't remember saying anything that would put him on his guard, but as I couldn't remember a lot else, that didn't mean much.

'Like the name Donleavy,' he answered promptly. 'Who's Donleavy?'

'A missing person,' I said glibly.

'Another missing person?'

Another? If I was asked whether I'd enquired about Alan and Amy, or May, I would have said that I had not. I would not have been lying: I simply wouldn't have remembered doing so. But neither would I have been able to deny that I had asked about them.

'Yeah, another missing person. People like me get asked to look for people like them, you know.'

'And are you looking for him within The Accord?'

'No. Should I be? Do you have anyone in or around it called Donleavy - Joe Donleavy?'

'I don't know everyone in every Segment in The Accord; there are many, and many do not stay with us for long. Those I do know, I know by their chosen names.'

I noted that he had avoided a direct answer.

'Did you bring me up here to talk to me about Donleavy?'

He smiled, but a half-smile, like something was troubling him - maybe making him sad - and it wasn't me.

'No. I brought you here to ski. Ready?'

* * *

I invited Rupert, Felice and Mercury to join me for dinner at the hotel. I wasn't prepared to venture into their domain again. They didn't come. Saul and Sarah came instead, to say that the others had left for Paris suddenly and they were only staying behind to clear up the chalet before they, too, would depart. I invited them to eat with me, only marginally hesitant at the impression they would make in their outfits, in front of most of the residents: the previous day, the hotel had been next door to empty when they came in for their coffee and toasted sandwiches. From the look that passed between them, I thought for a moment that they had instructions to refuse, but they accepted.

'Where will you be going on to?' I asked.

'We don't know yet. We're to go to Paris for assignment.'

'Will you be re-assigned together?' I was probing how much they were a couple, mostly from idle curiosity, perhaps a little bit in order to shift the conversation gradually towards their accounts of the night before. If they were a couple, what did she think while Rupert was tearing him apart, *if* that was what had happened?

'I don't know,' Sarah answered. 'In the first phase, it's sometimes necessary to change one's surroundings and circumstances fairly frequently, to see what one best becomes.'

'Becomes? Best becomes?'

'We are what we do,' Saul recited. 'We all have conflicting impulses, all the time. We're all constantly confronted by choices. There is nothing we do one hundred percent apart from being born and dying: they're the only acts we perform with the whole of our beings - body, mind and soul. Often we don't know what we really want to do until we do it, until we commit ourselves to the extent of action. Thus we are defined by the action.'

'Sounds like The Diceman to me,' I said, only half-humorously.

They looked blank. Too young when it first came out to have heard about it from the publicity it attracted, Luke Reinhart's Diceman had, I knew, remained fairly constantly in print since, but most people of their age group or younger didn't know it.

'It's really about psychological fascism, the dominance of the strongest impulse. What he says is that in any situation, there's a range of choices, towards some of which there are stronger inclinations than others. So he lists his choices, giving more chances to those towards which he is more strongly inclined and fewer to those towards which he is only faintly drawn, but in the end he throws the dice to see what course of conduct to adopt. That way, even the minority impulses get a chance - if only slight - of being acted on.'

They didn't look much clearer after my explanation than before, though I was confident Rupert, if not already familiar with the thesis, would have understood and enjoyed it. It wasn't, as I recollected, a great book: I seem to remember that there's a couple hundred pages in the middle that could and should have been reduced to about ten; but it was a book that had made a considerable impression on me at the time. I said, probing:

'A bit like last night.'

Sarah's expression remained impassive, but Saul was still too inexperienced completely to conceal his reactions. He flushed:

'It isn't usually like that, you know.'

Sarah flashed him a look across the table that told him to shut up. I smiled sweetly at her and asked him:

'Like what?'

He seemed not to know where to put himself. He was part of The Accord and she was, by however slender a margin, further up the hierarchy; on the other hand, he knew me from before, not long distant, had slept at my club, had spent Christmas Day and night in my house, was eating dinner as my guest and, whatever hidden writ they were carrying from Rupert, it did not extend to outright rudeness or hostility. Saul found an answer and mumbled:

'You were very honoured. You were treated like one of the seniors.'

Maybe it wasn't so much a dream as a meditation upon a favourite theme.

'I drank a lot,' I confided, as if I wasn't used to more than the occasional drop which, from his time in my house and at my club, he knew not to be the case, though could hardly say without being exceptionally rude. 'I can't remember the whole of the evening.'

Sarah said:

'Does it matter? What happened happened; it's what you were then; what you are now is what you are now.'

Om? *Hare hare*? It was a distorted version of the westernised Zen that had been popular in the sixties. I said:

'Do you know the sound of one hand clapping?'

They looked more confused than when I had referred to the Diceman. They exchanged a quick glance.

I said, speaking directly to Sarah:

'Silence.'

The way I said it was an order, a reprimand for her interference, and it was her turn to flush. Then I sucked out the sting.

'Silence. That is the sound of one hand clapping. It's an old Zen question.'

I suppressed a smile at the memory of the time I'd told Carson the same story. She'd listened closely then snorted:

'One hand clapping, one eye reading, one finger picking a nose.'

It gave Sarah time to come back off the ropes.

'Isn't that the best approach to last night?'

'Surely we are not only what we do, but what we have done,' I suggested. 'Isn't that is how we are defined by our actions?'

What I was doing, instinctively rather than by design, was latching onto Saul's remark that I had been treated as if one of the seniors, meaning one of the seniors in the hierarchy of The Accord, and talking to them - or, rather, down to them - as if I was someone they were bound to listen to and learn from. I was taking the friendship Rupert had extended and abusing it by reflecting it right back into his own organisation to see what I could find out.

It was scary how easily I found it to lapse into the lingo. Maybe the reason I always despised organisations like The Accord is because I was suppressing an attraction towards them, though the only attraction I could identify was the fantasy early the evening before, of collecting around me a bevy of submissive beauties to carry out my every horizontal command. Sandy used to criticise me for surrounding myself with women: herself, Carson, Natalie. Maybe it was the same fantasy. If so, I'd done it badly: submissive didn't come into the picture; each of them was, in her own way, as tough as the others, and twice as tough as me.

Both my tone and my eyes intentionally soothing, hopefully hypnotically so, I said:

'Tell me what you remember about last night.'

Sarah, formerly the stronger of the pair but somehow successfully weakened by my spiel, bit her lower lip to resist me. Saul had no such trouble. He had recovered his control.

'Dinner,' he said shortly. 'Dinner, some wine and conversation.'

'Like you said, you drank too much.' Sarah hid behind his lead.

I was going to get no answers from them.

I went up to my room. I rang home and suggested to Carson that she join me where I was going for the weekend.

* * *

It wasn't spring but it was Paris.

She had booked us into a hotel on Boulevard Haussmann, near to the *Opéra*, even nearer to the *Galleries Lafayette* and *Le Printemps* department stores.

The hotel allegedly had four stars, but from the looks of it, only by adding two and two. It was in the midst of renovation works, most of them centred on our room. The door to the bathroom was half-painted, the lavatory seat threatened to re-circumcise me every time I took a leak, the remote control for the television would only work sporadically, there were no glasses in the mini-bar and the male receptionist was as Franco-arrogant as they make them.

Malthus was not on duty but - with the help of his office - a message was passed through to his home for him to call us, which he did. With the traditional *bonhomie* which Carson had cautioned me to expect, he suggested he come back into town to join us for a drink. That or he wanted an excuse to get away from his family. Because Carson was still fiddling around and I was too impatient to wait for her, I went down to the Cancan Cocktail Bar (I kidkid you not) to wait for him instead. It lived down to the standard of the bedroom. It was a drab green lounge - a not dissimilar shade to The Accord - wholly absent in the sparkle and verve that its name promised. The waitresses were all waiters.

Her description of Malthus had been accurate and I hailed him the moment he entered.

Once we had found a table - there were no booths - and were downing the first drinks, he said:

'So you are the Woolf.'

'Just Woolf.'

'I have heard much about you from Timothy.'

'Just Tim.'

He looked as confused as the average Accord initiate, so I explained that Tim didn't use his full name, not normally.

'But you are not making a holiday with your pretty wife,' he said non-consecutively.

Pretty? Wife? If Carson hadn't arrived at the right moment, I would've thought he'd mixed me up with someone else. Unless a lot more had happened that night in the chalet at Val d'Isère than I had imagined. On balance, I hoped it'd be Dolly; only on balance; experience more than compensated for youth, Sandy had taught me early on and had never allowed me to forget.

Politely, Malthus rose and shook hands with Carson, clicking his fingers to attract a waiter. She had the same as us, Alsace lager. He ordered three. I picked up the conversation where we had left off.

'No, this isn't a holiday. Have you heard of a group - an organisation - called The Accord?'

He frowned, concentrating, trying to retrieve anything relevant that might be lurking between his sideburns.

'They're seen around the streets quite a lot, selling magazines, collecting money really, wearing dark green - they wear sort of uniforms, in dark green.'

'Yes. Now I connect. *Pourquoi?*'

The lapse into French was intentional, a reminder that - pleasant, comradely as he might be - he was the one with the right to ask questions on his terrain.

'I'm not sure,' I admitted. 'I'm looking for Carson's aunt - you know about her.' He nodded. 'And her kids, who she was looking for. And someone else. A man called Donleavy, Joe Donleavy.'

'Who is this?'

I wasn't about to tell him the truth. The merest mention of Leahy was likely to merit a short haul to the nearest nick and a long stay until I spelled out everything I knew.

'He's a solicitor - lawyer - well, almost. He's a trainee lawyer.'

'A law student?'

'More or less. But working with a lawyer, apprenticed, okay?' He nodded again that he understood. I continued. 'He's gone missing, too and, well, I think he's maybe got a connection to this outfit, The Accord. What do you know of them?'

He tossed his head in the air, blowing his lips out in what wasn't a kiss, but a Gallic expression of contempt:

'*Un culte*, yes. A cult for...' He looked around for the word: 'For the confused, yes?'

'Yes. And if they aren't confused when they go in, they probably are within a few minutes.'

'But...they are quite respectable. There is no crime. They have not been accused of abducting; not here, I think.'

'Nor anywhere else I know about, but I don't know that much about them myself. Anyway, one person's free choice is another's abduction if you work at it hard enough.'

To my surprise, he understood; his English comprehension was superb - probably better than mine.

'What is the connection?'

'It's thin,' I conceded: 'Could be coincidence. Could be nothing.' He waited patiently for my protestations to abate. 'He was working in Newcastle; his girlfriend said he was interested in the harbour at Blyth, that's a small town, a port, north of Newcastle; she didn't know why; his boss said he didn't either.'

Malthus picked up the quiet distinction.

'You do not believe him?'

'Not much, but I don't know what that makes of it.'

'Dave doesn't usually believe what day of the week it is unless it's Sunday and he doesn't have to get up.'

The French copper smiled thinly. I could read his eyes: the women, *oui*, they should be silent when the men are talking, *non*? I was glad he hadn't said it out loud: French lawyers are no cheaper than their English counterparts and I didn't want to have to fork out a fortune to keep her from the *guillotine*.

'I went out to Blyth; I saw two of these Accord people going on board a ship.'

'*Oui*?' French for the same reason as before.

'That's it.'

'You say, it is your word, thin?'

'Wafer thin,' I said, forgetting where I was and that I had probably managed a religious insult without intending it. I rushed on to play my sole remaining card. 'But Tim Dowell agrees there's maybe something in it.'

'And the relations? You think The Accord also?'

Carson had finally worked out what had happened before and asserted herself.

'I've got one thing in common with The Accord: I don't believe in coincidence. I saw them when I was here. Then Dave sees them in Newcastle. Blyth,' she corrected herself. 'What would a cult like that have to do with shipping? From what Dave's found out since, they're into first class flying, not cattle class ships.'

I translated for her.

'She thinks it's suspicious. It's not their style; it's not part of anything they would be doing - above board.' The pun was accidental but he didn't appreciate it anyway.

He looked sceptical and resolved his dilemma the way I normally do, by ordering another round of drinks: his and my third, Carson's second.

'What do you suspect?'

I shook my head.

'I don't have a clue. There seems to be a lot of money around it; more than they could be getting from selling their magazines or that sort of activity. I admit, it could be completely innocent - maybe they send their uniforms or magazines by sea to save money, I dunno. It just didn't look that way. Besides, you'd use a shipping agent, you wouldn't go visit the ship yourself.'

I was fumbling. The truth - so far as there was one - is that while I felt we were being pulled into the orbit of The Accord, I didn't know why or by whom. The Accord would say that there did not need to be a reason, it was its own purpose, but that wasn't enough for me - there had to be a reason, but I couldn't work it out without knowing more about them. Donleavy was part of it, though, I was certain but, again, I couldn't see to what end, what his game was.

The thought made me shiver; his father had said he was a gamer, that he liked to play with situations, take the long route that no one could follow. If that was what he was doing here, then he was succeeding. Even with Carson's family in the mix, it didn't tell us anything about what he planned to do with us all.

'And for the relations, just coincidence?' Like a good copper, Malthus had picked up my thoughts.

There was a scrap more, which I didn't expect would impress him.

'The cousin - Alan - May's son - called my house. He used the word "appropriate" in an unusual way.' Malthus' eyes glazed over as if my point wasn't obvious. 'Appropriate is a word they use a lot, like about every other word,' I exaggerated. He nodded encouragingly, expecting me to continue. 'That's all. I said it wasn't strong,' I added, though I'd actually said so in relation to Joe Donleavy.

'It is not strong,' he said flatly, almost without accent.

'All I want is to find out if you've got anything on them. It's just a favour.'

'This I understand.' The universal language of policemen. 'A favour for Tim?' He got the name right at last; I was relieved the entire visit hadn't been a wash-out.

'Sure,' I said without hesitation, inwardly groaning at the thought of what I might have to pay Tim back for it.

Perversely, as it seemed to me, Carson corrected:

'No. A favour for me.'

He smirked.

'Of course, a favour for you.'

After he'd left, I raised my eyebrows in surprise.

'You're mellowing, Cars.'

'I'll take you on anytime.'

Then she grinned.

'I'm mellowing. You're mellowing me. Is that okay? Boss? Dave?'

'Where you wanna eat, sweetie-pie?'

'I know a place in the Chaillot Quarter. I think they're open in the evenings. Might bump into some friends of yours.'

I wasn't sure I wanted to bump into any friends of mine while I was with her. There was a bunch of what happened in Val d'Isère I still hadn't begun to tell her, or decided what account to give of it. It wasn't a decision I wanted taken away from me by reason of some indiscreet observation on the part of any of my Alpine-found chums.

'It was pretty weird in Val, Cars. I'm holding some of it back.'

She had half-risen when she suggested where to eat but now sat back down again, her arms crossed, her eyes wide in anticipation.

'Go on,' she commanded.

'It'd be easier if I could,' I prevaricated. 'I'm trying to tell you the truth here, and I don't think you're going to believe me.'

I examined her face and eyes closely for any hint of incipient sympathy, or even marginal amelioration of her wariness. She didn't need Accord training to maintain her blank expression. She repeated:

'Go on.'

'I'm not sure what happened, and that's the truth. I got very drunk with them, by accident: I'd drunk a lot before I went to see them; I'd assumed there wouldn't be any alcohol; there was - sherry, red wine, you know what red wine does to me.' I'd feel more confident if I could get the pleading tone out of my voice. 'I really don't remember a lot of the evening, but I, uh, I think something sexual happened.' I held up a hand to forestall the inevitable request for - as we say in the course of formal litigation - further and better particulars. 'It might've all been a dream. Though,' I admitted: 'It'd have to have been a wet dream. And, uh, if I start trying to guess where it was at, I don't know which version would cause you - or me - more anxiety.'

I paused for breath and to study her face.

That woman never ceased to amaze me.

She reached out a hand and took mine in it.

'It happens, Dave. Things happen. Things you don't want to remember and eventually convince yourself to forget.'

'Like...' I only had to say the one word to remind her of a time of high tension when, Sandy about to deliver Alton, Carson and I hiding out after a night without sleep in what used to be Lewis' flat to avoid some heavy villains, we had made love - correction, we had fucked - long before the notion of becoming lovers let alone partners in our private lives was anywhere near fruition or practicality.

She withdrew her hand, her face sad.

'If you like, but it wasn't what I was thinking about.'

'What then?'

'No, I just said, it's things you've convinced yourself to forget.'

'Are we back in Australia here?' I probed.

'Damnit, Dave, I just said: it's things that never happened. If I can let you alone, why can't you do it for me?'

'Yes,' I said. 'I'll leave it alone. It's okay.'

But it wasn't.

I wondered if it ever would be.

CHAPTER SIX

The phone jangled heavily beside me.
Carson lay just as heavily on my other side.
It had been a heavy evening.
The day was going to be heavier.
Malthus' voice said:
'The aunt. She is dead.'

* * *

Dolly looked virginal. Her black curls positively sparkled. She was on duty at the desk when we arrived. I said:
'Hi.'
'Welcome to our house,' she said, as if she had never met me before.
'Hey, it's me, Dave Woolf, remember, from Val d'Isère?' It'd been all of a few days; I must have made a real impression on her.
'Yes. Welcome to our house.'

I exchanged a look with Carson, who asked:

'Can we go through to the Lounge?' Apparently this was what they called the restaurant. 'I've been here before. I know the way.'

'Please. Our house is your house.'

I shook my head in bewilderment and followed Carson through to the back.

As soon as we were seated in a booth, a member of The Accord came over. He had a wispy goatee, slightly pitted skin and straggly brown hair. He waddled rather than walked. He said:

'Hi. Welcome to our house. My name's Joab. I'm your host for this evening. Let me tell you about our specials today. We have a Melanesia, which is delicious, it's a wild rice dish, lightly fried in a scented virgin oil, with vegetables, sultanas and nuts. Then...'

'That will do, Joab.' Rupert had come up behind him, without my noticing. 'I'll take over from here.'

He sat down next to me, opposite Carson, uninvited, ignoring the confused Joab who, after a moment, went away looking worried: maybe he was concerned about his tip. Rupert held his hand across the table to Carson.

'I am Rupert. I lead The Accord.'

'I'm Carson; I follow the dufus.'

He chuckled, holding onto her hand until she pulled it away.

'He mentioned you in Val d'Isère.'

'I did?'

'You did,' he confirmed.

'What'd he say 'bout me?'

'What would you like him to have said?'

'You Jewish or something?'

For the first time, he looked confused.

'No. Why?'

'That's a Jewish habit, answering a question with a question.'

'It's also true of Jesuits.'

'You a Jesuit?' she demanded.

'Do I look like a Jesuit?' He answered her question with a question, laughing.

'No. You look kind of ordinary to me.'

'Why should that surprise you?'

'This,' she waved a hand around at the brightly lit room, with its three walls of pictures and images of war, horror and destruction, religion and the occult, sex and music, juxtaposed to leave unclear which was which, what was good and what was bad. The cult's logo was visible from everywhere: a green square with lines emerging from each corner, at a forty-five degree angle, which managed to make one think of a swastika without having anything in common with it. It was also on the menus, the napkins and the cutlery. 'And that,' she pointed directly at the fourth wall, containing only the one larger than life portrait of Rupert himself.

'It's a good likeness, don't you think?' He didn't wait for an answer. 'What about the pictures?'

'What's it all about, Rupert?'

'One way of putting it would be, bringing it all down - by embracing it, by becoming it, by taking it over.'

'It all seems a bit sick to me.'

He asked me:

'Are you really here just to get something to eat, Dave? The food is good...' He let the sentence trail away almost wistfully, as if it was a pity I wasn't.

'No,' I admitted. 'But it seemed like a good idea at the time.'

Three young women - somewhat Slavic looking - were ushered in one side of the Lounge and out the other. They looked confused, wary, anything but on their way to enlightenment; it would have been incongruous if the Lounge wasn't the soul of incongruity in itself.

'Forgive me not inviting you to eat with us upstairs. It wouldn't be appropriate. Not here,' he qualified. 'And what else was it that brought you in to see us?'

I thought about this one for a while, before answering:

'Curiosity, I'd say; my curiosity isn't sated yet.'

'About us? About me? About your troop of missing persons?'

'All of the above.'

He looked at his watch.

'I will be conducting the Midnight Meditation; perhaps you would care to stay for it?'

'Would that be appropriate?' Carson quipped.

'Oh, yes; it's open to the public. We ask for a small contribution,' he explained, as if he hadn't caught her sarcasm. 'Though of course it is entirely voluntary.' Green didn't just stand for spiritual sickness.

It was still only nine-thirty. I suggested we go elsewhere to eat - somewhere that served booze, I thought to myself - and return for the meditation.

* * *

The meditation was held on the first floor, in a room that half the house in Cloudesley Road would fit into, with high windows draped - in green, of course - from ceiling to floor. The curtains were drawn tightly shut. It was candle-lit and the walls were almost completely bare, save for the ubiquitous portrait of Rupert and the logo. The floor was hardwood. like the chalet in Val d'Isère. We sat cross-legged on cushions embroidered with the logo, amongst a motley collection of strays, mostly, from murmurs we could overhear while we waited for the show to begin, Americans and English, mainly male, a few women. There were two distinct circles; The Accord members who were acting as ushers kept all of us inferior, non-member types in the outer circle.

Shortly before midnight, the insiders filed in, maybe twenty, thirty of them, in their dark green uniforms, unexpectedly more appealing in force than when I had met them before in singles or pairs. I noticed than none of the Slav women were amongst them. I noticed that the members did not get cushions on which to sit. I saw that Sarah and Saul had arrived, though they were not sitting together, and pointed the latter out to Carson, who had not noticed him. We also saw Joab. I saw no one else I knew or knew of: not Amy nor Alan nor May; nor Joe Donleavy either. Carson whispered and pointed out two of them called Mordecai and Eunice, who she had met on her first visit to Paris.

On the dais, several cushions were scattered around a high-backed, leather chair, so finely wrought it might have been a throne. The inevitable logo was etched into its back. It reminded me for no great reason of a time when Tim and I had found ourselves together in the middle of the night, alone in the dining hall of one of the Inns of Court, brooding over the most recent murder in the series we were each, independently - not to mention competitively - then investigating. It was the dais, the chair and the air of mystique that made the association.

I was still thinking about this when Mercury entered.

'We are honoured tonight that Rupert, our founder, is in Paris and has agreed to conduct the Midnight Meditation. This is a rare occasion for us and I'm sure you will all have sensed our excitement in the air.'

She nodded to someone at the back of the room behind us. A few moments later, the procession began. Rupert was preceded and followed by seven acolytes, not including his wife, but Dolly amongst them. There were two other women, like her young and of some beauty and apparent innocence, all three of them dressed alike in green sweaters and skirts, bare-legged, sandals. The other four were men, slightly older, rougher looking: they served to accentuate Rupert's fine features. The men were in slacks, but otherwise, as the women, sweaters and sandals.

Rupert, however, was resplendent in full dress uniform: flowing robes and a cape of dark green, on his fingers sparkled rings and around his throat, a necklace of green gems that couldn't possibly be real - could they? As they entered, all The Accord members rose, as - more slowly - did the rest of the congregation until, reluctantly but unwilling to sit it out, Carson and I followed suit. Rupert's nymphs and nymphets distributed themselves - including Mercury who had remained on the dais - in matched pairs around the chair into which Rupert settled himself comfortably, far more comfortable than I was on the floor when we all sat back down again.

'Welcome to our Midnight Meditation. The theme of this evening's meditation is...' Rupert paused for effect and looked around the room until he caught my eye: 'Trust. We all find it difficult to trust others, and we all need to be able to trust. How good it feels when you are with someone you trust.' His voice was gentle, caressing, gradually there were longer spaces between his words. 'What a weight lifts from our shoulders. How light we feel. It is like floating. Don't think about this; feel it. Close your eyes now. Close your eyes. Let it begin.'

* * *

'Come in now. Open your eyes. Come in. Open your eyes. Come in.'

I won't pretend what I had been doing had anything to do with meditation, but I'd be lying if I said I didn't feel spaced, light-headed, even calm. Carson's face was rapt, intent, her eyes only barely open, as if she was emerging from the meditation with reluctance.

'Turn to a neighbour, someone sitting beside you but someone other than a person with whom you came tonight. Hold both his or her hands. Tell each other that you trust him or her. Keep hold of each other's hands; keep saying it, keep saying trust, find different ways of expressing it, recapture all the ways of saying it that represent the feelings of trust you have just experienced.'

I was intending to cheat and hold hands with Carson, but she was already exchanging vows with an acned youth who needed a shave and a bath. Because of my hesitation, everyone else within my reach had already found a partner and it seemed that there was no one left for me. I was relieved and embarrassed in equal proportions. I wondered if I ought to wring my own hands together and tell myself how much I trusted me. It didn't seem right to lie.

I had noticed Felice's absence from the procession and had not seen her in the wider gathering of Accord-ites - Accordions? - in the inner circle between the public and Rupert. I had not, however, realised that she had slipped into the room after the procession but before the meditation began. I knew it now because I saw her stepping carefully between the trusting couples, from a spot near the door towards where I was sitting, and knelt down to take my hands.

'I trust you; I trust you, Dave; I trust in you; I trust in your eyes, in your smile, in the strength in your hands.'

Lady, you don't mean a word of it, was what I thought, but said nothing until she stopped and waited for me to tell her something in return.

'Yeah, sure, I could trust you. Maybe.'

Her eyes held mine. They had been slightly glazed over while she had been spieling, but now they were sparkling clear - and laughing at me.

Rupert said from the dais:

'Now this.'

People swivelled around on their cushions, letting go of each other's hands. Felice made me move up so she could share my cushion, but she kept hold of my hand, sitting between me and Carson. I felt uncomfortable for a whole new reason. We were squeezed tightly together. It stirred a memory. It stirred more than a memory. I wanted to pull my hand away but our fingers were tightly intertwined and her only response to my initial efforts to extract them was to intensify her grip as if she had misunderstood the meaning of my movement.

Rupert repeated:

'Now this.'

One of the young women on the dais with him rose gracefully, willowy, speaking so softly I almost could not hear her:

'I am the light.'

At her feet, her partner spoke:

'I am the dark.'

Rupert said:

'I am the light, I am the dark.'

The woman spoke:

'I am the light.' She raised her arms above her head to form a spire, then brought her hands down, palms pressed together, in a straight line between her eyes, then her breasts, turning them through one hundred and eighty degrees at the end so that they pointed directly down between her legs. Her partner reached up his own hands, as if pleading, imploring:

'I am the dark.'

They froze as our attention was diverted to the next pair, one of them Dolly, who rose as her partner remained seated, speaking:

'I am the fruit.'

The response from below followed:

'I am the poison.'

Rupert repeated:

'I am the fruit, I am the poison.'

Dolly put her hands on her breasts and parted her legs:

'I am the fruit.'

Her partner stretched his hands up under Dolly's skirt, clutching her legs:

'I am the poison.'

'I am peace,' spoke one half of the third corner, rising.

'I am war,' hissed her partner from the floor.

'I am peace, I am war,' Rupert intoned.

And:

'I am love, I am hate,' following the fourth pair, of whom Mercury was one, before they repeated their lines and formed their own position.

'Now this,' Rupert said.

The four frozen tableaux came writhing to life. Though there was no single act to which a censor or a prude could have taken strong objection, they were engaged in a performance as erotic as any more overt imitation. As they danced, leaning out from each corner as if a live embodiment of the logo, they continued to chant their lines, initially quietly, rising in a crescendo until they were shouting frenziedly and other members of the organisation had joined in, choosing the line that most suited them and sticking to it. Soon, members of the audience proper also began to take part. To my consternation, Carson did so too, though quietly, murmuring through clenched teeth, adopting poison for herself, until the only three people in the room not given wholly over to the ritual were me, Felice swaying but silent by my side and Rupert up on the dais, utterly impassive but humming or chanting much as he had done - or had he - in the chalet at Val d'Isère.

* * *

We didn't hang about afterwards. Rupert, Felice said, would be too tired to talk; we should come back the next day, Saturday, around midday. It suited me: I wanted to find out what was going on with Carson. We walked silently back in the general direction of our hotel, the nearby residential streets quiet, until we found a bar that was still open. I needed one: there had been a point during the meditation proper when trust had become Sandy and melancholy threatened, which didn't suit what was my first spell in Paris with Carson.

She wouldn't talk much about it. She was embarrassed to have been caught up in it.

'That was the wife?'

'Right. Felice.'

'I'd like to look that good at her age. I'd like to look that good now,' she added.

'You look fine to me,' I said, meaning it. 'You don't need something like that,' The Accord.

'I don't figure on joining up if that's what's worrying you.'

'You could've fooled me for a few minutes back there, Cars.'

'It was like going back to church.' Half-Italian, she was, of course, a Catholic.

'If I'd belonged to a church like that, I would've stayed.'

'I didn't mean that,' she said crossly, knowing I was referring to the dancing girls with their swirling skirts and bare legs.

'What do you mean?'

'Just... Oh, just, belonging, sharing something, losing yourself in a congregation of voices, losing yourself to the priest.'

'Emphasis on losing yourself, right?'

'Don't psychoanalyse me, Dave, you're not qualified.'

I'd seen her in this sort of mood enough times before to know there were only ever two ways to handle her. I could be soothing, agree with everything she said, change the subject and, if I got lucky, she wouldn't actually beat me up. Or I could respond and within five more minutes we'd be bitching at each other like there was no one we hated more.

'I'm qualified enough to know how you work, Carson.'

Which is another reason it had been a heavy evening.

* * *

Carson made the identification.

She did it at the site, where May still lay, her neck at an angle she could near as dammit have looked down her spine. She was found under a bridge, by a tramp, clothing torn, raped but as yet unclear whether before or after she had been murdered and whether the rape was connected to the killing. Behind us, incongruously, floated *Bateaux Mouches* sight-seeing boats, their multi-language taped guides bouncing tinnily across the water, and, less oddly, working barges.

Malthus - angry at, ashamed of the people who inhabited his city - muttered that they were animals, the tramps and bums and drunks and junkies who hung out below the surface, along the banks of the Seine, preying on tourists and each other for their primitive needs: money, clothes, something that passed for sex.

Carson was numbed, not so much by May's death - which we had both known was a possibility ever since she disappeared - as by her condition, by what had been done to her. By the time we arrived, Malthus had already put together some information about her recent whereabouts, a hotel in which she had stayed, a couple of places where she had eaten, though there were plenty of gaps yet to be filled in. In particular, he asked if we had a picture of May's children.

'There was a visitor. A man, a young man,' he elaborated. 'Perhaps who come for her baggage to the hotel with Carson.'

'He wasn't wearing dark green, was he, by any chance?'

'No.' He had asked.

I had a photo which I held out and onto before yielding it up to him.

'Did you find out anything about them?'

'This Accord?'

'Yes.'

He waved a hand around him:

'I have been occupied. I have made enquiries. Lavelle,' he called to one of his *gendarmes*: '*Le téléphone.*' He took a mobile phone from him: to my untrained eye, it looked like the same model Leahy carried. That was one coincidence I could live with. He punched only a couple of buttons before he began yammering away in French, too quickly for me to catch a word I could understand. Then he listened for a while, spoke some more, pressed another button, tossed it back to his officer. 'Nothing here; we are awaiting Interpol. I will tell you. Now, we must to the office, my friends, to make the statement.'

Which is why we didn't make our midday meeting with Rupert.

* * *

Carson had a lot more to say than I, in particular in answer to Malthus' questions about May's financial worth. A female officer was present. It was tempting to leave Carson and try to catch up with the cult, but every time I moved away, even to wander down to the lavatory, let alone to stretch my legs, Carson's eyes implored me not to leave. I didn't know what was going on in her head, only that it was heavy.

It only belatedly occurred to me that Malthus was unaware of her past so did not appreciate just how sensitive the situation was: the woman he was interviewing had bumped off the victim's old man, even if in defence of her father. Standing behind her, I used my eyes to signal I needed to talk with him alone. He didn't respond at once, and I began to wonder if he had got my message, but then he suggested:

'Carson. Go now with the officer, and refresh yourself, yes?'

Listlessly, she obeyed. As soon as she left the room, I gave him the outline.

'She was in England; she can prove this, no?' He meant at the time of May's death which it was by now known had occurred before her arrival yesterday afternoon.

'Yes, sure. That isn't the only reason I'm telling you.'

He waved a hand airily.

'I understand. It is distressing.'

'More so, you know?'

He nodded, frowning.

'What are you thinking?'

'I am wondering about the connection,' he admitted.

'What connection? Between that and this? There isn't any, Malthus, how could there be?'

'I do not know. We all, we do not believe in coincidence.' He was reminding me that coincidence was the only reason I had for wasting his time chasing up The Accord. 'May is talking with Carson, she is being friendly; the children are not,' he said flatly.

'Oh, come on, that's hardly a basis for murder, Malthus.'

'I have seen not so much motive. And there is money. I am waiting for you to think of the money and your friends.'

'Huh?' I crossed my legs and lit a Camel, ignoring the frown that crossed his face. Somehow, I never really thought about the French worrying as much as the rest of us about lung cancer: I mean, they all smoked, didn't they?

'The Accord. These organisations, they prey on the discontented young people of the wealthy classes, I think.'

'Some of them, I guess; most of them, maybe. But I don't think many of them, uh, actually urge the process along.'

He studied me through puzzled eyes, his sideburns twitching.

'I do not understand you, Dave. I think this is a line of reason that will appeal to you. I think you will adopt it.'

'I don't know,' I confessed. 'I'm ambivalent about them; yeah, sure, I'm suspicious, but, uh, I've gotten to know Rupert, their boss-man, a bit over the last few days and, well, I quite like him and I just don't think murder is his trip. Just an instinct. That's all.'

Carson returned and overheard the end of my remarks.

'Not whose trip?'

'Rupert.'

'The man isn't the whole organisation, Dave,' she reminded me. 'I saw that woman: the wife.'

She had seen Felice squished up next to me on the cushion; later, she had remarked how good she looked. For all her cool acceptance of my possible sins at Val d'Isère, she was as jealous as any other woman I've known, as jealous even as Sandy, for whom infidelity was the only crime which she sincerely believed still merited the death penalty.

An officer came in and whispered in Malthus' ear. He asked us to excuse him and left the room. When he returned, he looked grim.

'Now perhaps we have the connection.'

* * *

I'd been to the *Bois de Boulogne* before, many years before, in the autumn it must have been, when the trees were full and the grass was luscious and the lake splendid and shining and couples walked hand-in-hand or smooched against a tree and friends argued good-naturedly, Gitanes or Gauloises drooping from lips or fingers, an open bottle of red wine in a bag or basket to the side.

You'd have thought I'd be familiar with the sight of death by now: I've seen more dead bodies than most people I know put together - live dead bodies, I mean, not the ones on the news, which are in the same class as the television or movie dead and don't count.

These bodies were not twisted, nor had they been abused, other than by a single bullet in the back of each head. Nor were their clothes torn. With a quick dry-clean in a one-hour, street-front store, their dark green uniforms would be pristine and fit for re-use by the next Accord member of the same approximate shape, size and sex.

I felt less for her, for Sarah. I had seen her in the street, shivering as she sold their magazines, and been rebuked by her in the hotel bar as she drank coffee and gobbled toasted sandwiches I bought her. I had seen her cross-legged on the bed, chanting in a green nightgown. Maybe I had seen a bit more of her than that. Then I had rebuked her back, across a dinner table in the same hotel. Finally, as I told Malthus to help him with time-of-death, I had seen her last night, at the Midnight Meditation. That was all. I wouldn't've cared if I never saw her again in my life; I didn't particularly expect to do so; it shouldn't matter to me that she was dead.

Colin - I didn't have to call him Saul anymore - was another story. I knew him first as the toy boy of my friend Natalie. He had spent Christmas in my house. I had followed him to Val d'Isère deliberately, as a way in to The Accord. To that extent, I had used him and it was therefore possible that I had some responsibility for his death. Certainly, I had thought he and I would meet again, and talk, and maybe I would find out what he had to hide. I pitied him. He was not a strong man, and certainly not a clever man. He had first come to Europe in the employ of Burger King. Maybe he had eaten too many and it had addled his brains. I had a real hard time thinking of him as truly wicked: it just didn't fit.

Nor did much else.

* * *

I ought to have been shocked but wasn't by what awaited us on our return to the city centre. First, we learned that Rupert, Felice and the remainder of the top structure of The Accord had that morning all disappeared, it was believed had flown out of the country by private plane; secondly, Tim Dowell had arrived by train.

Malthus had called Tim before he had called us at the hotel. He had not, however, despatched police to the headquarters of The Accord until he was told of the discovery in the *Bois*. The men who had gone there had insufficient information to know what or who they were looking for, or to know who might be missing. They either did not know, or had been told to say nothing, about the bodies. Their instructions were to do no more than keep everyone inside until Malthus arrived. It was only when, from the car on the way back to town, he telephoned to ask specifically if Rupert and Felice - the names I had given him - were there that we found out that they had gone, the top staff with them. Mercury was one of those who had left; Dolly remained behind.

Tim was settled comfortably in Malthus' office, slurping coffee.

'Next time you two go away, why don't you go somewhere interesting, exotic - Bahamas or West Indies, you know?'

'Why? Too far away to bother you?'

'So I get a good trip out of it.'

'Sorry, thoughtless of me. Anyone know where they've gone?'

'Filed a flight plan,' he grinned: 'For...'

'Southend Rochford,' I snarled, guessing. It was the small airport from which the late Mr Justice Orbach used to fly; from where, once, he had taken me up for a spectacular night-flight

I'd just as soon forget but would never be able to; where, once, I had watched him take off on another spectacular flight that he wasn't intended to enjoy any opportunity to remember.

'Yeah, but they've got no record of arrival.'

I glanced at my watch. On any basis, by now they should have arrived. I asked:

'What do you know?'

'Enough to justify this trip. Morris. Let's talk Morris.' The Newcastle brief. 'Like a lot of small solicitors, he does a range of work, not all of it strictly legal work. I don't necessarily mean he's bent. What I mean is, work that you don't need a solicitor for but someone else could do as well. Some property management, some accounts work, some trustee work, even some shipping work.'

'Shipping?'

Carson, who had been calling Natalie at the club to break the news about Colin, heard my question as she hung up.

'I've got a feeling Nat'll get over this one.'

'Took it hard, huh?'

'Yup. Hard as nails.' Actually, Carson said later, she had revealed one moment of vulnerability: she wanted to know if Colin had liked her at all, if it had all been an act or if it had been nothing more than a ploy in a game with me. Carson had reassured her: so far as we were aware, it was the one genuine coincidence around. 'What's this about shipping?'

'The ship you saw at Blyth: cargo space was reserved by Morris. It wasn't the first time. It was a regular run. It's a North Sea tramp, fifteen hundred tons, non-unionised, privately-owned: the skipper's got a slice of it - pops in and out of Norway, Denmark, Germany, Holland, France, Belgium, maybe on a long haul into the Baltic Sea. There used to be hundreds like it, but they're dying out: containers are taking over, even on the short runs. This sort of ship takes something on here, drops it off there, keeps moving, mostly loads on pallets. Cargo not worth building a new ship for but as long as there's life left in the vessel, it's worth keeping it in service.'

'So what was on it?'

'According to the manifest, literature, records, videos and other supplies for The Accord at its branches...'

'Segments,' I corrected, to distract attention from the fact that it was exactly what I had assured Malthus they weren't likely to have been doing.

'Fine. Segments, verses, volumes, I don't care. Its Segments, then, in Europe.'

'Just how many has it got? How big is this thing?'

When I'd asked Rupert, he had been vague. When I'd asked Colin and Sarah during dinner, they had disclaimed knowledge.

Malthus now chipped in, reading from a fax:

'Twelve. Twelve permanent centres, seven in Europe, four in North America, one in Antigua. So reports Interpol.'

'Interpol? They've got them on file?'

Malthus shrugged.

'It doesn't mean much. Some complaints from family, missing relatives. One suggestion of drugs. Nothing fixed. No crime proved. Interpol,' he hesitated, looking for the right words, not so much because his English was wanting but because he wanted to be tactful. 'With information, it is excellent; it has records; it has many, many records.'

'But it couldn't catch a villain for love or money,' I finished off for him.

Tim said:

'It's not really its job, Dave; it's only there for information pooling and dissemination.'

'Fine, what they've provided can be tossed straight into the pool.'

'What's up? I've made your connection for you: Donleavy to The Accord.' Donleavy as Morris' trainee.

'Mm. I asked Rupert - he's the head honcho - about Donleavy. Claimed he'd never heard of him. Said he didn't know everyone in the organisation and some of them he only knew by their inside names.'

To be accurate, I should have said that Rupert only implied that he hadn't heard of Donleavy, but I didn't want the attention to settle on him. I also explained about the 'inside' names they took on once they joined. Tim shrugged: it didn't bother him what people called themselves.

'So?'

'So if he knew Donleavy as a solicitor, he'd know him by his real name, right?'

'If it's legitimate, why would he be dealing with it? It'd be some flunky.'

'Yeah, but if it was legitimate, why would members be visiting the ship at all?'

'We're waiting for the Geordie Queen to dock before we can ask the captain that question for ourselves.'

'Which is when, and where?'

'When is tomorrow night; where is Harwich.' In Essex, not far from Southend, nor from London.

'Which is where you'll be?'

'Hell no, I'm staying here to co-operate with Monsieur Malthus for as long as I can and eat and drink as much as I can - you think I'm crazy? Wally will meet the ship. He's got nothing better to do on a Sunday evening anyhow.'

It might be enough to drive him back to his wife.

'That means you're staying over?'

He beamed.
'Won't that be fun?'
Carson groaned.

* * *

We visited The Accord together. The police had searched it from top to toe without turning up anything suspicious. The woman at the desk was new to me, though it was possible she had been amongst The Accord members within the inner circle during the Midnight Meditation. She had a pleasant, slightly round, face, black hair and was a little overweight. She said, as if we were not backed by a brigade of armed *gendarmes* and as if they had not been kept prisoner in their own premises for some hours without explanation:

'Hi. I'm Lois. Welcome to our house. How can I help you?' She addressed her remark to me in English with an American accent.

'How come you all seem to know immediately what language to speak in?'

She laughed merrily.

'That's an easy one. I don't speak French.'

'What would you have done if I didn't speak English?'

'Gesticulated a lot, I should think. How can I help you?'

'Are you the most senior member left?'

'Oh no, not at all. That would be Hiram. He's the Segment leader.'

'Would you tell him we're here, please? This is Inspector Malthus.'

'Of course.' She picked up a phone and told Hiram that an Inspector had arrived. 'He'll be down in a moment, if you'd like to wait.'

I sat across the desk from her. I asked her how long she'd been with the group and where she was from. She answered politely, precisely what she was asked and no more. I asked her why she had joined, wondering how easily she would be able similarly to confine her reply.

'It was appropriate.'

I had the idea this was not going to be an easy interrogation so I wasn't displeased when a fat, squat man with a completely bald, gleaming white head and wire-framed Coca-Cola bottle ends for glasses descended the stairs from the first floor where the meditation had been held. He held out a hand not to shake any of ours, but to usher us ahead of him back up the stairs. He looked too old still to be carrying a biblical name but, hey, what did I know? Maybe this was his second time around.

The meditation room had been transformed and looked now like an ordinary conference room, with the logos doubtless representing the tentacles of enterprise stretching into as many vulnerable economies as could stand the competition. I introduced Malthus and Carson but left Tim out of it for the time being, along with a couple of Malthus' uniforms whose names I couldn't pronounce. Malthus asked immediately, in English:

'Hiram. This is your correct name?'

Hiram smiled serenely.

'It is now. But I suppose what you mean is whether it's the name I had before I joined The Accord?' From his accent, Hiram was about as upper class English as Rupert himself.

Malthus smiled back just as sweetly.

'Are you familiar with French criminal procedure, *monsieur*?'

Hiram shook his head, adding:

'I have nothing to hide.'

'I was not thinking so much of hiding. To fear, perhaps.'

The smile departed his face about as swiftly as Colin and Sarah must have departed this mortal coil.

'What do you want, Inspector?'

'Some answers. Where is your leader?'

'Look, I'm not trying to be difficult, but can't you tell me what is going on? Surely I'm entitled to some explanation.'

Tim coughed. Malthus turned, glanced at him and nodded. Tim said, in his best 'I'm-just-a-copper-doing-my-job-sir' voice:

'Two of your members are dead, sir.'

Hiram blanched, his face as pale as his pate.

'I don't understand. Who? How?'

'A man called Colin. Colin Wrighton. But his, er, Accord name was Saul. And a woman called Sarah: that was her Accord name.'

'How did they die? Were they in an accident?'

Our looks told him. He lowered his face into his hands, close to tears. We waited in silence. When he looked up, his eyes red and hollow and scared, his glasses streaked, he said:

'Look, I don't know anything about all of this.'

It was enough to guarantee him a long and private session with Malthus, until he had been drained dry of everything that might identify what 'this' was. For the meantime, though, there was a more pressing question yet to be answered. Malthus repeated:

'I ask you, where is your leader?'

'Felice? I don't know.'

We exchanged puzzled glances, then I asked:

'Why did you say Felice? The Inspector meant Rupert.'

For the first time since we broke the news, he recovered sufficient composure to smile spookily as he said:

'Rupert is no longer a part of The Accord.'

CHAPTER SEVEN

Tim's information was wrong in one material respect: the 'plane did reach Southend Rochford, but later on, after a detour through Hamburg where Rupert - and, apparently, Mercury - had disembarked or disappeared. Anyhow, they weren't on the manifest when the plane landed in England.

* * *

I was less surprised at the schism in The Accord than I might have been. Generationally, I had been around cults and the like most of my adult life; though not unique to the sixties, the sudden abandonment of so many conventions and norms - the social revolution - had led to an upsurge in cults as people struggled to find new ways to exist.

Someone - the hell if I know who - once told me that if a cult is exclusively led by one strong person, he - or she - can stay in control forever. If there is more than one, even if a couple, even if married, however, they will eventually fall out and one of them will triumph while the other will be excluded.

It's about total control; it's about being bored with commanding the allegiance of those whom the leadership has become accustomed to view and treat as followers and inferiors and wanting to tackle the only other equal; it's about being the only one who can say what it all means.

* * *

We did not leave Hiram a happy or contented senior of The Accord. Malthus and Dowell pumped him with a zeal for which I could only account in one of two ways: each was trying to outdo the other in this almost unprecedented display of Anglo-Franco co-operation; or, neither of them had much time for quasi-religious cults.

After a while, I went back to reception to ask Lois to ascertain the whereabouts of Dolly. Carson decided to accompany me; I couldn't imagine why. Lois decided which way the cookie was crumbling and did not check with Hiram before complying. Soon enough, Dolly joined us in the otherwise deserted coffee lounge. The non-member guests had been allowed to leave shortly after we arrived: the remaining members must've got fed up playing waiter - sorry, host - and customer with each other and were nowhere to be seen. Who knew where the Slavic-looking girls had gone.

Dolly was scared, nervous, fidgety. No sooner than she had sat down, she asked whether we wanted anything to eat or drink: she would fetch it for us herself. I figured activity might calm her down and asked for coffee and a roll of some kind, any kind, which latter earned me a sharp dig in the ribs from Carson's elbow even though - for once - the pun was unintentional.

'What's going on, Dolly?'

'I don't know what you mean,' she said dully, as if drugged, anything but the assured child-woman who had taunted me with her looks in Val d'Isère and again, along with the other meditators, in this very building about eighteen hours beforehand.

'Why did you all leave Val d'Isère so suddenly?'

'I don't know. I go where I'm told. I do what I'm told.'

Carson barely suppressed an 'I bet'. I frowned at her: she was allowing jealousy to obscure her professionalism; also her empathy - Dolly was clearly distraught.

'Dolly, where do you come from?'

'My parents are from the States, but my father worked for the government but abroad a lot of the time. I guess, all over.' It accounted for the accent. 'Why? Why do you want to know?' It was an automatic, Accord-style question for question and I ignored it.

'How old are you?' Carson's curiosity had been piqued.

'Twenty.'

'How long have you been a part of The Accord?'

'Forever,' she answered dreamily. 'It's been the best time.' A nervous tic flickered across her face, as if she knew that it was all over, collapsing around her, but didn't yet want to face up to it.

'Are your parents still alive? Are you in touch with them? How do they feel about The Accord?'

'My mother left my father a few years ago. I stayed with him. We didn't know where she went; anyway, we lost touch. It was difficult for him, for us. I think, well, he doesn't mind mostly, because, well, he doesn't have to look after me anymore. But it isn't that he doesn't care; whenever he can, he comes to see me.' She was Liza Minelli as Sally Bowles in *Cabaret*. 'Really he does.'

'What does he do for the government? I mean, is he in the military or the Diplomatic Service?'

'I can't say. I don't always know.'

'But what does he think about this?' Carson asked, her sympathy finally awoken by the shared childhood trauma of a mother who deserted them.

'What do you mean?' she asked, wide-eyed, grabbing Carson's revised attitude like a life-line.

'The Accord,' I snapped, tiring of the poor-little-me routine.

She stared at me. For a moment I could not decide whether she was on the verge of tears or anger. Then she said:

'He was angry at first; then he came and visited and met Felice and then he said he thought it was alright, for a while, if it was what I wanted.'

'He didn't...' I hesitated. 'Well, didn't he find it a little strange? Wasn't he worried about it, from your point of view I mean?'

'It was easier. Like I said.'

'What's your real name, Dolly?' I held up a hand to forestall her protest. 'The police will ask; you'll have to tell them.'

She pondered this for a moment and realised it was more likely true than not. She said defiantly:

'I don't care. I can tell you. Dolly's my real name. Really. When I joined, I took another name, but then when I met Rupert and Felice, Rupert said I didn't need it, it wasn't necessary, it wasn't appropriate.'

'Your last name?'

'Demonica,' she said, her eyes flashing. 'Appropriate, too, huh?'

I shook my head sadly: at one moment, she was a lost child; then a demon; then she could be witty, bright, self-mocking. She had everything going for her in life: looks, smarts, family. What the hell was she doing in an outfit like this? As if to confirm that she wasn't dumb, she answered my unspoken question.

'You've met Rupert. You were taken with him. Weren't you?'

'But I wouldn't sign up for life.'

'You're you; you do what you want. I wanted something different. I want to belong.'

Beside me in the booth, I sensed Carson shiver: she, too, wanted to belong. Was it true of more people than I might have imagined? Was it, perhaps, true of all of us?

'Tell me what's going on, Dolly. Hiram said Rupert's no longer in charge. Is that right? And that Felice is?'

She glanced around her to make sure no one could hear her.

'That's what's being said.'

'Meaning? Do you believe it?'

'I don't know. Rupert's gone away before.'

'But has he quit before? Has Felice taken over before?'

'I don't know. I'm very junior.'

'But you've been very close to them, to both of them.' I reminded her I was one of the few people with whom she could not hide behind her lowly status. 'Is that right? To both of them?'

She smiled thinly, understanding exactly what I wanted to know.

'Both of them, that's right.'

Carson raised her eyebrows but didn't speak.

'Then you must know what's going on, Dolly. Whose idea was it to come back from Val?'

She thought before answering.

'Felice. After you were there, they had a huge argument. It went on for hours. It was the worst argument I've heard them have, but I don't know what about.'

'Was it about me?'

'I'm not sure. A bit, maybe. Rupert liked you but Felice didn't trust you.' Not even after the meditation? My my. 'She didn't want you around. But Rupert said you were a natural.'

'Natural what?' Carson snapped before I could divert the course of the conversation.

'You had a natural understanding of things.' Dolly looked puzzled, as if she couldn't think what other interpretation the expression could have been given. 'Rupert said that.'

'But they were arguing after I went? When do you mean? The first night, or after we'd been skiing together?'

'Both. They argued during the night. Then more after you'd been skiing.'

She was proving so co-operative that, but for Carson, I would've taken the chance to press her for an account of that night that might have told me how much had happened and how much had been a dream. On cue, Carson slid out of the booth and headed for the *Mesdames*, casting a shrewd glance back over her shoulder at me. I seized the time.

'Dolly, tell me what happened that night? I'd drunk a lot. Things happened. I'm not sure.'

It was a mistake. It put her back into a position of power, mystery. It gave her back control. She leaned across the table and stroked my cheek amusedly.

'What do you want to have happened, Dave?'

I gripped her wrist.

'It's not all games, Dolly. People have been hurt. You know that, don't you?'

'Rupert? He's alright, isn't he?'

She was a better actress than I imagined if she was only pretending not to know about Saul and Sarah. I played on her concern.

'Perhaps. What makes you think he might not be?'

'I know it's wrong to say it; I know she's now The Leader; but I don't trust her, not the same way I trusted Rupert. Or Mercury.'

'Mercury?'

'Yes, don't you know?'

'Know what?'

'They're close, too; very close; close like...like you asked me. But differently. Much deeper. Spiritually. More than Rupert and Felice. She's gone too, of course. You know that, don't you?'

It accounted for Mercury's non-arrival in England. What had Rupert said the last time we saw him in the coffee lounge? Something about bringing it all down. But who was bringing it all down? And why?

Carson returned. Dolly glanced at her watch and got up.

'You have to excuse me now. I have to prepare the evening meal for the members.'

Carson sat in her place, opposite me instead of next to me. She sunk her chin into her palms and rested her elbows on the table with a thump that hurt me more than it hurt her. She waited. I waited. She sighed and gave in first.

'Well?'

'Well what?'

'Well what did you find out happened that night?'

'Whatever I wanted to, according to Dolly.'

'Fine,' she snarled. 'You wanna play games, I'll play games. Now tell me what you wanted to have happened.'

* * *

Fortunately, we were joined almost at once by Tim Dowell, before I had time to reply, frustrating her to the point that I feared for my life or, at least, my favourite parts.

'You finished up here?' he asked. 'You want to get something to eat?'

'Sure, why not?' Tim was a good friend and a close friend, to both of us; he was also an experienced man and worldly with it, but he was not sophisticated he would've needed to be to listen to my account of Val d'Isère, and Carson knew it. Expecting a scowl and a hissed threat that she was not about to let it go, she surprised me by taking my hand as we followed him to the entrance of the building. While we waited for Tim and Malthus to exchange their final vows and make their arrangements for the morning, she kissed me lightly on the cheek and admitted:

'I don't think I really do want to know, Dave.'

'I can't keep up with you, Carson,' I sighed. 'You change from minute to minute.'

'But I'm better than I used to be, aren't I? It used to be every second.' It wasn't a joke.

'Sure, kid.' I squeezed her hand. 'Better than before.'

Tim refused to discuss what information he had obtained from Malthus until we had found somewhere to eat. He was, I think, frightened that if he did so, we'd want to take off in several different directions at once and he would be deprived of his night on the tiles. He had conscientiously purchased a guide to Paris eateries and now announced that he wanted to try something called *Ambassade d'Auvergne*, fortunately, like most of Paris, within walking distance, not far from *Les Halles*. It turned out to be a cheery, family-run establishment, with a bunch of local wines of the Auvergne that meant nothing to me but that Tim dithered about before selecting two, both of them red. I groaned at the thought. Did it mean I would dream of sex with Tim? The thought was too horrible to bear. He looked up and grinned at Carson.

'No tell.' He meant Sheila, to whom Carson was close.

He wasn't about to cheat on her, though, because he selected a cassoulet with a dish called *aligot*, comprising mashed potatoes with some sort of cheese, reeking so heavily of garlic no one could spend the night at his side. To start, he had a fish soup. I'd been in France for the best part of a week and my stomach was feeling the effects, both inside and out. I stuck to *stek fritte*, no starter. Carson was an Australian and, as such, as unimaginative an eater as I; she followed my lead for main course, but his for *hors d'oeuvres*.

'Well, where do we go now, children?' he asked, once he'd sunk a full glass of wine.

'The alcoholics' ward, I imagine,' I said dryly.

He guffawed:

'Coming from you, Dave?'

'Alright. Tell us what you got? Word on the Geordie Queen?'

'Yup. That's what Malthus was telling me. It's arrived. Neither Rupert nor the other one...'

'Mercury,' I reminded him

'Right. Mercury. Neither of them's on board.'

'What is?'

'What, or who?'

There were times I could kill him. Through gritted teeth, I said:

'Who?'

'Crew-list includes one...' He paused for dramatic effect: 'Alan Yavitch. Countryman of yours, I believe,' he said to Carson: 'Relative, even. Turns out he signed on in Hamburg, just this trip.'

* * *

It was by then too late to catch the last train back to England, which was Tim's intention when he insisted we go to eat before he share the news with us. By the authority invested in him by no one in particular, Wally Wadd had effectively quarantined the ship and its crew, threatening that if they did not co-operate he would file a contagious disease complaint which would put them back out in the harbour, flying a black ball, unable to leave and unable to dock, until - on Monday at the earliest - the medical people could find time to board and investigate. The cost of losing dock-time and the hands standing by to unload was more than the Geordie Queen was worth. The local police were co-operating and mounting a twenty-four hour guard.

Tim wanted me to wait before returning, to go instead to Hamburg. His plan was to take Carson back with him, to interview Yavitch about his movements during the past few months, the whereabouts of his sister and his relationship with his mother. Working backwards, it was possible that Yavitch had himself wacked off his mother, which was Malthus' money motive: it would leave him at least a day, maybe two, to make his way to Hamburg and sign on. I was destined for Hamburg for the good reason that I knew Rupert and Mercury by sight.

'Nope, no way, no how.'

'Come on, Dave, you don't need to see him. Carson'll be there. She knows as much as you, more probably.'

'You do Hamburg,' I said flatly.

'It doesn't make sense,' he shouted, causing the owner to glance up to make sure we weren't about to break his Auvergne-proof dishes.

'Yes it does,' Carson said, taking my part, and my hand, to calm me down. 'I understand.'

Dowell scowled. I explained:

'I've been there - Germany - once, Tim; it gives me nightmares. I can't help it. I know it's irrational. I know any of them still alive would have trouble lifting a finger to press the start button on a microwave, but I can't stand it. I'm just looking around and around, thinking where were you, what were you doing, are they waiting to get me.'

He muttered something prefixed with a 'bloody' and that rhymed with 'muse', but he understood. He was only angry because he'd forgotten how I felt about Germany even though, when re-unification was on the agenda, we'd talked about it and I'd admitted it was something I hated.

'I don't care,' I'd stormed. 'I don't care how wrong it is, I don't care how much they suffer; let them suffer for ever; it's not long enough. We should have nuked them at the end of the war. Just for the hell of it, just to kill 'em.'

I once asked a well-known, communist Jewish barrister how he felt about Germans.

'Let me put it this way, Dave; some of my best friends are Germans, and I hate them all.'

Which is why the next day, Sunday, Tim went to Hamburg while Carson and I flew home to London and popped home to change our clothes and remind Alton we hadn't forgotten him, thanking Jada and Frankie for looking after him, before driving to Harwich for another family re-union. We were pretty well hungover: too much booze, not enough sleep.

After dinner, we had strolled back to the hotel, stopping at a bar for a nightcap or two. It was maybe two thirty by the time we got in. I asked at the reception for an alarm call for eight thirty and tea for two at nine. At seven thirty the phone rang and the jabbering began. At seven forty-five, a room-service waiter arrived with the tea and Carson had to restrain me from throwing him out bodily, and only succeeded because I was stark naked beneath the sheets. At eight thirty, the alarm call arrived. At eight forty-five, they gave us a second blast for luck. At nine, they re-appeared with the tea and an order form without a time on it.

* * *

Though it was a Sunday, most of the half-dozen or so crew of the Geordie Queen were at work. Some of them were scraping rust and painting, a bright orange, anti-rust undercoat that clashed violently with the pale grey and blue of the topcoat. Others were uncovering the hatches, preparatory to unloading. As well as the police guard, Customs and Excise had decided to join in the fun, just in case. Wally was leaning against the rails, smoking.

'I didn't know you smoked.'

'Used to. Quit. Started again. And, uh, hi, Dave, it's nice to see you too. Carson.'

Alan was isolated in the crew mess. He was dressed in work jeans and a check shirt, only the collars of which were visible above a thick, knit sweater streaked with paint. He was drinking black coffee from a mug. He hadn't shaved or, I suspect, taken a shower since he came on board. He was surly. As we entered, he snarled:

'Get her out of here. Get that bitch out of here before I kill her. Like she killed my father.'

Taking his cue from Wally, Carson smiled sweetly:

'Uh, hi, Al, it's nice to see you too.'

'I'm Dave Woolf. We've spoken on the phone.'

'You're that bitch's bloke; I'm not speaking to you either.'

Wally said soothingly:

'I don't much like her either, Mr Yavitch, or him. But I've got my orders and he's the one who is going to question you. Just pretend you never met them before.'

'I never did meet him. I wish I never met her.'

'Alan,' Carson tried reason. 'It was all a long time ago; do you think I haven't spent as many sleepless nights as you? The court acquitted me; you know Nate, your father; you know how he could get; what choice did I ever have? I was just a kid, man.'

'Not that much,' he said, and spat on the floor.

'How long have you been a sailor, Alan?' I asked.

Before he remembered he wasn't talking to me either, he said:

'I used to sail, at home, in the vacations. Not sea-going, but I worked the harbour ferries.'

'Why? Your mother had enough money. Why did you have to?'

Because he'd answered me once, he recognised that he had to continue, at least until I asked something at which he could find a reason to take renewed offence.

'I liked it. It was good. Get about among different people. Not just my mates from school, or my sister's from uni.'

'Where's Amy, Alan?'

'I dunno.'

'Don't you care? I thought you were pretty close?'

'We were. Till we got to Paris. Then I dunno what happened. She was hanging about with this guy she'd met on Facebook, which I'd expected, but he wanted her all to himself and, well, she liked that, she liked being the centre of his attention'.

I sat down opposite him on a swivel stool fixed to the deck, across the narrow, Formica-top table where the crew ate and, I supposed, drank and smoked and swapped stories and gang-banged the mess boy and watched television when near enough land to catch a signal and DVDs the rest of the time. Carson remained standing behind me, as did Wally.

I was feeling queasy. Though tethered to the dock, though well protected by the harbour, there was a slight movement, enough for me to realise we weren't on dry land and for my stomach to wish we were.

'When did you last see her?'

'In Paris. At the end of October. I was bored. Lonely.'

'So you got hooked into The Accord? For something to do? Because they took an interest? Because it's littered with other lonely people, some pretty lovely lonelies too, eh, Alan?'

'What're you talking about? What accord?'

'Alan, you were positively IDed at the Chapter house in Paris.' This was the only lie. 'You signed onto a ship that carries their wares through Europe; you came on board in Hamburg, the same day The Accord hierarchy - the seniors - were in Hamburg. Don't treat me like a fool. Better still, don't behave like one.'

He pondered this collection of putative coincidences for several moments before he asked:

'What accord?'

'You ever hear of someone called Donleavy, Alan?'

'I knew a bloke called Donleavy, back home, Patrick Donleavy, that who you mean?'

'Try Joe Donleavy, in Europe.'

'No. I've never heard of him. Can I go now.' It was a gesture of defiance, not a question.

'Is he Amy's Facebook friend?' I had not the first rational basis for asking this, yet I knew it; maybe I did have natural understanding after all.

'I said, I've never heard of him,' he hissed.

He was lying and a whole part of the plot fell into place. What did his father say? Too clever by half, takes the long way round, negatively 'interested in' me and Carson. I might not be able to use a computer much, but I'd heard what they could do. A story like Carson's left a trail easy to pick up; crumbs would include her uncle's family. He was using them to get at us. Using The Accord too, though I was not yet sure how.

'When did you leave Paris?'

'A few days ago. I hitched to Hamburg. Took me a while. Slept out one night. Nearly froze to death.'

'Passport?'

'Captain's got it. But it won't help. They didn't stamp it. They hardly ever do now.' The European Union; free movement of labour, the detective's worst enemy. Actually, as he wasn't an EU national, he ought not to have benefitted, but once within the community no one bothered anymore. 'Why does it matter?'

'Oh, well,' I flashed on a line I'd once heard a barrister keep using in court. He'd say, in order to disarm his cross-examination: 'Now, officer, it may not be important...' Then he would continue: 'But you weren't actually at the scene you've just described, were you?' So I said now:

'Oh, well, it may not be important, but I just wondered if you were still in Paris when your mother was murdered.'

I studied him closely, trying to ignore Carson's tightening grip on my shoulder. His expression was unfathomable. He bit down on his teeth, pulled his lips in against them, his hands clutched the coffee mug as if it was a lifeline, and his bulging eyes were fixed to mine with superglue. He could have been controlling his emotions - the way according to Carson butch Australian men are supposed to do - trying to take it in his stride, or perhaps he was making a bad job of trying to look shocked, or perhaps he was concealing either his glee or his guilt. What he said was:

'Very funny. Very funny, I don't think. My mother's in Australia.'

'You didn't see her in Paris?'

'What are you talking about? I said she's in Australia.'

'Why did you call me?'

'Amy said she'd been over.' He wouldn't refer to Carson by name.

'Where'd you get my number from, then?'

He flushed, but with embarrassment, not guilt.

'My mother wanted us to take it. She wrote it down for us. We told her we didn't want it. But Amy kept it anyhow.'

Carson leaned down and whispered in my ear. I brushed her away. I'd already got it. I said:

'And you didn't see your mother over there, right?'

'I've said,' he insisted.

'And you don't know Donleavy, and you don't know The Accord or anyone in it?'

He nodded.

'So how come you asked for me when you rang? You might've known she worked with me, but how come you asked for me at her home number? And how come when we came in here you referred to us as lovers, Alan? Where'd you get that bit of information from?'

This time, when he flushed, I didn't have to wonder what it meant.

* * *

Except for the leathery face and casual clothes, Captain Bynoe looked more like a businessman than a sailor: he was slightly balding but well-greyed, bespectacled, smooth shaven, about fifty-five years old, with a waist just beginning to thicken. He saw us in his cabin, the only private place he could be sure we wouldn't be interrupted.

Wally led.

'How did you come to sign on the Yavitch boy?'

'I had a message waiting for me in Hamburg, telling me he was coming, asking if I would sign him on.' Full co-operation was his by-word.

'From?'

'Felice Hayat,' he replied promptly.

'The Accord woman, right?' I checked, and spelled it out for Wally.

'That's right. I've been carrying their supplies for years, sometimes people, like this.'

'How come?'

'We're a small outfit. There's only this and the Geordie Princess left. When they pack up, we're finished. Everyone knows it; it makes it difficult to keep officers and crew, especially officers. I'll be alright. I've got a few bob put away; I wouldn't go on another ten years anyhow. We're local. What we do, when we've got spare capacity, we'll ring round customers - old customers, occasional customers – and offer them a good rate. That's how we first got to know them. Frank Morris sent us some business over the years; he's my solicitor, as a matter of fact. He said, oh, three, four years ago, he did some work for a religious foundation, a trust, an organisation, I can't remember exactly how he put it; they were a bit strange but harmless, I always thought. I never looked too closely. After that, they said, anytime I had spare, let Frank. They didn't always want it; they wanted it more from Europe to here, which is when they'd ask me first.'

'What're you carrying this time?'

'A couple of crates from their Hamburg church, house, what do they call it?'

'Segment.'

'Yes. C. & E. are looking at it now.' Customs and Excise.

'Who did you deal with there? Felice Hayat and who else? The boss man, Rupert de Villiers?' I asked.

'I never knew him. Didn't even know his name. They called him The Leader.'

'And what did you carry for them?'

'Just crates and people. They told me it was religious clothing and literature, things like that; some of their members. Understand, Sergeant, I don't really care what's inside a crate or a container. I'm not responsible. It could be drugs or guns or whatever. As long as it's sealed before it comes on board and delivered like that to Customs, it's not my responsibility. Long as I don't know. Likewise, as long as someone has a passport. Don't get me wrong, I would care if I knew anyone was doing anything wrong; I'm just telling it like it is for me, for any skipper, any shipper; we can't examine our own customers' goods, or their intentions, come to that.'

'You said Frank Morris was your personal solicitor. Did you do all these dealings through him personally?'

'Sometimes. Sometimes one of his staff.'

'Would that be Joe Donleavy?'

Wally cast me a glance. Tim had not - for reasons I well understood - briefed him on Donleavy. He didn't say anything, though.

'Yes. When Frank wasn't available. He would call me. He once came to see me about a load for The Accord.'

'With them?'

'No. After it was on board. Said he was in the area, thought he'd say hello, see if everything was alright.'

'Where was it going?'

'That load? I can't remember. I'd have to look it up in the office. No, I remember. Rotterdam for onward to the United States. Then I brought a load back here.'

There was a rap at the cabin door. A policeman poked his head inside and eyed Wally out. He left us for a moment, then returned, grinning.

'I think it's time we all went to watch some TV.'

* * *

We watched in the mess-room where Alan was still waiting to learn whether he was going to be released or arrested. He looked paler than before; I took it the news about his mother was beginning to sink in. I hoped so. I hoped it would incline him towards a little more candour.

A couple of Customs men were also waiting for us. There were introductions and handshakes all round. I was beginning to worry. I was on the side of the establishment this time, instead of against them, and it wasn't a comfortable feeling. One of them pulled the blinds and punched the remote. A DVD was already loaded, though there were more on the floor. Pardon me, the deck.

Once The Accord logo had flashed up on the screen, the Customs man started to fast forward. I asked him to give it a minute or two. Rupert's features filled the screen.

'Hello. I'm Rupert. I'm the spiritual leader of The Accord. Today I want to talk to you about violence. Violence. There is violence in all of us. There is violence in many of our actions and most of our thoughts at some point every day. There is violence even between ourselves and those we love. Why? Why do we feel we need violence in order to express ourselves, in order to communicate, in order, even, to love?'

I think that was the point I realised what was to come. I gestured for the officer to wind it on. Rupert continued to talk - at several times normal speed - for another few seconds before the officer took his finger off the button just as Rupert was saying:

'Is it perhaps the case that we need violence to love because we do not trust it, do not trust love, do not trust ourselves in love and with those we love?'

The camera pulled back so that, for the first time, we could see the location. It was either the meditation room in Paris or one very like it. Rupert was robed, as he had been that night. A door opened and he turned as if surprised. An Accord woman who I did not recognise but who could, I supposed, have been one of those of Dolly's ilk who had joined him on the rostrum during the meditation I had witnessed, entered the room. She said:

'Leader.'

Rupert's face was already turned away from the camera so that we could see only his back. The zoom closed in on the girl. At first, I had thought she was wearing a skirt and sweater or blouse - in dark green of course - but now I saw it was a single piece, which she pulled over her head un-self-consciously, wearing nothing beneath.

The girl knelt down in front of Rupert. Presumably he, too, had been naked beneath his robes. She licked his prick and took it into her mouth. The camera, which had moved round to the side for this candid cut, held steady - steadier than I could have held it - as she took it in deeper and deeper with each swallow. And then he was thrusting it into her, hard, violently, holding onto her hair and the back of her head as she struggled to breathe, to get it out of her mouth, thrusting harder and harder until I thought she was going to choke until she was doing none of the work, making no independent movements of her own, like a lifeless doll. He jerked her head to and fro until he roared and flung her backwards unconscious onto the floor face down, flinging himself after her and pumping into her from behind without break.

That was, as they say, just the beginning. It got worse. We watched the rest of it at double speed but there were still several faces I recognised, including Hiram. But none of the names I knew well, like Felice, Mercury, Sarah, Colin or Dolly. Not even Joab or Lois. The climax was a Satanic sacrifice. When I realised who was in it, I told the officer to wind it back and replay it at normal speed. I didn't even look at Alan as he watched himself riding the victim from behind, doggy style, buggering her, not even as he pulled her up by her head while someone - Rupert, we were intended to presume, as it was his cult and his movie - repeatedly thrust a dagger between her breasts. I didn't even have time to make out her face before it was covered with spurting blood, before Alan was... Rupert was... the screen was filled with it. Fadeout. End with Rupert talking shit again.

* * *

We had to hang around for an hour while the enforcement agencies argued jurisdiction. Because there was no longer any question of Alan being released, Wally asked me not to question him further until it was decided who had charge of him. We watched them debate. None of them was the least bit interested in the filmed events, let alone appalled by them. They just wanted the credit for the capture.

Customs and Excise wanted to keep him for smuggling, so that any other ensuing charges could also be laid to their credit. On the basis that I would get more out of the police than out of them, I pointed out that there was no legal connection between Alan and the smuggling activity. Just because he was in the movie, and it was now safe to assume in The Accord too, didn't give him responsibility for smuggling the porn. He was on board in another capacity. He had neither access to the crates nor responsibility for them, nor had he loaded them or picked them up. He had been questioned too soon, even if he was intended to deliver the DVDs somewhere, so that, to this extent, we had already spoiled their bust in favour of our own. They could, I conceded, keep Bynoe, who I was convinced was innocent and would walk away without more than a warning to be a bit more selective about his casual customers.

This led to a brief intermission while one of them went off to call their Legal Division, which I coincidentally knew was located just outside the Inns of Court in London. The grim-faced return made the grudging concession that I was correct almost superfluous. All that was left was for Wally to see off the Essex Constabulary, and though there is no theoretical authority on the part of Scotland Yard over other - quite independent at law - police forces, I could see from the outset that he would win his argument that they had been doing no more than lending him assistance, so that it remained his bust. So complete was his victory that he managed to persuade them to deliver Alan to Chelsea nick on his behalf.

I didn't bother asking why Chelsea. I knew that the Yard had no facilities for other than incidental incarceration, so he had to choose somewhere. And if he had, as he assured us as we left the ship, had quite enough for a while, and if he was, as we knew, living back in the Section House, where else would he want to go but to a certain drinking club on the Old Brompton Road, where he could booze and if he asked nicely even eat for free, and which was, as coincidence would have it, very near indeed to Chelsea Police Station.

He drove us back at record speed, enough to scare the shit out of me. We were all silent for the first few minutes, each re-examining our own reactions to what we had witnessed. There was one question we were all afraid to ask. Eventually, I did so:

'Well?'

Wally shrugged; the wheels wobbled, the car swerved, but we remained on the highway.

Carson said:

'It looked so terribly real. It's difficult to believe it wasn't. But it's just as difficult to believe that it was.'

'Appearances can be deceptive.'

'Yeah,' she snorted. 'Like you thought Rupert was alright. A weirdo, maybe, but alright.'

'So?'

'So that's your idea of alright? You're lucky I was on the other side of the table, Dave.'

'Personally I thought it was the earth moving,' Wally remarked non-consequentially.

'Shut up, Wal. This is between him and me.'

'He and I,' I murmured.

'What did you mean?'

'I meant, so what had happened to change your mind?'

'Yeah, that's what I thought you meant.'

The rate Wally was driving, the conversation was now about fifty miles back on the motorway.

I explained:

'It wasn't Rupert. None of it was Rupert except the opening and afterwards, which were entirely innocent. Remember the surprise on his face when the woman came in? That was genuine. After that, it's a cut-out.'

Carson asked:

'How do you know?'

Wally asked:

'How do you know?'

I said, face reddening:

'Ah, uh, that's something I can't really tell you. Just trust me on this one. It wasn't Rupert,' I repeated firmly.

* * *

It was after two in the morning when we got home after visiting the club and Natalie. We waited for Wally while he visited the police station and Alan, until he returned to the club to visit with Joannie and our presence proved not merely unnecessary but distinctly unwelcome.

Just before we dozed off to sleep, I asked Carson:

'What was that about? What Alan said, about not being that much of a kid?'

CHAPTER EIGHT

Tim came home from Hamburg, mission unaccomplished. There was live bait awaiting him in the person of Alan but not as much as we would all have wished. Felice Hayat and the remaining top structure of The Accord were in England for less than three hours, time only to cab to Gatwick and thence straight out to Boston, Massachusetts.

By the time Tim got back, Wally had secured a warrant on the group's London base and turned it over without result. There were only a couple of members in occupation at the time and nothing incriminating, not even a nude centrefold of Rupert. Whatever plans they had to expand had not progressed beyond the first stage: their landlords denied any knowledge of a wish to take over more of the building they occupied.

We briefed Tim fully on the interview with Alan and left him to enjoy the video alone. He let me sit in on his own interrogation of Alan, however, though not Carson because she was, he reminded us, the boy's first cousin. Rather than hang around the station, Carson went up to the office to let them know we were still alive even if not awfully active in the firm's affairs, and to explain to Ruth that when I'd said I'd either give up investigations or give up the firm, I really did mean it; it was just that I didn't mean it for now.

The evidence on which to hold, let alone charge, Alan was flimsy. If the woman in the video was English, and if she had really been attacked, he would have committed an offence wherever the movie had been made. If the scene had been shot in England, though there was no reason to believe it had been, he could at the least be prosecuted for buggery, whatever the woman's nationality, and if it could be shown that he had participated in the session for gain, or in knowledge that it was to be sold, he could also be susceptible to additional charges; the most serious charge would only follow if the ending was no act and he had known it was coming. For the time being, he was held at the ostensible request of Inspector Malthus of the *Sûreté*, in connection with May's murder, though there was likewise no hard evidence to link him to it and, personally, I didn't doubt his innocence in that matter.

Though Alan was still a youngster who had just spent a night in the cells reflecting on what he by then believed was his mother's death and on his now public participation in the film, he was still affecting the brashness of yesterday. But his face was translucent, his eyes bloodshot and he was shaky on his feet. Wally took the notes but no part.

Once the boy was seated, Tim asked:

'Did you sleep?'

'Not much.'

'Can you help us at all with the whereabouts of your sister? The French police are looking for her, to tell her about your mother.'

'I told him,' he gestured in Wally's direction. 'I told him everything I knew, all the names I know. I haven't seen her since soon after we arrived in Paris. I've only spoken to her on the phone. And I didn't have a number for her,' he added quickly. 'She always rang me.'

'Where? At The Accord?'

He shrugged then nodded. He could hardly continue to deny that connection.

Tim asked:

'How did she get your number there?'

'I dunno.' If he'd been on a polygraph, the needle would've left the sheet.

'Tell us about The Accord. How did you get involved?'

He glanced at the floor as if embarrassed or ashamed.

'It was pretty much what he said.' This time I was the target of a flick of his wrist. 'It was Donleavy we were going to meet up with; Amy and he had developed a thing through Facebook. We met him at the coffee lounge. He wasn't living in it but he had a lot to do with it. It all happened very quickly. Amy went to stay with him, I don't know where. I moved out of the hotel and into a rented apartment where a lot of them lived, people around The Accord, people maybe still deciding whether to go into it full-time or not. Outside members. I got with this girl there, the one in the film.' He flushed yet more fully. 'We went into it together.'

'What's her name, Alan, her real name?'

'Becky Vintner.'

'English?' Tim asked casually.

'Yes.'

'What happened in the film, Alan? What happened at the end?'

'You saw.' His face was by now red enough we could have switched off the solitary light by which the room was lit.

'I meant, was it real?'

He was shocked: it had not occurred to him we might think so. He shook his head vehemently.

'It was just an act, you know. I mean, alright, it was a pretty weird scene, but it wasn't all at one time, like it looks. It's put together from different scenes.'

'Where did it take place? The part you were in?'

'In Paris. In the Segment House.'

'When?'

'A few weeks ago.'

I interrupted to ask:

'While Rupert and Felice were away?'

'Right. Yes. He wasn't there when I was. I've seen the film the opening talk came from before. There's a few of them, teaching videos. They're used in the Segment Houses and they're available for sale. That's why, you know, when the Customs Officers started to look at the tape, I told them it was nothing, just religious talk. I was shocked when, well, you know. I don't know when the bits he was in were made.' He was taking for granted that it was Rupert.

'You knew you were being filmed?'

'Yes, of course. It wasn't the first time.'

'What was it for, then? What did you think it was for?'

He looked at the floor again and didn't look up. He mumbled something. Tim asked him to repeat it. None of us could make it out. He said:

'It was part of the teaching, you know. We had to act things out, bad things as well as good things.' It was consistent with some of what I'd been told. 'But I thought, well, it was for internal use only. Like, we'd seen other films, from elsewhere, from other Segments. They showed us one just before, I mean before the one you saw. Look, I know it all looks stupid and crazy, but you see, when you were inside, when it was all part of something else. When everyone took part, it didn't seem that way. Not at the time; not in context; not when they were telling you it was alright and everyone else believed them.' The crass psychology of just about every kind of weirdo group, sexual, religious or political - fascists, communists, Scientologists and social workers.

Tim shook his head in silent dismay.

'How regularly did these, uh, sessions take place? How much was sex a part of this, uh...' He hesitated, then concluded reluctantly. 'This...philosophy?'

'It was part of it,' Alan acknowledged with equal reluctance. 'I figure a lot of the people who got involved, they did it for the sex.'

'Like you?' He shivered. It wasn't an image of himself he enjoyed. He didn't answer. 'Why did you go to Hamburg?' Tim asked.

'I didn't know,' Alan said non-consecutively. 'I didn't know about the films. I didn't know how they were being used. I didn't know they were on that ship.'

'Why did you sign on?'

Again, he followed his own line of thought rather than Tim's direction.

'I knew, you know, there was a lot of in-fighting in The Accord. Some people, some of the older members, said there'd be a bust-up, that one was coming; I think they were preparing us for it.'

'Between Rupert and Felice Hayat?' I asked only my second question.

'Yes, that's right. They said it was inevitable, that it was necessary, a re-arrangement.'

'Did you know Colin Wrighton? Saul, his inside name was. Sarah?'

'I've met them. When they came back with The Leader, after New Year's.'

'They're dead,' Tim said flatly. 'Murdered.'

His eyes widened so far it seemed like he was trying to see out of his ears. Tim said:

'You're in a lot of trouble, Alan. I'm trying to help you. But you have to tell us everything you know. I can't help you otherwise. You're involved in something serious here, son.'

He nodded once to say he knew. He gulped.

'Could I have some water? Please.'

'Would you like some tea? Coffee?'

'Just water.'

Tim glanced at Wally, who went out to fetch a paper mug of tap water. None of us spoke during his absence. After Wally returned, Tim repeated:

'Why did you go to Hamburg?'

'Amy rang me; she said I should get out of it, get out of The Accord. She told me to go to England. She said she'd meet up with me here. I was going to leave the ship here.'

'Why not take the train from Paris?' Tim asked. Alan didn't answer. 'Did you take anything to Hamburg?' Same silence. 'Getting onto the ship, was that her idea?'

'Yes, that too, she told me I'd be able to get on board.'

'Why did she tell you to get out? How did she know you'd be able to get on board? What's her connection with The Accord? What's her connection with Felice Hayat? Who told you about Dave and Carson?'

Alan gnashed his teeth together. He was frightened, and who could blame him? His mother and two others had been whacked out, Rupert had turned out to be, so far as he currently believed, a porn-movie stud, his sister was who knew where doing who knew what and he himself was on General Public release as a small part player; he was in over his head. He took his time before responding.

'Can I see a lawyer? Please.'

* * *

For the second night running, Wally came to the club. I was there, too, avowedly to console Nat for the loss of Colin, mostly because I couldn't sit still at home or respond to Alton's incessant demands for attention. From the expression of smug delight on Joannie's face when he arrived, they'd bridged the gap the night before. While she worked, Wally confessed that he had spent what was left of it with her.

'It's really over, your marriage I mean?'

'It's better. She never really liked me being on the job. Ever since I've been working for Tim, she's been going on at me about it. Complaining I'm never there - which is true - that I'd rather be working with him than at home.'

'Was that true?'

'It became true'. Self-fulfilling prophecies.

'And Joannie? How much was she a part of it?'

'I'd like to think not much, but, well, who can say.'

Without asking, he extracted one of my Camels from the pack I'd left lying out on the table and took a deep draught of his beer.

'What do you think, Wal?'

'About this mess?'

'Mm.'

'I don't know. I don't know about the kid. There's feelers out all over Europe for the sister, the Donleavy boy, this Rupert chappie and his woman. The Americans are looking for Hayat. I'm not sure how it puts together.' I noted that he passed over Joe Two at a pace that suggested he hadn't put one and one together.

Natalie came to fetch me.

'There's a call for you, Dave.'

It was Leahy, Donleavy's father, calling from his car outside on the Old Brompton Road. I apologised to Wally and left the club - without offering any explanation - to go and talk to my client.

* * *

He flashed the lights twice then drove slowly around the corner into Bina Gardens while I followed on foot. He double parked while he waited for me to catch up, ideally placed for a quick take off, which is what he did almost before I'd shut the passenger door behind me and well before I'd strapped on the seat belt. He didn't say anything until we were heading west towards the Chiswick roundabout, then asked only:

'Well?'

'I don't know, Leahy, but I've got some ideas.'

He grunted and waited for me to elaborate. I was still turning over in my mind how much to tell him when he pulled into a dark road behind some industrial units and parked so close to the wire-mesh fencing behind them that I wouldn't be able to open my door.

'Well?' he repeated.

I laid out for him the slice of information I had obtained from the girlfriend in Newcastle: that he was close to some of his clients; that he had an unexpected and unexplained interest in Blyth; and that he sometimes handled shipping for a nutty, pseudo-religious outfit called The Accord, possibly along with other affairs of theirs.

'What's that?'

'One of these cult things.'

'Not my boy. His mother brought him up a Catholic. He wouldn't have anything to do with that sort of thing.'

'I don't believe in coincidence a whole bunch, Leahy. I go to Blyth, see some of these creeps clambering on board the Geordie Queen; next thing I know, they're all over Paris; next thing I find out, their solicitors are the firm your boy was working at.'

'What has Paris got to do with it?' He was growing gloomier by the minute; knowing how much more there was to come, I was almost feeling sorry for him.

I told him next about Carson's aunt coming to see us, the missing cousins and the Facebook arrangement, how May's body had been found and how Alan had turned up in a feature-movie made at and by The Accord, which was hidden inside - literally - a teaching DVD.

'Joe? Was he in this?' Leahy had turned about as red as had Alan that morning. It didn't surprise me: the man was a prude.

'No, not that I saw. I don't think so.'

'What then?' What did I think?

'I'm thinking it's what you said - that it's about us. But I'm not sure how - I'm pretty sure he was using The Accord to get at us but I'm not sure how. You know what you said, about gaming and complicated routes to an end - that's what it fits, but I haven't managed to work it out yet. I don't think I've identified all the pieces, all the players, that's why'.

'What about the mother?'

'I could go either way with it. After May went missing, Carson came back here - maybe he had no further use for her.'

'You're saying he killed her?'

I shrugged.

'You said he wasn't a killer. Then there's the other thing that doesn't fit: Colin and Sarah.'

'Who're they?'

I back-tracked to Natalie and fast-forwarded through Val to the *Bois de Boulogne*, concluding:

'I can't see how they connect to your son.'

'It must be another player,' he said confidently.

'Are you saying that because you don't want to think, uh, that...?' I let the question tail away; he knew what I meant - that his son was the author of all the deaths.

'No. I saw what I saw in him, I told you that. It scared me enough to pull you in. This seems like something else and it scares me worse.'

If it scared Joe Leahy, it had to terrify me.

'Who, then?' I asked.

'That's the question.' He paused for thought. 'I don't understand people like this.' The Accord. 'Tell me what you think of them.'

'I think The Accord's pretty weird. At the least, it's a vehicle for manufacturing, transporting and selling porn.'

'I don't get that,' he admitted. 'It's easy, open, available everywhere.'

'Not as easy as you think, not all of it. You have to find people and locations, especially actors - they're expensive, at any rate for the way-out stuff, and this was pretty way-out. They've got a neat way to find actors who they don't have to pay and who're a damned sight fitter and cleaner and healthier looking than the junkies who're usually available for this sort of thing - neat, fresh, middle class, could-be college kids - and they've got the locations, and they've even got their own theme. I mean,' I admitted in exchange, 'it was pretty sharp stuff, the whole linkage between the opening, which was this serious talk by the cult's leader, and the substance, added a whole dimension of fantasy brought to reality. Like,' I hesitated: 'Like it gave it a veneer almost of reasonableness, anyway not something the viewer had to be ashamed of.'

'These films.' He pronounced it 'fil-ums'. 'You think this is all they're into?' He was gloomy again; I could almost feel sorry for him; he knew somewhere, deep in his heart, if he had one, that his son had crossed a line, even if he wasn't sure which.

'I don't know. There may be other stuff; the skipper talked about people signing on and off his ship, so that may be something else. But as I say, I just don't know yet.'

* * *

Carson was still up when I got home. She had been drinking on her own, which was unusual, but only white wine, which wasn't. I kissed her lightly on the lips and went upstairs to kiss my sleeping son before trotting back down to join her with a Southern Comfort for myself. I gave her a brief résumé of my encounter with Joe Leahy.

'He gave me your gun back, by the way: I put it in the study.' Where I also kept my own souvenir of our previous association with him. She shrugged indifferently. 'He's going to see Morris,' I concluded. 'Thinks he may be able to get something out of him,' I added, meaning she knew exactly what I meant.

'And you're not going to warn him?' she asked dully.

'No, I'm not going to warn him. Nor Tim.'

'Why not?'

'What do you want, Carson? Leahy behind bars, from where he'll find a way to reach out to us, and sweet fuck-all resolution of what's going on between The Accord and your family and his son? Because that's what it'll get us: a life sentence of worrying about our backs.'

'Some of us already do,' she said moodily.

'What's up, Cars? Is this about Alan's crack yesterday?'

'I don't know what you mean; I don't know what he meant. He hates me, you know that, you know why,' she complained petulantly and unconvincingly.

'Do I? Do I know why?'

She sat upright on the sofa:

'I don't want to fight, Dave. I'm frightened, that's all. I'm frightened of what's happening. It's close, too close, closer even than Orbach.' When we'd suffered a similar threat of a life-long sentence of fear. 'What's our next move?'

'Wait and see, I should think. We've got to wait and see who the police pick up, where and what for. I take it Tim didn't ring?'

'No. I had a chat with Sheila. He was still out. He'd only rung to say he'd be late.' It would be more economical if he rang those evenings he planned to return before midnight.

As if he'd been listening in the wings, the door-bell rang and I knew it was going to be him even before I switched on the outside lamp and looked through the peephole. I left him to shut the front door behind him, muttering that it was a fine time to come calling. He followed me to the living room, tossed his head at Carson and helped himself to a glass and the bottle of Southern Comfort. Finally, he spoke:

'Ice?'

'Fridge,' but I went to get it for him.

He sprawled out in the armchair in which I had been sitting, so I went and sat with Carson on the sofa, carelessly draping an arm around her shoulders. She snuggled closer as we waited to be told to what we owed the visit.

'We're going to let the boy go.'

'Why?' Carson was shaken.

'Nothing to hold him on?' I assumed.

'Mostly; he's got a lawyer now. The Yanks found Hayat and have been interviewing her and some of the others. They're frankly admitting that some of The Accord sessions have involved sex: apparently, and I believe this as little as you're going to, sex is prohibited for long periods, and then they engage in group sex as a sort of ritual coming together, pardon the pun, which isn't quite what the boy told us but the difference isn't worth a damn. Anyway, they're saying it's your friend Rupert's set up and when they found out what he was doing with the films they booted him out of the group, and since Val d'Isère they've been going round the Segments in order to explain to the members why.'

'But...' I protested.

'But what, Dave? But you say it isn't Rupert. You still haven't told us how you know.' He was close to smirking: he had his own idea and I didn't think it was a million miles from the truth.

'What about the boy? Getting him onto the ship?'

'She says it wasn't her. Denies knowing the sister, so there's another contradiction we could try to exploit, but it's minor, not enough to hold anyone on.'

'They're not holding them either,' I muttered, meaning the Americans.

'Nope.' He glugged his drink and poured himself another. 'I had a chat with the detective on the case. We agreed; it was too early, we didn't have enough.'

'It was your decision to let Alan go?' Carson asked, surprised and angry. 'I thought you meant the lawyers.'

'No, it was me. I think we'll get more out of him if he's out than in. Obviously, we're going to keep a close watch on him. As they are on her.'

'And May? What about May?' She was as near hysterical as I'd ever heard her. 'Are you all going to just forget about her?'

'That's Malthus' problem,' Tim said dourly. 'But I'm sure he'll keep us informed.'

I frowned. It wasn't that I didn't like what Tim had done: I might have done the same. It was more that it was becoming clear that he wasn't fully levelling with us, that he'd gone back to his old way of working with me, holding something back, usually in order to manipulate me into doing something he couldn't himself properly do, of which he would, in the end, be able to take lawful advantage. I thought we'd gotten beyond that, to a level of trust where - if needs be - he would ask me outright. I asked slowly:

'How much of this is to do with Leahy?'

'Who's Leahy?'

* * *

I decided to work from a new angle. I went back to Paris. Before I even found a hotel for the night, I returned to the Segment House. It was half-deserted. The remaining few put on a brave face, but there could be no doubt that the split at the top had caused a chasm all the way down to the bottom. For example, Lois had quit, according to Dolly, with whom I was granted an audience by a reluctant but not yet sufficiently authoritarian Hiram.

I was gentle with her. The traces of brashness that had marked our last encounter had faded. She was even more of a kid than Alan. And she was prettier. I said:

'You know about Saul and Sarah, don't you.'

It wasn't a question: they had all been interrogated by Malthus' men.

'I don't know anything; I don't understand anything.' She looked around the coffee lounge, worried who might be listening. 'I'm frightened. What if it happens again? It could be any of us.'

'When did you see them last?'

'After the Meditation. You were there. Everyone was there. We had a party afterwards, we always do.'

'What sort of party?'

'Just a party.'

'Dolly. I know about the DVDs. I've seen one.'

Across the table, she seemed visibly to shrivel:

'That's not possible. You're not a member.'

'You've taken part, haven't you? You've taken part in a sex scene.' I knew this for sure. 'A scene which has been filmed, haven't you?' Which I didn't.

She took a long time before answering, her voice as tiny as a school-child trying to guess the correct solution to a problem she hadn't prepared for in her homework.

'Yes.'

'With Rupert? I mean on film.' She had already admitted she slept with him.

'No. He would never...'

'But Felice would.'

'You don't understand,' she cried petulantly. 'Rupert was good; Felice was supposed to represent bad.'

Finding calm in familiar dogma, she explained:

'There are different elements in all of us. Everybody is more one thing than either of the others, though we've all got bits of each. It's the combination of the elements, across different people, that dictates what happens. It was Felice's...' She searched for the right word. 'It was her job to do things like that, just as it was The Leader's to keep it all together. Do you see? By being all ways within The Accord, we had a perfect balance. Do you see?' she repeated.

I did and I didn't. As when Sarah and Colin had given me their explanation, it had overtones I could relate to intellectually, although only objectively, not personally. It was faintly reminiscent of the crude definition of psychoses and neuroses, elements of which are said to be present in each of us.

The theory - as I have understood it - goes that a psychotic believes in the primacy of his own perceptions as against those of the outside world, while a neurotic accepts the primacy of the outside world and is struggling to suppress his own impulses so as to accord with it. I'm not sure if it was intended as a compliment or not, but someone once told me I was the only person he had ever met who was exactly equally psychotic and neurotic. I also don't know if he was right, but it would explain a lot. What was right, though, was that any and all of these theories - within reason - can strike a chord and find a degree of response in most people, especially the young and questful.

'When your father was here, did he meet both Rupert and Felice?'

'Just Felice, I think.'

'Where? Here? In the Coffee Lounge?'

'No. In her own room.'

I wasn't thinking she might've seduced him, but he was a man of some influence and blackmailing him for future use was a different matter. I thought out loud:

'Colin - Saul - and Sarah were with you in Val d'Isère. Felice and Rupert argued when they were there. The only other people there were Mercury and you. Right?'

'You know that. It was a Christmas holiday party.'

'And we had a party, when I was there. Right?'

She was too scared to play any more games.

'Yes, sort of.'

'What do you mean sort of?'

'You watched for a bit then passed out. You didn't really take part. We pretended with you, just a bit. But really it was just us, doing our own things.'

I let out a sigh of relief. She'd said 'passed out' rather than 'blacked out'; if you pass out, nothing happens except dreams; if you black out, anything can have happened but you don't remember. I'm an expert in such matters, though I doubted she knew the difference.

'Was it being filmed?'

'I don't know. I don't think so. It was private.'

'Then why were they trying to involve me?'

'I think...' She hesitated, then continued nervously: 'I think Rupert liked you.'

'Liked me? Sure, I know he liked me.' Then I understood what she was saying. 'He swings both ways?' Well, I knew that: I'd seen him with Colin; I had never thought that was hallucination. 'He liked me,' I repeated, grasping the nettle.

I'd thought he was pretty weird before. Now I knew he was barking mad.

'She did too,' she murmured.

'Oh, great, me and my body beautiful.' I assumed she meant Felice but it might as well have been Mercury. I decided that, for once, I was better off not knowing.

She struggled to explain; as I'd remarked before, she wasn't stupid.

'Most of us, in the group, we're young. Younger than them. It's…it's not a challenge; they know so much more than us. Like Saul: that's why they took to him, too, that's why they brought him to Val. He was the same as you, older, more experienced, like…' She looked around for something different but did not find anything: 'Like, more of a challenge.'

'The rest of you, you're easy meat?'

'That doesn't make them wrong. It doesn't make it wrong. It doesn't make us wrong.'

'No, but it doesn't explain why you let it happen to you, though.'

'I told you,' she whispered. 'It's been the best time.'

I reached across the table and took both her hands in mine.

'Dolly, Dolly. You're a beautiful girl. You're bright. You've got so much potential. Why don't you go home? Go home to your father, Dolly.'

Her eyes were filled with tears.

'I don't know where he is.'

'I can find him. I will find him. I promise, I'll find him and send him to get you. Will you go with him?'

'I don't know,' she whispered. 'I don't know anything anymore.'

Half-formed minds, half-formed wills. They took them, hooked them into something larger, mysterious, beyond their control and their grasp, and drained them until they had nothing left but to cling on for dear life, knowing nothing on the outside could make sense of what they had become within the group.

It was the way of all cults.

* * *

I didn't stay at the Hotel Screw You. I wasn't a masochist. I stayed instead at the hotel at which Carson had lodged with Auntie May, the *Hotel Saint-Germain-des-Prés*, with three stars vastly superior to the other's four. Before I left Dolly, I showed her the photograph of Joe Donleavy. She admitted he looked familiar but insisted that he was not - to her knowledge at any rate - a member of The Accord, and couldn't for the time being place where she had seen him.

'It might just have been out bestowing,' she apologised.

'And these two?'

'That's Esau,' she said of Alan. 'Who's she?'

'His sister. Have you never seen her?'

'No. I'm don't think so. She's beautiful,' she said wistfully, as if she didn't know that she was too.

Finally, I tried a picture of May, who she also failed to recognise. Even with the half-hearted identification of Donleavy Minor, I had secured nothing I didn't know already.

I checked into the hotel and called Tim at his office. I told him to use his contacts to try and track down an American government employee called Demonica and laid the blackmail theory on him. Though he was at first dismissive, once he thought about the sort of people who might find themselves in

The Accord he accepted that it might add a new dimension and an extra source of income.

'And protection,' I reminded him.

'That too. What do you want from Demonica?'

'Whatever you can get, plus tell him to go get his daughter out of there. I think she'll leave with him.'

'Why not have Malthus deport her?'

'He won't let any of them leave the country. If Demonica works for the US government, he might have the clout.'

'Why do you want her out?'

'I like her. She's a victim, Tim, not a player. Besides, I owe her.'

'For what?'

'For explaining something that's been bugging me. I'll, uh, tell you when I get home. It's not important.'

I could hear his silent derision cross the Channel down the telephone line and land like a mortar with a whoosh and a thump in my ear.

'Have you checked in with Malthus yet?'

'Nope. I will. How's Alan doing?'

'Staying in a hotel near your club.'

That wasn't suspicious: there were plenty of hotels near my club, and many of them not too pricey.

'Paying how?'

'Cash.'

'But he didn't have enough to go to England from Paris?'

'Or didn't want to come in through a regular point of entry.'

'What's he doing with his time?'

'Sightseeing. That's all. He hasn't been near anyone or anywhere.'

'What about The Accord's London place?'

'It's just a couple of rooms in the basement of an office-building. He hasn't been there.'

'Does he know you're following him?'

'He might. I've got good men on it, but if I was him I'd make the assumption, at least for a while. I'll call the States, try and get a line to this Demonica, let you know.'

In accordance with our custom, we hung up on each other without any of the costly courtesies.

* * *

As instructed, I told Malthus I was back in town. He didn't seem thrilled. He didn't offer to meet me for a drink as he had done when I was with Carson, but agreed to see me the next morning. I was bereft of company for the evening and fast running out of ideas. Colin Wrighton was on my mind. The more I thought back on him, he didn't even fit as an Accord recruit. Natalie had accepted his desertion of her for the tender loving arms of The Accord with equanimity, but that had more to do with her eagerness to see the back of him. I called her at the club and waited patiently for Joannie to fetch her.

'How long did he say he'd been with Burger King?'

'I don't know. What's it matter?' She didn't want to be reminded of him. 'Not long, now you mention it.'

'Did you ever see him at Burger King, ring him there?' He'd claimed to be working out of the main London office: management training.

'No, not really. I only saw him once in any sort of working context.'

'At that catering exhibition?'

'Right.'

'Which is where you think he met The Accord people?'

'I think that's what he said. Honestly, Dave, I wasn't paying much attention at the time. It wasn't what I had on my mind.'

'Okay, don't worry. I'll see you.'

I could also recall the look of horror on Colin's face in Val d'Isère, when I'd watched him being fucked by Rupert. At the time, I'd put it down to pain, or the natural embarrassment of anyone caught quite so clearly in the act, unnatural or not. Now I was focusing on him, the embarrassment seemed excessive. I called Tim back, but he'd already left for the day. I would have to wait until tomorrow to see what Malthus knew about Colin. By then, he ought to have a full profile.

Meanwhile, I reconciled myself to eating alone. As I'd suggested to Carson, I went to *L'Alsace à Paris*. It was a shame it was too cold to eat in the courtyard outside, as I'd done when I'd been in Paris years before. The streets of Paris are an entertainment in themselves; it would have been as good as watching TV while I ate. I gulped Alsace lager and scoffed oysters laden with tabasco just for the hell of it and because Carson had done so, but I got less enjoyment out of them than usual.

I was about to leave when they arrived, she leading him by the hand, he looking confused - like someone had fetched Christ down from the cross and was pulling him away through the crowd long before the resurrection was due - both of them every bit as hauntingly, magnetically attractive as I remembered, though perhaps not as impeccably turned out. She scanned the room determinedly until her eye alighted on me, then she crossed over, still pulling him along after her, and they settled into a pair of chairs opposite me.

'I'm supposed to be looking for you, not the other way around,' I complained. 'How'd you find me here?'

'We saw you leaving the Segment House this afternoon.'

'From inside or out?' I asked Mercury, since Rupert seemed to have lost his voice entirely.

'Outside.'

'Why didn't you approach me then?'

Rupert said sadly:

'We didn't want any of them to see us. You took a taxi.'

'So how'd you find me here?' I repeated. 'In the restaurant.'

'I remembered you talking about it, in Val d'Isère.' His eyes widened greedily. 'Did you eat all those oysters by yourself?'

'Yeah, sure. You're hungry, I imagine. It's an expensive city and you haven't got any money left, have you?'

'Not much,' Mercury admitted. 'We'll get it back.'

'The money or The Accord?'

Rupert brightened visibly, flicking his hair back from his forehead with the tips of his fingers.

'The Accord. It's the only thing that matters.'

'And a meal, like, uh, now? On me?'

The band played 'Do you really need to ask'. It wasn't a contest. They exchanged a token glance before nodding enthusiastically in unison.

At least I now had someone with whom to eat dinner.

CHAPTER NINE

It was all darker, much, much darker than I had thought, so dark it wasn't surprising I hadn't spotted the players hidden in the shadows or read the secret script. Porn was just part of it: they were into people trafficking, drugs, moving money about, anything and everything you could hide in open sight in a cult so weird that nothing looked odd. When you had access to hundreds of passports for every age, sex and weird demeanour, there was no better way to move people between countries; if you had explainable access to small cargos loaded onto pallets, how easy to move bales of cash or hide tabs and tablets; if you had friends in low places, they would be sure to deal with anyone who got in their way.

Donleavy was not a killer; that didn't mean he'd mind if someone else did the deed for him. His revenge - sought the long and complicated way round - was to use Carson's family to suck us in to The Accord where others would take care of us for him. It was at least as clever as his father had said he was; it was as bold a manoeuvre as ever I had encountered, even at Orbach's hands. It was also dangerous: he was using The Accord for his own purposes when it was designed to be used for others who were far, far tougher than he.

* * *

Amy was in my hotel room when I returned alone and not a little bit lonely for it.

She was every bit as beautiful as in the photograph I had seen of her and her brother Alan. For the first time, I could see the resemblance to her mother May. They had a lot in common. Time does that: time and circumstance.

She was not tall, but because she was so precisely proportioned it took a moment to realise it. Her legs seemed longer than they really were, her breasts fuller, her body lithe, her skin smooth, her dark locks rich, her face a study in perfection.

I have omitted to mention that she was naked and lying stretched out on my bed, on top of the covers instead of beneath the sheet, the weather notwithstanding.

I have also omitted to mention that she was dead. Small wonder she reminded me of her mother.

* * *

When I made the offer to feed them, I had initially meant us to remain at *L'Alsace*. That way, they could eat solids while I could continue the nourishment that has kept me going longer and more contentedly than daily vitamins, veganism, plastic sandals and a rigidly controlled protein intake. Looking at them across the table, robbed of their institution and their authority, sensing their desolation, I wanted to do something special for them, something that told them not merely that I was not their enemy but that I was positively their friend, something that would diminish the fraught fear that all who have ever tasted success, power, wealth or mere happiness have to live with and that is captured in the old saying 'How are the mighty fallen'.

'Feel up to a walk first?'

They weren't in a position to argue: it was my treat. I called for the bill, checked *l'addition*, and led them out to the street.

I clocked the location and followed my feet, pushing through the noisy, young, ill-kempt, multicultural, colourfully-dressed gathering on the streets outside, hoping they were keeping up. Where I had in mind was a restaurant Carson and I had noticed but not eaten in, not far from the hotel on the *Boulevard Haussmann*, to be exact on the *Place de l'Opéra*. I didn't tell them where we were going, mostly because I could not recall the name of the restaurant, nor even that it was - as we were to discover - located in the Grand Hotel.

It took far longer to reach than I had anticipated. I've remarked how small Paris is, but I forget that it doesn't mean that to go from one place to another is like crossing the village green, and I also forget how very hard the streets are on the feet. I told them only:

'I've got a nice restaurant in mind. This area - Left Bank - too many people who know you might see us.'

They smiled at me and at one another. I realised something else that was going on. They were - for the first time, probably - doing something every other couple in love does: enjoying walking, hand in hand, without responsibilities, just being together as an end in itself. I'm not sure they realised what was going on themselves. One the one hand, they still wanted to get their group back, The Accord. On the other, and perhaps because they had only recently been ousted, they weren't yet ready to admit that it was probably more of a relief than a disaster. Like a bad relationship that breaks up just too soon, when all attention is on its recovery and it is impossible to recognise that beneath the despair and the anguish lurks that same, secret suspicion that it is far more for the best.

We didn't talk much as I led the way across the *Pont Saint Michel*, along the *Boulevard du Palais*, and then the *Pont au Change*, to reach the Right Bank via the *Île de la Cité*, beneath the portals of *Saint Chapelle*, perhaps all of us - notwithstanding our varying degrees of familiarity with the city - overawed by the luscious architecture. From there, we passed the silent, sleeping shacks of the *Châtelet* flower market before crossing the green dominated by the spot lit *Tour Saint Jacques* to turn left along the famous *Rue de Rivoli*, soon reaching the enclosed, arched pavement, the other side of the road from the *Louvre*, with its mixture of - now closed - garish tourist shops selling t-shirts, Kodak film, tourist videos of Paris and its environs, photographs from the banal to the baroque, and expensive, fashion-name boutiques with clothing that cost enough to bring up an Ethiopian baby from birth to an adulthood of penury or armed revolt. Somewhere around the *Palais Royal* my instincts twitched and I swung vaguely right up a broad avenue that, when I saw the street sign, told me I was heading for the bullseye: *Avenue de l'Opéra*.

The restaurant was where I thought it was. It was one of *Les Restaurants de la Paix*: the *Café de la Paix* and the *Restaurant Opéra*. We had crossed from the fifth to the ninth *arrondissement*. I noticed as we approached it a certain tension creeping into Rupert's stride, because we were for a while moving in the general direction of the quarter where The Accord was, which superficially contradicted my suggestion that *L'Alsace* was too vulnerable a location for a lengthy talk. Pride prevented him from saying anything, and I suspect he was relieved he had not done so as I led them not into the café but into the grand, high-ceilinged, old-fashioned restaurant itself where the tuxedoed staff outnumbered the customers and there were more *maitre d's* than choices on the menu or silverware on the tables.

'*Monsieur?*'

'Hi,' I said. 'We'd like to eat. Just the three of us.'

Fortunately, though Mercury's and Rupert's wardrobe reflected their current want of resources, I had dressed - for me - relatively neatly for my night on the town. I was a walking advertisement for Timberland, and I don't mean the shoes alone. As I handed my jacket to the hostess, I took out my wallet and cigarettes, and, about as subtly as Saddam Hussein exhorted his population to allow themselves to be bombed into ignominy, ostentatiously checked to make sure my brand new credit card was to hand. American Express Platinum was still rare enough to cause favourable comment in the occasional store, and familiar enough from its long-established American sibling that no restaurant or hotel was going to turn its owner away. Carson was pissed off: I had a choice of supplementaries - another Platinum at the same annual fee I had to pay, or a Supplementary Gold at ten per cent of the cost which is what she got.

They looked around them in ill-concealed delight. Then Rupert, understanding what I had done, said:

'You've done us proud.'

'That was the idea.'

'Why?'

'If I've got to eat two meals in one evening, the second one's gotta be good?'

'No, that's not it.'

'Dolly. She said you liked me. I felt that in Val d'Isère. Let's say it's reciprocal. Let's say there's few enough who do that I can't afford to ignore them when they come around.'

Mercury, considerably the more cynical of the two, interjected:

'Felice quite liked you too, in her own twisted way. You going to bring her here to eat?'

'I doubt it. She comes back to Paris, the first place she's going to eat is the *Préfecture*.'

Without awaiting our order, they brought us each a small platter of pastries.

'Which is not where we're eating,' Rupert reminded me there was no ostensible reason for me not to have belled *le bon* Malthus.

'You don't order, you don't eat,' I mumbled, suddenly embarrassed by my own generosity.

Whatever the origins of my instinct to treat them regally, I was about to enjoy the rewards. Notwithstanding the dozen oysters I had eaten at *L'Alsace à Paris*, largely forgotten by my stomach during the unaccustomed exercise between the two restaurants, this was one of the best meals I ever ate. I abstained from another starter, but encouraged them to indulge themselves. He had an ensemble of eggs and seafood. She had a salad of similar orientation. For main course, I always find it difficult to resist lamb and my eyes and stomach darted in unison on *carré d'agneu Sisteron au basilic, courgettes fleurs farcies*, while they demonstrated their own brand of harmony - and hunger - with the beef dish for two: *côte de boeuf grillée ou poelée a la moëlle*.

There was only one thing to drink with it, and a magnum was the size I ordered from the youngest *sommelier* I could recall ever encountering in a first-class restaurant. He had earned his credit: he poured as it is supposed to be poured, holding the bottle from the bottom without touching the neck.

Once we had settled into the meal, Rupert - with frequent interruptions from his paramour - told me about it.

* * *

The group had its origins, of a sort, in Scientology. It had evolved from Scientology not in a derivative sense so much as by way of reaction to a philosophy and a discipline that the original members of The Accord viewed as in equal parts oppressive and repressive. I knew - and know - little about Scientology, and want to know less. I can recall a time when I could not pass its shop-front on the Tottenham Court Road without a - usually bespectacled - young man or woman asking whether I had time for a 'personality test'. I invariably replied that there was nothing there to test and went testily on my way.

Others, I suppose - students, visitors, tourists, local office workers or shoppers - would take anything that cost them nothing and filled some time, provide them with some company and persuade them they really were a lot more interesting, worthwhile and dynamic than their mothers had allowed them to believe. Last time I passed, it was still there, proving that nothing could dry up the supply of cult-fodder.

I don't like organisations on principle, and I like those which prey on human weakness, insecurity and feelings of inadequacy least of all. Mostly, probably, because I have at times of my life been vulnerable to all of the above. But I'm a core conservative at heart. If I could get by - as I did at that time in my life - on booze and cigarettes, drugs, decadence and short-term borrowing, I didn't see why everyone else couldn't do so too.

This principle had made me approach The Accord with similar heady contempt and cynicism, and everything I had learned about it reinforced my prejudice. Liking Rupert and Mercury was a different matter altogether. I didn't know what they had done with and in The Accord, and I doubted I would think much of it if I did. That didn't stop me liking them, nor did it stop me believing that maybe - just maybe - their intentions were, when Rupert established the outfit, more honourable than otherwise.

Which is more or less what he told me.

'I didn't want anything to do with Scientology myself, but Felice was interested in it. I'm not sure that's quite the right word. Captivated by it, I think. I had come out of the army, oh, about two years before. I was finding it difficult to settle down. Qualities such as leadership - which is the essential thing you learn in the army - were no longer in demand, admired or even respected.'

'How did you meet Felice?'

'At a party. My younger brother was in advertising. Advertising, pop music, the arts, drug dealers, bread-heads as we used to call them, publishers, fashion-designers, they all mingled freely. The beautiful people. She was a fashion-designer of sorts, though after one brief season of success she didn't have anything new going for her. She had been married, to a black American baseball player. It had turned sour. It wasn't even supposed to work. It was...' He struggled for the right word, which Mercury supplied.

'It was a joke,' she said flatly.

'That's right. In someone else, it might have been called a protest or a gesture, but Felice was above either: it was a joke. She gave the impression of coming from a wealthy family: remember her claim that she skied in Val when she was young?'

I didn't remind him that in fact it had been his claim on her behalf.

'Actually, her mother was in service with a wealthy French family who owned a chalet outside Val, and that's when she learned to ski, with the children of the family. That and other, similar experiences gave her a taste for the high life, for wealth, for power too. But she never concentrated on anything, not for long.'

Mercury sneered.

'As long as each fuck took.'

'I, uh, get the impression you and Felice don't quite get along,' I said.

'Oh, well,' she drawled, examining a chunk of beef on the end of her fork for dramatic effect: 'I don't go down on snakes either.' She shoved the meat into her mouth and snapped her teeth down on it so loudly for a moment I thought one of them had broken.

Rupert laughed.

'Mercury doesn't mince her food or her words.'

I shuddered; I was glad she hadn't gone down on me either.

He continued his tale.

'Felice stayed in the States for a while after that. She was involved - and I do mean involved, closely - with some extremely insalubrious types: gangsters, mobsters, that sort of thing. Then she came back to Europe. I don't really know why we got together. Yes, alright,' he hastened to beat Mercury to the punch. 'She was sexy, not just good-looking but incredibly sexy. And I was bored, and perhaps a little lonely, and I was, compared with most of the people around that scene at that time, a little different. I should have explained: my family have money. Money wasn't the problem; I was the oldest; I had a private income.'

'Had is right,' Mercury said. 'It's all in The Accord now.'

'We'll get it back.'

'Will you?'

'I think so. The Accord is incorporated in the United States as a religious charity, but I never covenanted my income to it there; in England, though I diverted the money to it, it has no legal personality so probably I can stop it. You're a lawyer, what do you think?'

'I think you need a lawyer,' I told him. 'I mean, like, one who can read. You think I do investigations because I'm good at law?'

'I think you do them because they're a way of doing good, and because you're good at them.'

I started to protest, but Mercury, seated next to me, took my hand.

'Let it go, Dave,' she was recovering her style and her humour with my champagne. 'You can afford to let an insult get by you once in a while.'

I batted my eyelids.

'Promise not to do it again.'

Rupert ignored us.

'Felice had a friend - a woman friend - who was involved with Scientology. She was another divorcée - dismal, depressed, intermittently suicidal. It was doing good things for her. Well, things that seemed good at the time. But they were heavily into segregation, getting their members to congregate only with one another, building up a strong membership unshakeably committed to Scientology - to L. Ron the Hubbard man. Did you know Hubbard had a lot of connections back to the

American fifties, the beat poets and writers, through Burroughs, William S. Burroughs?'

'Vaguely,' I murmured. Burroughs had enjoyed a revival not too long ago to have forgotten. Sheer physical survival over a long period of time - against odds greater than those I had struggled with - had bestowed on him a literary status that defied my comprehension.

'Anyway, this friend - I can't even remember her name now - wanted Felice to go with her to a Scientology meeting. There was an implied threat of disconnection and Felice figured she at least owed it to her to take a look. Anything new was of definition interesting to Felice.'

'Where were the two of you at by then?'

'Living together. We didn't get married until well after we'd established The Accord. It was convenient - she was American, I am English, it allowed us to develop on both sides of the Atlantic.'

We finished the main course and they brought the desert menu. I couldn't do it to myself but ordered another bottle of champagne - single - instead. I don't know how she kept her figure if this was normally how she ate, but Mercury had a fruit tart on an almond base and even Rupert graciously accepted a bowl of fruit salad. They also graciously shared my champagne. I was surprised - and relieved - to note that, though it was nearly midnight, the restaurant showed no signs of emptying out. So far, Rupert had yet to reach how they'd set up The Accord.

The journey from Felice's first visit to Scientology to the assembly around them of a caucus of acolytes with whom they travelled abroad to Antigua in the Caribbean where they formulated the first cardinals of the cult was a briefer tale than might be expected.

What Scientology had done for Felice was to introduce her to the idea of setting up some sort of organisation of which she could be the boss, the Queen. If she did not have the patience or ability to excel in the world around her, she would create a new one. Nor would it be difficult to find a supporting cast. Like The Accord later, and like, I daresay, several other such outfits, there were always a few misfits for whom their organisation of the moment didn't quite suit, looking for something new.

Her biggest task was to convince Rupert to apply those 'leadership qualities' to the formation of an institution which would provide people with a real home and a chance to fulfil themselves psychologically and spiritually without leaving them prey to any competitors.

'In other words,' I contributed: 'You did the same as everyone else, but because they were your intentions, they were honourable?'

'Something like that. Is that unusual?'

'I suppose not. Tell me about Antigua.'

* * *

Antigua, in the Leeward Islands, is a low-lying island of little more than a hundred square miles and considerably less than a hundred thousand people, with a different sandy beach for every day of the year, fringed with palm trees, nestling in coves and natural harbours which are the former craters of volcanos whose anger had long since expired.

'The point is, there is nothing in Antigua, nothing to do, no one to do it with, just long, hot, dry days. Even the rainy season involves no more than a few, brief, gentle showers, and it's peaceful, peaceful and calm, and they let you alone so long as you don't disrupt their order. When we were there, it hadn't been governing itself for that long and it achieved full independence while some of us were still there. Of course, it was crooked and corrupt as only these tiny islands can be. The first Prime Minister's cabinet included quite a few members of his own family and took fifteen of the seventeen seats in Parliament, several of which were later the subject of successful legal challenge but his party just stood again and re-took them.'

He smiled: he felt right at home. A whole country to do his thing in would have been even better.

'I suppose that's where it all came together. For years afterwards, we continued to go back periodically, until it got too hot.'

'Too hot?'

'There was scandal, arms-smuggling, which came to a head a few years ago, but everyone who was familiar with the island knew all about it for years beforehand.'

My ears pricked up. Arms-smuggling was, to my mind, a bunch more interesting than porn, and linked back to my client a lot more easily. But it was Israel smuggling arms to the Medellin drugs cartel, not Nicaragua or Cuba to the IRA. Nonetheless, I asked:

'Could any of your people have had anything to do with smuggling arms?'

'I wouldn't have said so, but then I wouldn't have said they would have anything to do with other things,' he added. It had already long gone unsaid but was well understood that I had more than a vague clue about the organisation's most recent activities. 'The other big thing about Antigua was banking. It was both a tax haven and a safe haven for people who didn't want too many questions asked.'

'Tell me about then,' I invited, still seeking a handle on the man.

So he told me how they had struggled and argued and wrestled - he and Felice and the early members, including, as they visited mainland America, more and more from the States - there were so many names I couldn't recollect any of them afterwards - to structure some sense out of the mad, collage-philosophy of the times.

'We were different, you know. We were the generation that got away.'

'Doesn't every generation think that of themselves?'

'Perhaps, but I believe it was true of us. I think it was the media that did it. Remember, television was invented before the war, but it was artificially delayed because of it. It was the fifties before it began again properly, but because it had been held back, it sprang on us with a special ferocity, and developed with a frightening speed. By the seventies, the evolution of the mass media had brought people into contact with one another - across national and geographical boundaries - in a way that couldn't have been imagined even ten years before. The music, the images, the influences: Vietnam was our war, too,' he addressed his remark to Mercury - the American - more than I. 'We could see it at the same time as Americans, our own contemporaries, listening to the same music we were listening to, idolising the same heroes, and getting shot to death in the Far East, which we watched on the news each evening the same day it happened. Media; immediacy. It was a giant change in the demography of culture.'

I shook my head, confused. Maybe I'd had too much to drink. Maybe I didn't think he was making a lot of sense. He said:

'Come on, Dave, you were there, you're not much younger than I am. How old are you?'

I told him. He said:

'Well, I've got five years on you, that's all, nothing. What I'm trying to get at is, most progress, especially mass progress, is something worked out fairly well ahead, with the establishment - or the forces of power, the grey forces if you like - in command of it. They have their systems, their institutions, their own prophets, through which to foresee it. It's not surprising or a controversial proposition: it's what learning and power are about. What happened in the sixties and seventies was like an explosion, and it wasn't until the eighties that they began to get it back under control.' I didn't ask who 'they' were: that much I understood. 'All I'm saying is, we weren't subject to the same extent of psychological or mental domination - dictatorship; they weren't on top of it, of us; they hadn't foreseen how it - media - would impact. How could they? It was unprecedented.'

'Which is a good thing, right?' I needed to check my bearings. 'That they weren't on top.'

'Sure, by and large, for most of us. But it also left a lot of people confused, looking for something, vulnerable.'

'There were plenty of gurus around,' I confirmed and then, for no particular reason, feeling cruel: 'Looking for groupies.'

Mercury laughed.

'That's alright, too. That's about right. But she was the one looking for groupies, not Rupert.'

'I didn't get the impression, in Val d'Isère, that you were exactly abstemious that way.'

He laughed too.

'Are you?' Seeing that I had not followed his point, he explained: 'It's your own hang-up. You've still got the deep-seated notion that someone or something serious about anything - philosophy, politics, psychology, religion - shouldn't also enjoy sex as much as you do.'

'Who said I enjoy it that much?'

'Okay, then as much as you'd like to.'

'Great. If you're going to give me psychoanalysis, you'll owe me a dozen sessions for what this meal is costing me.' I began to think that treating them well, feeding them and boozing them, honouring them, had back-fired on me: it had restored all his composure, all of his command, that I had felt in Val and suffered from intermittently since.

So he talked instead about looking for common threads, common needs: attitudes and ideas that would strike not merely a response in their members and supporters but one so powerful, and so original, that it would stimulate them to take The Accord so much further forward into action and effect. Anyone could be one step ahead of the next philosophical vogue: the trick was to be so far forward that the movement's unique qualities - what would today be called its unique selling point - could last a lifetime.

'Don't underestimate it. It was a terrifically difficult task. Liberation through self-knowledge is old hat, as is self-knowledge as a first step towards change; but I wanted something more for them, a method - an Accord - by which they could retain, rather than cast off, deep-seated attitudes and images of themselves and remix, remould them into not just one new persona but an ever-changing sequence. What happens, so often, is that people go through some form of therapy, or group, or awakening or change, and they think they've got themselves together but, you know, after a while, it doesn't work, and they're not way back at the beginning but much worse off, just because they've tried and failed. My thesis was that the trying mattered, the changing, the awakening mattered in its own right.'

'It's the journey not the destination that matters?'

'Almost. Not quite. Because there was an end implicit in the journey, that of achieving accord and bringing it to others, for others to share.'

'So what went wrong?' I was suddenly bored with this abstract account. I wanted the dirt.

* * *

What went wrong was Felice. The Accord had been her fantasy, one she had persuaded Rupert to go along with. He had proved adept at it, which she admired, but his aptitude was based on sincerity, even integrity, which she did not. It had only, like her previous marriage, been a joke.

Of course, this is to reduce to a couple sentences a process that took some years. At first, she had been excited, had taken part. Whether by reason of her relationship with Rupert, or by force of personality, or by virtue of her role as an inventor of it, or perhaps merely because of the personal inadequacies of their followers, she had appeared to grow with it, to find as much for herself as they purported to be providing to their trusted courtiers. As they progressed, it ceased to be important that, after all, she wasn't so smart; as they passed into the higher reaches of the obscure, the whims that derived from the brevity of her attention span became messages from the beyond. It would not be quite right to say that no one had the courage to announce that the Queen had no clothes, because that was probably her most common state. It was, rather, that her nudity was perceived as a blessing not a curse, a state of sainthood not sensuousness.

By the time Mercury, through her own unhappy, tortuous route, wove her way into the inner circle of The Accord, Felice and Rupert were already far apart. There had been neither sex nor love, neither passion nor compassion, between them for so long that their estrangement had of necessity been absorbed into the institution like two points of an essential and inevitable dialectic. The range of elements they had identified provided them with an ample selection of costumes to wear without either one of them needing to show up the other as a fraud. Rupert was The Leader; but Felice was the source. It was in the nature of the roles they played that she, far more than he, should draw around her a coterie of intimate initiates, a counterweight to Rupert's ethereal insularity.

'Mercury and I knew how we felt about each other - and what we were to become for one another - for several years before we ever made love. Felice never believed that. It was a self-fulfilling prophesy.' Him and Wally Wadd both.

'What about Dolly, then?'

'I loved her like a daughter.'

'Daughter-love like that gets you sent down,' I answered.

'Sometimes you have to fight fire with fire.'

'If a child puts his hand in the fire, you don't stick yours in after it.'

'How was I to prevent Felice taking complete hold of her?'

'Why keep her in The Accord?'

'Why not?'

* * *

So far, what he was telling me was what he had understood at the time. Felice - and her closest cohorts - were in charge of the management of The Accord, the daily operations, the movement of members, the funds. They were solvent, more so than might be expected; they were able to enjoy the good life, which Rupert did not deny suited him well. It might have gone on indefinitely.

Did he know she was using The Accord as a front for other activities, those of her former friends in the States? Did he know she moved money, she moved drugs, sometimes she moved people for them? Did he know they could not afford their lifestyle on magazine sales and meditation income alone?

'No, I didn't,' he insisted. 'I didn't know, but I suppose there were times when I suspected, asked, she'd brush me off with a half-explanation that...' He paused, then sighed: 'A half-explanation I knew wasn't true but that it suited me to believe or ignore.'

It worked for a long time; it had worked until very recently, when Joe Donleavy got more involved in some of The Accord activities than he was supposed to. Most of what Rupert and Mercury now knew and told me was guess-work, speculation, but informed, knowing the parties involved.

I challenged him.

'You denied knowing him.'

'I didn't know him. I had,' he hesitated: 'I had seen the name. On papers, in documents, in her diary. I didn't know who he was or what he meant. I was trying to find out. I thought you might help me.'

'If she knew him, she was playing a dangerous game with me,' I said as much to myself than to them.

'Was that supposed to be a question or an explanation?' Mercury contributed one of her cryptic insights.

'It was the catalyst, though,' Rupert said: 'For what happened after.' He glanced down at his empty dessert plate. 'I suppose you could say you owe us this meal; your arrival brought it all down; it cost us The Accord.'

I too could be cryptic when it suited.

'Was that supposed to be a complaint or a thank you?'

Neither of them could state with any certainty when first Felice had started to abuse The Accord to her ends beyond immediate psychological or physical satisfaction. Anytime within the last five years, at a best guess. At some point, she had realised that far more of the senior founder members paid her allegiance than they paid Rupert, and that she had been sufficiently close to them for long enough that to get them to do her will, even where it flew in the face of Rupert's, was child's play.

She would have used whatever technique suited each of them. Sex, often, though for some in abundance and for others by withholding it altogether: no rationing, only extremes. She had acquired inside knowledge of individuals derived from histories they had conveniently forgotten. This was what passed for intellectual power within the cult. To describe her as a spider at the centre of the web would be accurate, but would fail to reflect that the web is far more dependent for its existence on the spider than the other way around.

'Where did the sex come from?'

It sounded a stupid question out of context, but he knew what I meant.

'I don't deny that at times The Accord, or people within it - I, Felice, Mercury too,' he added, a little unnecessarily: 'We've enjoyed ourselves. There wouldn't be a lot of point in it all otherwise. It didn't have to be sexually. We played around with continence,' he said, which I would have thought was a contradiction in terms. 'But I didn't know about the films until very recently.'

'What did you learn about the films?'

'That, on a few occasions, Felice had made films of particular groups, on particular occasions. That quite a lot of the senior hierarchy were involved, both as participants and in the making of them. That quite a lot of the younger members had also taken part. That they had been circulated between Segments.'

'I gotta admit, it would've been a damned sight more interesting for the Galatians than Paul's letter home.'

'Actually, it wasn't a letter home,' Rupert corrected me. 'It was written in order to set right the error of their thinking.'

'While these films showed the right way to gang-bang, right? You ever see one of these films?'

'Yes. I asked to see. Felice sent me a couple. They were, well, fairly innocuous.' I doubted he'd seen the production I'd watched in Harwich.

'Sent you?'

'Yes. For about three years - until a couple of years ago - I spent little time in the Segments.'

'Where were you?'

'Antigua for some of the time. The States. I travelled a lot. I knew things were wrong. I felt we'd grown too big too fast. There were too many Segments, too many people - people I didn't know, wasn't close to, couldn't get close to. The Accord had lost its original thread and purpose. I was trying to work out where it should go, how to bring some of that back. I felt, well, I suppose, with hindsight, I knew that it was going wrong, that Felice was turning it into something it wasn't supposed to be, just another cult, I suppose.' He sighed, martyred. 'I was weak. I let it slip away from me.'

I asked gently, remembering what I'd thought as we wandered to the restaurant:

'Did you maybe want to let it go?'

Mercury's eyes shone and I knew I was right: it was something she'd thought, maybe wanted, but didn't dare suggest to him yet.

He smiled wanly, just short of pathetically:

'I must have, mustn't I? Otherwise it wouldn't have happened.'

* * *

By that time, we were the last of the patrons and the servants of the *Restaurant Opéra* were ready to rewrite the menu to offer our various bits up, delightfully encased in a delicate pastry, to the next day's diners. I flashed my Platinum the way a detective flashes tin and signed away the firm's profits for the next three financial years. The hostess handed us our jackets and coats and hovered politely. I suppose I might have tipped her anyway if she hadn't informed me that there was a five Euro charge. I shook my head, bemused: these frogs don't got much style; the meal topped three hundred quid and they wanted another few pounds for hanging up our outer garments?

I was going back to the Left Bank. They were, too.

'Where are you staying?'

They gave me an address that didn't mean anything, and explained that it belonged to one of the few friends around The Accord who had thus far come down on their side of the division. We stopped off at a bar just the other side of the Seine - a few doors down from Shakespeare and Company, the bookshop Carson had visited chasing my memories - for a nightcap, and for them to complete their account.

Over brandies for them and *marc* for me, which I had been drinking in those establishments which wanted for both Southern Comfort and *Genépi* but which I had great difficult pronouncing in a way any French waiter could understand, they filled me in on the argument as it had come to a head during the day after the three of us had last been together, on the slopes above Val.

It was the argument Dolly had overheard. Rupert demanded to know what was going on with Donleavy - who he was, why I was looking for him. Felice was evasive, uncharacteristically unsure of herself. What she admitted was that Donleavy - who had worked for their English solicitors - seemed to be hanging around The Accord. Pressed if she meant he was coming into membership, she conceded not; rather, he was hanging around some of the more peripheral activities - films, people, money. Things, Felice challenged, that had helped keep The Accord afloat but to which Rupert had turned a blind eye.

For the first time, Rupert demanded details of these activities and of Felice's involvement with them and with the solicitors and, in particular, with Joe Donleavy. He got little in return.

'I had only heard of these solicitors a couple of times. They had done a little bit of work for us, conveyancing, trusts, that sort of thing. They're not the sort of firm my family used. I know how we were first in touch with them. Abraham,' he smiled at a pleasant memory. 'He was one of our early members. He died. Cancer. He was only thirty-four. He had a little money, which he left to us. Left to the group in America, actually, because of what I said, that we're not incorporated in England, which was why it was a little complicated. Anyway, his family's solicitor was Frank Morris, and Felice and I had a number of dealings with him over the estate. Later, we used him here and there. He pretended to be quite interested in us, fond of us in a patronising sort of way. He just wanted the work. But there had been no recent dealings that I knew of, and I ought to have known of any. During the day, I found a bill from him, and a letter that didn't make a lot of sense, that had Donleavy's reference on it, and another scribbled letter from him which referred to an encounter between them - he and Felice - and I also found an appointment in her diary to see him.'

'For when?'

'For after we went back to Paris from Val. And then, just like that, you dropped Donleavy's name into the pot. From then on, it's been like a whirlwind. I think you spooked her; I think she's panicking; I don't know why or what about, but I can see it in her eyes - she's pretending to be in control, but she's not. If anyone is, it's her friends in America.'

'Do you have any of their names?'

'No,' he shuddered: it was the last thing he'd want to know.

The idea that I had been the catalyst was, however, less of a surprise - or burden to bear - than it might have been: it's what I do; it's what I've always done in order to get to the truth - thrown everything in the air and seen where it landed.

I knew about the films at a different level than Rupert had known about them or, for that matter, yet understood. He had referred to 'people' as one of her activities; likewise, he did not fully understand what they were about, but there had been too many of them who had come briefly into The Accord then disappeared from the scene. Some of them had not seemed at all appropriate - his word; others had seemed suitable - youngsters of the sort with which I was now familiar - but had also passed through in haste. It did not take much to imagine the price some of those Accord lovelies could fetch in another kind of market.

'Do you know anything about the other people I asked about?' I still hadn't told him about Alan: that he was a member of The Accord, albeit briefly; that he had featured in a DVD; how he had arrived in England; that the police were on his ass closer than he had been on his girlfriend's in the movie or Rupert had been on Colin's in Val. Nor yet had I asked or told him about Colin and Sarah. The evening thus far had been for background: we were only now beginning to focus on current events.

'I didn't at the time,' he answered honestly. 'But I've seen her since.' Amy.

'Where?'

'In Hamburg,' he said. 'In Hamburg with Donleavy.'

'In Hamburg. Where you went from Paris. Why?'

Mercury gently explained:

'We were virtual prisoners, Dave. We had no money. The group was abandoning us. Rupert was... He was shocked. He didn't know what to do.'

'And you? Why do I get the feeling you weren't that shocked by it all?'

'Because I wasn't.' My residual suspicion of her melted like ice-cream over hot pie. 'What you really mean is, why didn't I take over, if Rupert couldn't cope?' We were talking as if he wasn't present.

'Yup, that's what I mean.'

So she told him, not me:

'I want to spend the rest of my life with you. I don't want to do that carrying the burden of losing you The Accord. I couldn't save it for you, I wouldn't have if I could. It had gone entirely rotten. But you've had to find that out for yourself, and deal with it yourself, or you'll wonder forever if it might have been different, if I stopped you getting it back. I followed you while we were inside The Accord; I've followed you out of it; now we'll go forward together. Okay?'

Neither Rupert nor I answered. I said to either of them:

'So what you're saying is, basically you just let them do what they wanted with you?'

'More or less,' she said.

He said:

'I wanted to see what that was. What they did with us.'

'Which was?' I prompted.

'To take us to Hamburg,' he shrugged. 'That's all. That's all I know. They gave us our passports, two tickets to London, the clothes we stood in and a handful of cash - less than a hundred pounds.'

'But you came back here instead? Why?'

'Because they wanted us to go to London,' he answered flatly. 'Wasn't that right?'

In England, they could and would have been tied to the DVDs which we were intended to find. He and Alan were both being set up and taken off the board, superfluous to the game, not its object. Donleavy had Carson and me on it instead and, at that stage, he still had Amy as a piece to play. It was finally beginning to take shape.

'When did you see Amy? And Donleavy?'

'They met us off the plane. They were the ones who had our tickets and the money. The others took straight off again, I don't know where.'

I did, but I didn't tell him. Instead, I asked:

'When did you get back to Paris?'

'We came straight back. We've been here since. We've been trying to see some people. We haven't succeeded yet.'

'Who're you waiting to see?'

'Did you meet a woman called Lois?'

I nodded and asked:

'You haven't managed to see her?' He shook his head. I explained: 'She's gone. From what I can tell, she's left the group.'

Mercury shot Rupert a quick glance of satisfied triumph.

'I told you.'

I asked:

'That she would leave?'

'That most of them would leave, but, yes, her especially.'

'What about Dolly?' Rupert asked eagerly, hoping I'd tell him she was gone as well.

I told him what I knew and, trusting them, what I had planned for her. Only then did I ask about Alan but, though they must have been around at least some of the same time, neither of them could identify him from within, even by the name Esau. Only then did I tell them about Colin and Sarah.

Funny thing is, Mercury was the stoical one. Rupert cried. But, then, he was the one who'd been in the bedroom with them; but then, he was the one who'd delivered Felice's fantasy so successfully hundreds of lives had been caught up in it, along with quite a few deaths.

I didn't tell them how many. I didn't tell them about May: I wanted her in reserve. I didn't tell them about Amy: I didn't know about her until I got back to my hotel half an hour after I left them.

CHAPTER TEN

Malthus had Rupert and Mercury picked up at the address they had given me. Also, he had them incarcerated in a couple nasty little cells in the basement of the *Sûreté* building. Also, he had them fear for the rest of their lives when he informed them that not only did he consider them likely candidates for Amy, but for May, Colin and Sarah too.

Colin in particular, Malthus explained.

'He was a private investigator.'

'Where'd you get that?' I asked idly, sitting on the bed from which they had recently removed Amy's body.

'The FBI. Fingerprints.'

'Right.' PIs get printed when they get their licences. 'Who was he working for?' I wondered if he charged extra for taking it up the backside, or was it his idea of a bonus. I've heard of deep cover before, and of deep shit, but never the two in tandem.

'Albert Demonica, the little girl's father.'

My first thought was that I hadn't needed to waste Tim's time tracking him down: that would cost me. My second, that I had been correct about blackmail. My third, that he had allowed his daughter to remain in The Accord knowing what she was getting up to, or what was getting up her, while he worked himself off the blackmail hook. My fourth, therefore, that with a bit of luck, he'd get bitten by the snake Mercury didn't go down on and die a slow and painful death.

I wasn't surprised about Colin, though: I'd felt something didn't fit. I was narked he hadn't confided in me, a fellow of the order, but that was probably why; he wouldn't want my cases and his to get confused; he wouldn't want me trampling on his turf. Poor sod, I thought and said out loud.

Malthus was phlegmatic.

'He would know what he was doing.'

'Which was what?'

'I am told, from America, to produce the evidence for the revenue. Do you understand?'

'Yeah, sure. Demonica was being blackmailed with porn movies of his little kiddie; he was going to get the dirt and blackmail them back, by threatening their religious status with the tax people. Tax exemptions and benefits. We have the same sort of things in England. It would hit them where they hurt, in the pocket.'

'I will hit them where it hurt,' Malthus said grimly.

'I don't think you're right about them,' Rupert and Mercury. 'How long before they give you a time of death on Amy?'

'By this afternoon, I think so.'

'You want to wager it was while they were with me?'

'It does not matter. If I am not right, I shall.'

Notwithstanding the missing 'be', I got the message: Rupert and Mercury would be guilty of what he decided they were guilty of, and would probably claim the honour with pleasure once he'd, as he put it, 'hit them where it hurt' for long enough.

* * *

In the morning, I rang London. I rang Tim first, postponing the time when I had to break the news to Carson that cousin Al was her sole surviving relative. I caught Tim at his office. He had already spoken to Malthus, so he knew that the search for Demonica was off.

'Colin was his investigator,' I added.

'Yeah, I know. I got that too.'

'How?' He didn't answer but, on reflection, I realised that his name would be on the list for FBI information in the case as much as that of Malthus, which raised the question of what he had known and when. I was getting more suspicious of him by the minute but for the time being I played along. 'What else you got?'

'Alan is in Newcastle as of this a.m. He went up by rented car last night. Staying in the County.' Where I had stayed; where everyone who doesn't know Newcastle stays, just because it's directly across from the train station.

'Who's with him?'

'Wally,' he said with ill-concealed glee.

'You really don't like her, do you?' Joannie.

'I like Anne,' he said: Wally's wife.

His own marriage was so close to perfect, he believed the same was true of everyone else's and if Wally's had gone wrong, there had to be an external explanation - like Joannie. If Sandy hadn't died, he'd never have let me look at another woman. As far as he was concerned, he planned to bury me and Carson next to one another.

I was too tired to argue. I filled him in on my conversation the night before.

'What's going on, Tim?'

'It's clearly not only about porn.' He was giving me a little bit at a time.

'So?'

'There's a heavy frame around your friends,' Rupert and Mercury. 'Is it justified by her wanting to take over The Accord? Is it worth it?'

'What's a house worth?'

Every lawyer ever acts in a house purchase - which is every lawyer - gets asked by a client whether it's a good buy, and gives the same answer: a house is worth what you're willing to pay for it.

'What's a body worth?'

In both our experience, not very much.

'Someone's telling me to stay away - that's not Donleavy, but I don't see how it could be Felice either.' Dumping Amy in my room was the message. 'Who sends messages like that?' I asked out loud, both a question and an answer. 'Her friends.'

It was another piece of the puzzle. Was it complicated or simple? It was a bit like a mathematics problem that seems complicated until you get the answer, when - in hindsight - it seems obvious. I wasn't kidding when I likened Donleavy to Orbach, a man who had - it was widely believed by those in the know and as Jada had insinuated in her book - killed his best friends in order to adopt their daughter.

Donleavy had enlisted the family Yavitch to draw Carson and I into The Accord's orbit, in the expectation that if we screwed with The Accord, its backers would screw with us. If I accepted his father's belief that he was not a killer, which was consistent with how he had manoeuvred Alan into trouble but not a coffin, then somewhere along the line he had lost control of his own plot and May and then Amy had paid the price: in all likelihood, Colin Wrighton was the unanticipated wrinkle which had upped the ante but not far enough to take it out on us. Donleavy needed to be careful; if Felice realised how he had used them and fingered him as the person who had set the ball rolling, his father was probably the only man alive who'd be able to save him. Sure as shit, I wouldn't be able to.

'Let's see what the boy gets up to in Newcastle, take it from there,' Tim said calmly, as if my revelation was anything but news.

I was about to agree when he terminated the call by hanging up.

Out of excuses, I finally rang home. She absorbed the information better than I expected, maybe because she was still half asleep; no breast-beating, *mea culpa*, statements about all who come near her being doomed, just a flat:

'I see.'

'Is that all you have to say?'

'Do you want to talk to Alton?'

I did and I didn't. I did, because I missed him and if I stayed away much longer he might forget who I was; I didn't, because I was tired and irritable and tense and I couldn't cope with tales from his front as well as my own. So I told her to give him a kiss from me instead.

'Sure,' she said, equally flat.

'You're taking this well,' I eventually accused her, unable to take the strain of such uncharacteristic calm.

'What are you going to do now?'

'I have to hang about here for a while, Malthus says. At least till they finish the post-mortem. Have you talked to Tim?'

'Nope,' she answered tersely.

I briefed her on his information in full and selected material from my dinner with Rupert and Mercury the night before. Instead of commenting on the features salient to the case - Amy's proven link to Donleavy, Alan's whereabouts - she seemed only interested in Tim's remark about Wally.

'Wally's been hanging around the club a lot, Nat says.'

'How is she?'

'Who? Nat? Joannie?'

'Both, either.' I didn't really care: neither of us was making a bunch of sense. I was also beginning to wonder how much sense it made for Demonica to put a PI into The Accord just to play blackmail poker. According to Malthus, Demonica was on his way to Paris to collect Dolly: I was hoping he'd spend a little time with me first. 'Look, are you really okay?'

'Sure, sure, stop worrying. My period's late, it's making me ratty.'

'Well,' I said dubiously: 'I'll speak to you later. Take it easy, huh?'

Like Tim, she too hung up without answering.

* * *

Despite Malthus' ominous threat, Rupert and Mercury were truly in the clear for Amy: she had been killed at approximately the time we were slow-footing it from *L'Alsace* to *L'Opéra*. Also, they could prove they were still in Val d'Isère at the time her mother had died. Malthus was angry that that the investigating magistrate made him let Rupert and Mercury go. That was not all he was angry about.

'How much trouble you bring me. I am wondering,' he snarled, without needing to spell out exactly what he was wondering. 'Perhaps I am trusting you too much.'

'Give me some motive here, Malthus? What's in it for me?'

'Perhaps you also are being blackmailed,' he suggested, only half-joking. I winced: notwithstanding Dolly's declaration of my innocence, I wasn't sure I'd want to send copies of that evening in the chalet to all my friends, well, either of them. 'And perhaps you are not telling me all.'

I wasn't: if Tim didn't want Malthus to know about the connection from Donleavy back to Leahy, I wasn't about to spill the beans.

'When's he arriving - the father?'

He glanced at the wall-clock.

'Perhaps he is arrived.'

'Are you meeting him at the airport?'

'His people will do so.'

'The consulate?'

'The embassy.'

It was interesting: he worked for the government but his visit was allegedly personal, to fetch his daughter and explain to police what his hired hack had been up to.

At Malthus' suggestion, I took Rupert and Mercury away with me: he did not consider it politic for Demonica to see them around the building; nor was he willing for me to sit in on his interview with him. He did, however, agree to meet me later when he would tell me whatever he was willing to share. I figured a jump ahead. I told Rupert and Mercury I was going to The Accord Segment House where to await the elder Demonica in the company of his daughter.

'We're coming with you,' Rupert announced.

'You figure that's a good idea?'

As neither of them replied, I figured for myself that they did.

We cabbed it, a short journey that was a lot shorter than it ought to have been the way the driver cursed and cut, slipped and slid, tyres screeching the way my head was splitting. I led the way in so that if they slammed the doors to keep out their former *Fuhrer* and his moll, I'd already be inside.

The place was in an evident state of disarray. Though the door was open, there was no one on the desk. A thief could have stolen all the publications on display if he was crazy enough to want them. I called out:

'Hallo? Welcome to your home? Anyone appropriate?'

A blonde-haired, bespectacled woman whose face I recognised from the Midnight Meditation but whose name I didn't know peered down the stairwell and started towards me until she spotted Rupert and Mercury, gasped, covered her mouth and ran back the way she'd come without a word, as if she'd seen the devil. I said:

'They really love you, huh?'

'Rachel,' Rupert said, as if that was explanation enough.

Mercury smiled.

'She's always been a bit on the nervous side.'

Hiram came down the stairs, flanked by a couple of bulky Accord bouncers.

'What are you doing here?' he hissed at them, ignoring me altogether. I guess he knew what I was doing there. 'You're not supposed to come here; that was the agreement.'

'There was no agreement,' Rupert snapped. 'And as a matter of fact, I am the leaseholder of this house. I think my lawyer here will confirm...'

'Whoa, there. I ain't that good at English law, and I sure as hell don't know anything about French.' Nor did I take kindly to being described as his lawyer: friendship was one thing, but he hadn't paid me a *cent*. 'But, uh, if he really did sign the lease I'd say he's got a bunch more right to be here than you have, Hiram.'

'Everyone's got more right than you have, Woolf.'

I thought about explaining that if Rupert was the leaseholder and had invited me in, I had at least as much right as Hiram, and more if Rupert asked him to leave; I also thought about the two toughs at his shoulder and the way he'd called me Woolf. I shut up.

'Hiram, Hiram, Hiram,' Rupert sighed. It sounded like a ritual: as in, say it thrice and they were divorced. 'I want to talk to you, just talk. How can you be so frightened of me that you won't talk to me? How long have you known me?'

Hiram had the grace to flush.

'I don't know what to believe, Rupert.'

'Whom, is what you mean, isn't it?'

One of his cohorts leaned down to whisper in Hiram's ear. Hiram nodded.

'We'll talk to you. Upstairs. In the office. Just you, though, Rupert: not her.'

Mercury chuckled.

'The wicked witch of the West? Come on, Hiram.'

'That's our terms, Rupert.'

I turned so they couldn't hear or see what I said:

'Watch it, Rupert.'

'They won't hurt me, Dave. All I need to do is talk to them.'

'Yeah?'

* * *

Dolly was allowed to meet with me and Mercury in the Coffee Lounge. As on the last occasion I'd been there, there were no customers.

'It's all but closed. Just members, inside and out.' She studied Mercury curiously, like she was a creature from another planet. 'How is it, Mercury, being out?'

'It's fine, Dolly, fine. And he's fine, too,' she said, knowing Rupert was who the girl needed to hear about. 'Your father's coming,' she added.

Dolly brightened.

'When?'

'Soon,' I said, cutting off Mercury. I didn't want Dolly too comfortable. 'Has Felice been in touch?'

She hesitated.

'I'm not supposed to know, but I think she telephoned. I heard them talking about it amongst themselves.'

'Them?'

'Hiram, Chad: they're in charge now.'

'Doesn't sound like there's a lot to be in charge of,' I said.

She glanced at Mercury but answered me anyway:

'They're going to change it all, even the name.'

Mercury laughed:

'To what? Channel Four?' I shook my head, confused. The only Channel Four I knew was English TV, and there was nothing on it worth watching since they'd recently re-run the complete Hill Street Blues. Mercury explained: 'Channel Four is French TV. *Accord*.' She laid into the last word like a sworn enemy. 'The one that shows the so-called "adult films" on. The porn Accord,' she added, as if I might yet not have her point.

Dolly whispered:

'The Endowment.'

It hardly seemed apt: Rupert was the well-endowed one, and he was gone.

'Yeah, I like it,' said Mercury. 'Endowment, as in charitable foundation, and the name of the charity is Felice.'

'Dolly, I want you to tell me something,' I cut Mercury off again: this wasn't the time to indulge either bitterness or bitchiness.

I wanted, and was about, to ask her about Colin: I needed to pin down how far he'd gotten before he was gone for good, to identify those with the greatest interest in his departure; also, where Sarah fit in.

I didn't get the chance because just then yet another familiar-looking Accord woman entered the coffee lounge, fraught and worried and anxious to speak to Dolly. Politely, we pretended not to listen as they crossed the room, arms around each other, whispering together. But neither of us could avoid hearing Dolly's cry, as she broke free and swung around sobbing:

'They're hurting him, they're hurting him.'

I was on my feet - as was Mercury - both of us realising immediately who Dolly meant, before I remembered that I didn't have a gun, a knife or a medieval spear, and that there were at least three of them who had gone upstairs with Rupert and who knew how many more lurking in wait. I sat down again with a thump. Horrified, Mercury snapped:

'Come on, you're coming with me.'

Who, me? I thought.

'Who, me?' I said.

She grabbed one arm while Dolly grabbed the other: I got the idea they weren't about to take no for an answer. Reluctantly, I let them lead me to the bottom of the stairs, and give me a general - but not at all gentle - shove from and in the behind. I was still contemplating my choices on the half-landing at the turn in the stairs when I heard a crash from the main room on the first floor - the meditation room - and saw the door fly open and Rupert fly out backwards. I rushed up and caught him as he bounced off the opposite wall but before he landed on the floor. His eyes met mine, he groaned, and he collapsed in my arms. He had been badly beaten: he was bloody and bruised; there was an open gash on his cheek and a piece of loose skin flapped away from the cut; he had lost one shoe in the struggle, and his shirt was half torn off.

I stood, dazed, and turned to face the room, where Hiram was standing in the doorway, his expression half-defiant, half-ashamed. I ignored the sight of Mercury and Dolly ascending the stairs, in tears. Hiram said:

'Get him out of here.'

'Help me get him up, will you?'

Hiram shrugged and came out of the room, bending down on one side of Rupert while I bent down on the other. I waited until he was looking where to grab a hold of his former mentor and - for all I knew - best friend, before I struck him across the head with the whole of my forearm. He fell back, shocked, as I jumped across Rupert and kicked him first in the face then in the balls, not quite sure which was the more gratifying sound: his nose breaking, the squelch between his legs or his high-pitched scream.

I swung around in time to see his comrades emerging outraged from the meditation room. Rupert had recovered a measure of consciousness - and, I dare say, the unconscious residue of his military training - and managed to grab the ankle of one of them as they came to Hiram's rescue, upending him with a jerk that flung him face down directly in front of the two women.

The odds were a bit more even now: I only had one left to deal with, while they lashed into the man I was later told went by

The Accord name of Elijah, taking their cue from me and aiming at the parts even Heineken wouldn't try to reach. My own dance partner, whose name I similarly did not learn until afterwards, was Sarakiel, the prince of ministering angels whose job it was to officiate when the angels met in judgment. Certainly, he was contemplating judgment on me and his first blow to my forehead was almost the last one he needed because as I reeled backwards I, too, tripped - over Hiram - and nearly lost my balance.

Only nearly, though. Sarakiel flung himself after me, across the now crowded and well-littered landing. I dodged to the right, he led to the left; I ducked, he roared; I used Hiram's body like a starting-block, rising up at the right moment for my head to connect with Sarakiel's stomach leading to a rush of breath so foul-smelling he had to be a vegetarian. He doubled over and for a split but sufficient second his neck was exposed to my elbow, which came crashing down on it so hard I feared for a moment that I had broken it. His neck, I mean, not the elbow.

I stood up, my back against the wall, looking and lashing wildly around me as if I couldn't wait for the next comers. But the only audience was friendly: Dolly, the woman who had come to fetch her, Rupert, Mercury, against whose lap he was leaning, Malthus and a bulky stranger in a herring-bone suit, wing tips and smartly pressed hair who I took to be Dolly's father. We hovered for several more seconds in total silence as Malthus took it all in. Hiram was half-conscious, Elijah was crying, and Sarakiel was out cold.

Malthus applauded politely:

'*Pas mal, mon brave, pas mal.*'

* * *

His men removed the offending angels and their ilk, though it was unclear whether to hospital, the morgue or the jail. One of his men also took Rupert, accompanied by Mercury, to hospital, but in a different car. We removed ourselves to the Coffee Lounge where the woman who had come to fetch Dolly - and who in acknowledgment of her own future life outside The Accord now introduced herself by her real name and origin, Melinda Metcalfe from Baltimore, a town I knew well from a previous case but loved little for the same reason - set about revivifying the kitchen sufficiently to brew up a pot of coffee for our diminished party: Dolly and her father, me, and Malthus, who said:

'Mr Demonica expressed the wish to meet you.'

His tone failed to conceal his surprise that my fame should have reached ears across the Atlantic.

I wasn't surprised. I studied Demonica with equally ill-concealed distaste. Just in case I had missed the point, Demonica said:

'So you're Woolf.'

I knew just about everything I needed to know. My mind went back to a terrifying time in a house in Barnes, West London, while I had been looking for Tim. Four men had taken me prisoner, along with the wife of a recently deceased ex-client from long before. Of the six of us in that house overnight, only three of us left it alive and of them I was the only one who did so in anything approximating to a vertical position.

'And how are Bob and Dick?' We never did get beyond pseudonyms.

'I don't know them personally. Different department. But I know a lot about you, Mr Woolf. Seems you must have made some people back home pretty angry with you.'

Bob and Dick had been ONI: Office of Naval - alternatively, Negligible - Intelligence. Demonica, I presumed, though he was later to deny, was CIA, who had loaned Bob and Dick the house in Barnes. It was Bob and Dick who crawled out of the house in Barnes instead of walking, and I was why; hence, as he put it, pretty angry people.

'You gonna lay it out for me, or you want me to do it for you?' I allowed my eyes to drift pointedly in Dolly's direction. I wanted to hear how he lied his way out of how he'd used her; I wanted that almost more than I wanted her to know the truth; I had no wish to inflict on her the pain of finding out.

Demonica asked me:

'Who's Joe Donleavy?'

Malthus' eyebrows raised. He recognised the name from our first meeting. Hedging his bets, leaving unclear to whom his question was directed, he asked:

'Who's Joe Donleavy?'

It seemed like a good answer, so I asked:

'Who's Joe Donleavy?'

We all waited to see whether Dolly did the same. She bit her lower lip, then said:

'That was who you showed me a photo of yesterday?'

I began to have second thoughts about wanting to save her the pain of her father's betrayal.

'Do you know him?'

'I remember where I saw him,' she admitted.

'Where?'

'Here. He came here. After we came back from Val. To see Felice.'

'Why didn't you tell me before?'

'I didn't remember,' she said, but with less defiance than her words suggested. 'I didn't know. I was frightened. I was confused. Was it important?'

'Perhaps.' I didn't attack hard for two reasons. First, because the only difference it might have made - and a slender chance at that - was that I might have reached Amy before she, as it were, reached me, and that wasn't a guilt trip I was willing to lay off on Dolly, however badly she had just landed me in the shit with Malthus and her father. Secondly, because she did not have a patent on withholding information in the case, as Malthus no longer hesitated to point out.

'Joe Donleavy is who?'

'I told you about him, the trainee solicitor.'

Malthus shook his head to say it wasn't enough.

I was on the verge of telling the truth - always a port of last resort - when Demonica, by accident not design, saved me.

'We believe,' he began, leaving wholly at large who the 'we' was: 'We believe Donleavy and his firm were working both with The Accord and with some very interesting people in the north of England.'

'How this is interesting?' Malthus asked. 'How this is interesting for you?'

Demonica paused to assemble his words. He spoke slowly, carefully:

'For a long time now, illegal money from my country - the proceeds of crime - have been moved across the Atlantic to fund crime in Europe.'

Malthus nodded:

'This is not new.'

'Fair enough, it's not new, but just because it isn't new doesn't mean it's no longer a problem. We have a lot of laws at home that allow us to catch criminals by working backwards from their money. But those laws are only effective so long as the money is within our jurisdiction, or those few jurisdictions which are, shall we say, compliant to my government's influence.' It was unnecessary to point that this did not include France. He was talking about money where there was no evidence of illegality on the basis of which to get a warrant. He was therefore referring to America's wholly-owned subsidiaries, in Central and South America, some of the West Indian islands not including Antigua, parts of the Far East, rather than its independent allies in Europe. 'The less money they leave lying around for us to trace, the less chance those laws have of working.'

'You're talking about laundering. What're you saying here?' I interjected.

'I'm saying that laundering is neither a one-off nor a one-class activity. Moving mountains of cash is one form. Another way is paying the right people over the odds for things like printing and clothing. That's how Gaddafi funded the IRA - paying huge fees for cheap print jobs. There's as many different ways to use dirty money as there are people who deal in it, and there's as much money which continues dirty until it's multiplied a few more times over as there is money which goes straight into stocks, bonds and Bahamian bank accounts. We believe...'

'Hold it,' I said. 'You're going this far with us, you might as well go the distance. Who is "we"?'

'My government,' he said shortly. 'Does it matter precisely who?'

'It might matter to Monsieur Malthus.'

He smiled patronisingly.

'I'm here as a private citizen, Mr Woolf. Why is it so important to you to know exactly who I work for?'

'Maybe I don't want a bullet in my back,' I reminded him how he'd opened our conversation.

'I'm not ONI; I'm not CIA. Is that good enough?'

'It'll have to be.' Treasury, Internal Revenue, maybe Department of Justice Organised Crime Task Force or Office of Special Investigations. 'Go on.'

'This is where I don't have a great deal further to go,' he admitted. He counted on his fingers as he listed: 'That there is a network in the London and the English provinces that is funded from the States and is its channel into Europe; that it has fingers in the usual pies, pornography, prostitution, trafficking, gambling, drugs, money laundering; that both The Accord and the people I'm talking about in Newcastle used the same firm of solicitors - Frank Morris; that - as I said - Donleavy seemed to be the common thread. Then, bam, Donleavy disappears and is sighted a couple of times in touch with Felice Hayat.'

'Sighted by whom?'

'Colin Wrighton, now also by my daughter,' he said, nodding a head in her direction.

'Which doesn't explain you hiring Colin Wrighton, does it?'

'Yes and no.'

Malthus snorted.

'The Accord wasn't on my horizon before Dolly got involved with it; I wasn't even aware of it as a client of Frank Morris. Once she told me about it, I looked into it before I came over to see her and began to suspect it formed part of what I was working on; I'm still not sure how far their involvement goes. Some coincidence, huh?' Maybe the only true one in the whole case, I thought but didn't say. 'Obviously, I was worried about Dolly. I, uh, decided that it was in my own interests and those of my, uh, employers to try and put someone else into The Accord - both to protect her, and to see what he could find out,' he concluded, trying unsuccessfully to sound defiant.

'You met with Felice,' I challenged. 'Why not pull Dolly out at once?'

His eyes met mine directly.

'I think you know the answer to that.'

The more he saw that I had worked most of it out for myself, the more his demeanour changed from confident to shifty, confirming my factual suppositions although not necessarily his motive: it wasn't about the blackmail, that was merely the currency. It was worse: he'd had a choice between letting his daughter screw up his big career-making case or using her to make it; if he was a pal of Bob'n'Dick's, it wouldn't've taken him long to decide.

Dolly was confused.

'I don't understand.'

Her father draped an arm around her shoulders.

'It's alright, sweetheart. Listen, why don't you go gather up your things. I want you to leave here with me today.' He glanced at Malthus. 'That's alright, isn't it, Inspector?'

Malthus nodded coolly.

'To leave this house, yes; not *France*,' which he pronounced the French way.

I noticed Demonica failed to confirm. I doubted Dolly would sleep again until she was airborne. I didn't say anything. I, too, liked the idea of her well out of the way.

Obediently, she rose and left the coffee lounge.

Demonica pleaded:

'Put yourself in my shoes, Woolf. What was I supposed to do? If I lifted her out of here just like that, it could have compromised my whole investigation'. If Hayat had made good on her threat to release a sex film with her in it, whether directly to his employers or not, or if they even found out that his daughter was a member of the group, he'd have been pulled out of anything to do with The Accord in a New York minute and - now that he had established a connection with his main case - he would probably have lost that too. 'I had to leave things as they were while I played along.'

Malthus pursed his lips, scratched his left sideburn and brought his fingertips together in a spire.

'I wish to understand. She was in this film?'

I'm not sure why, maybe because he had innocently gotten me out of having to reveal Leahy, or maybe because I didn't want to make things more difficult in the long run between him and Dolly, but I came to Demonica's rescue.

'Not the one we caught up with at Harwich. Probably nothing heavy. They had a habit of editing film, some of it pretty innocent stuff by today's standards.' I took a stab at humour: 'By the standards of your Channel Four.' He got the point about as badly as I had done when Mercury tried it on me. 'Spliced in with the far-out fucks.'

'Right. I was sure that was what had happened.' Demonica bought my lead with evident gratitude. 'But my being sure wouldn't have been the same thing.'

'The same as what?' Malthus was still confused.

'As his superiors,' I said, my tone now divested of sympathy: 'He'd have been off the case, compromised. Right, Demonica?'

'You've got to understand, Malthus; you too Woolf,' he said, acknowledging my disapproval, 'I've spent years working on it all. This is just a small part of a much larger case.'

'Cake, you mean?'

'Think what you like, Woolf; she's my daughter, and it's my conscience.'

Malthus shook his head in dismay.

'To stay on the case, then?'

Demonica, eager for re-admission to the brethren of the self-righteous, failed to spot the contempt.

'Sure, that's right, you understand, you're a detective.'

Malthus spoke heavily.

'No. I do not understand. Not a daughter.'

Maybe it would've been kosher for a son, but not a daughter.

I was tired of trampling on Demonica for the hell of it; nor was I as shocked as Malthus - I had seen first-hand what people like Demonia were willing to do; nothing surprised me any longer.

'It still leaves a lot of questions unanswered. What are you speculating?'

'Felice Hayat is using The Accord to help her friends.'

It was consistent with what Rupert had told me the night before and that I'd fed into the factual matrix of the case.

'So what've we got here? The Accord as a cover for porn: that I'll buy; I've seen it for myself. I can see the connection that way, back through Morris, or maybe Donleavy if you like, to these other clients you're talking about. Good marketing. Or are you suggesting that The Accord is also a laundry the other way around: bringing money in and out of - where? - the States, England, here? To do what with it? People, too?'

As I spelled it out, I realised just how credible it was, and how original and what a good cover: no one but no one would investigate cash movements of charitable monies between parts of a cult as small, in the global scale of things - say, in comparison to the Moonies or Scientology - as The Accord; likewise, the movement of their personnel is a matter of indifference; and, an organisation that small allows one person - Felice Hayat - with a clique of close comrades within it to keep transactions well-concealed and under tight control.

What The Accord had become was a confidence trick that fed all her needs for wealth and the good life and power over people, again as Rupert had put it the night before. He was her greatest achievement, and victim, because it was his personal wisdom and vision which had not merely constructed the imagery and ethos of the cult, but that had contributed the essential qualities of sincerity and integrity to it. There were many other victims, too: Dolly, maybe people like Lois and Melinda Metcalfe, who knew who else.

Demonica watched me absorb and answer my own questions. Malthus, too, was beginning to realise how well it fit together. The problem was, there remained a number of pieces which didn't seem to have any relevance.

'Why did Hayat boot Rupert out? And why now? How did the Yavitch kids get involved? Why kill May, why kill Amy?' I didn't bother asking about Colin Wrighton: if he was any good at his job, by the time they caught him at it he would have discovered enough to merit killing him; if, as I had understood, he and Sarah had partnered off in The Accord, she would have to go down with him, however much or little he had confided in her.

'Another question,' Demonica said: 'Would have to be why Donleavy got involved at all?'

I knew the answer to that one, but it wasn't information to share, so all I asked was:

'Was he?'

'Was he what?'

'Was he involved? Let's say,' I was fishing: 'Let's say more than a few months before he did a runner, what about then?' I meant, but of course did not say, before he was spun into orbit by the revelation about his father.

Demonica shook his head.

'*I* wouldn't be able to answer that. On what I know, I'd have to say maybe not, maybe Morris, maybe some running about for his principal, maybe some activities he began to put together, but it would be hard for someone in his position to have initiated the involvement. You're a lawyer, an English lawyer, you'd know better than I.'

'I'd say, yes, difficult; not impossible - trainees bring in clients; it makes them looks good, can help them get taken on once they qualify. But what you're saying makes sense: if Morris is bent, or even a little careless with the old ethical lines, I doubt he'd trust a trainee clerk, not at once anyway. Donleavy probably wouldn't have initiated the relationship or managed it, but he'd probably know enough to use it for his own purposes if he was minded to do so.'

It was where I had already mostly arrived: Donleavy was using The Accord to get at Carson and me; I had admitted I was looking for Donleavy; I was also acquainted with Colin-Saul; my presence freaked Felice and she turned to her sponsors to warn them there might be trouble; they stepped in to protect their interests and, maybe using the same resources as Malthus and Dowell - fingerprints held by the FBI, to which they would surely have access - they turn up Colin's identity and turned him off. Donleavy could in theory be responsible for May and Amy but I doubted it: they were loose ends and, as I had logged, a cheap and easy way to warn me to stay away.

Donleavy was probably still waiting for them to go to the next stage and kill me and Carson too, but I didn't think it was going to happen: while he might want us dead, they would be much more careful before bumping off a lawyer who, so far as they were aware, had no criminal skeletons in his filing cupboard, only empty bottles. It was a lacuna in his legal education, though given who he got it from, it was understandable: lawyers keep records in a way criminals mostly don't; if I was killed, or if Carson was killed and I went off the range, it could unleash far worse problems than knocking off a few Australians or the odd PI. The little shit had miscalculated: he had got it upside down - he didn't want anyone dead except us; what he was getting was everyone but us. He might have been too clever by half but it wasn't enough.

'There is something else to ask, Dave,' Malthus said gently. 'I think you know this.'

I had been wondering when someone would get around to asking. Promptly, I said:

'I told you; I'm working for Carson, my girlfriend.'

He shook his head, eyes wide and sad:

'No, I think that explains the cousins, the mother, not this Donleavy.'

I frowned, wondering how to answer him without finding myself spending tonight where Rupert had spent last.

'It's privileged. I was hired as a solicitor.'

Malthus snorted derisively.

'This will satisfy Dowell?'

For once, I had the man on my side.

'Sure. I guarantee it.'

I belatedly picked up the emphasis Demonica had placed in an earlier answer, on the word 'I', as in '*I* wouldn't be able to answer that'.

'Who's in charge of the English investigations, then? I mean, into The Accord.'

I guessed the answer before Demonica told me, surprise in his tone:

'Why, Dowell of course. I thought you knew that.'

At some level, I probably did.

* * *

That evening, I returned to London. I had Malthus' agreement to do so, which is more than Demonica could claim as, just as I had anticipated, he and Dolly flew out directly to the States, although the Inspector did not try to stop them. I had promised to return on demand, and at least five percent of me meant it. For the time being, however, I needed some answers from Dowell that I didn't anticipate achieving by cross-channel communication. I called ahead to ask him to meet me at the house. He wasn't in the office, but I left a message anyway.

I was at the front door, keen to see my loved ones, about to insert my key into the door when it was opened from within. Expecting Carson carrying Alton, I thrust out my arms.

'Sweetie-pie,' Tim snarled.

'You got my message?'

'What message?' He didn't wait for an answer. 'I came to see you about a wee problem.'

'Being?' I was tired and confused. 'Where's Carson? Where's Alton?'

I followed him into the living room.

'Good questions. Does Alton have an American Express card on your account? Has he learned to drive?'

He was doing nothing for my confusion, even if I was already alert enough to put my tiredness on hold.

'Explain,' I demanded as I dove into the kitchen to fetch some ice from the freezer: first things first.

He had followed me, clutching two glasses and a bottle.

'Wally lost Alan this afternoon. They were on foot at the time. Suddenly, car swoops up alongside Alan in the middle of Newcastle, boy dives in and away they go. Wally didn't see who was driving, but like a good lad remembered everything I taught him and wrote down the licence plate. A rental - Hertz must be doing good out of this case even if no one else is. Anyhow, they told us the card number it was rented on and from there, that'll do nicely. You wanna guess or you wanna drink?'

CHAPTER ELEVEN

I didn't respond to Dave on the phone because, by the time it had sunk in, I knew what I was going to do and I knew the lengths he'd go to stop me.

I didn't tell him either just how late my period was: that raised a different series of issues I didn't feel ready to confront.

I went through the motions of dressing and feeding Alton, delivering him to pre-school, then, instead of going into the office, I returned to Cloudesley Road and popped in to see Jada. I didn't make a big deal of it.

'I have to go out of town. I'm not sure when Dave will be home: tonight, tomorrow. I'll, uh, be back soon.' I couldn't look her in the eye.

She knew me too well.

'What's wrong?'

'Nothing.' I told her the same as I told Dave. 'My period's late. It always makes me moody.'

She didn't answer; she didn't believe me.

Dave's been too much like a father, or older brother, to her and she relates to me by association; she didn't have the confidence to push me into confiding in her.

'Shall I pick him up? Keep him here?'

I hadn't bothered about clothes and toys or food; we each have a key to the other's house.

'Yeah. Thanks.'

I went home to pack the few belongings I had when I went to live there, leaving behind most of the things Dave had bought me or paid for, feeling guilty I hung on to the Amex card but knowing I might need more than I had in the bank or could charge through Visa.

Also, from the study, I took the gun Leahy had returned through Dave, checking to see if it was still loaded.

It was.

* * *

Ever since the first time, I've been scared it could never happen again. Sometimes I say I don't want children. I say that a lot around Dave because I know he's low fertility and that he and Sandy never thought she'd get pregnant. It was why she hadn't bothered with birth control. He admitted to me one time that he'd been worried Alton wasn't his until he was born and they confirmed there was pure Southern Comfort running through his veins. I tell Dave I don't want a child because I don't want him to worry about not making me pregnant. But it isn't true.

For a long time, I was in two minds about it. One side of me wanted a child to undo all the fuck-ups of my own childhood; the other didn't, in case history repeated itself. I compromised by saying I wanted to have the choice and worrying I couldn't get pregnant, let alone carry to full term. I said it only to myself. I didn't want to have to tell anyone why I was worried about it. I didn't want to have to tell anyone about that first time.

Now I figured Alan knew about it. Alan and probably therefore Amy had also known. I don't think May knew, or if she did she had buried it so deep she would have sworn it was untrue.

It was the only thing that made sense.

* * *

I caught a flight to Newcastle with no difficulty at all. Hardly anyone wants to go there. I checked through my solitary case so the gun wouldn't show up on the x-ray. I owned so little, I could otherwise have carried it on board as hand baggage.

Last time I'd been there was with Dave. We weren't speaking at the time, though I can't remember why. It was after we had become lovers but before we started to live together. It seemed a long time ago, though it was less than a year. I was compacting the whole time I'd known him - and before him, Sandy - into these last few months of living together; I'd known him four, five years. They'd been good years; they'd been the only good years.

I rented a car at the airport. I knew where Alan was staying because Dave had told me and, even though the odds were against finding him at his hotel patiently awaiting my arrival, I headed there first. The only other points of reference were all Donleavy's: Jesmond, where he used to live; where his firm was; Blyth harbour.

I didn't figure Donleavy to have returned to Cramlington, where he'd been brought up. There was nothing left for him there. I did figure Donleavy was in the area, though, that Alan knew it, and that he was who Alan had gone to see. Why else would he have hung around London, then slid away like a thief in the night to a town he had no other connections with, unless it was where he'd arranged to meet up with Donleavy?

Donleavy and, I assumed, Amy.

I put it together like this. We knew Donleavy and Amy knew one another: they were the Facebook connection. We knew Alan had been led into The Accord. We knew Donleavy had connections back to The Accord - through the firm he used to work for - and therefore to the exotic import-export Blyth business, to which, of course, Alan was even more directly connected and to which he had been tied, according to what Dave told me he'd said at Chelsea Police Station, by his sister Amy.

Throw into the pot that Donleavy was Leahy's son and it was as obvious as the day: Donleavy had enlisted Alan and Amy, with their hatred for me, and The Accord with its twisted activities, into his campaign to execute the revenge he had assumed on behalf of his father.

That was why I had decided Alan and Amy knew about my abortion. It explained the extent and intensity of their hatred. I don't mean to say that they should have loved me, or that their resentment was incomprehensible, but on the face of it, they should by now have grown beyond their anger at me.

As the court had commented, I was a victim too, if not the greatest victim of all; it was I who would have to live for the rest of my life with the knowledge that I had killed my uncle, even if I had only done so in order to save my father.

If the court had only known. If anyone had known, what would they have believed of the fifteen year old who killed her uncle, whose baby she had aborted not three months before?

* * *

They say you always love the first one most of all. I don't know if it's true of everyone else, but it's true of me.

I was always a big girl, and mature for my age, and embarrassed by both amongst my contemporaries at school and in the neighbourhood - embarrassed with the other girls; more embarrassed with the boys. I'd had to grow up quickly once my mother disappeared, left alone to care for my father in his wheelchair, with the chip on his shoulder that would have prevented him rising out of it if ever he'd recovered the use of his legs and which did prevent him letting me alone for a moment - in part to punish me for my mother, in part pre-emptively, because he was afraid that if I slipped out of his sight I'd never come back.

Nate and May, and Amy and Alan, both much younger than I, were all the family we had within reach. There was distant family - of my father's - still in Europe, and a third or thirtieth cousin in Perth, and there were lots of people I had grown up calling uncle or aunt but who were just friends of my parents, friends mostly of my mother who stayed away, ashamed of her or feeling guilty by association, once she had left.

It was a morose house. I don't think it had been decorated since they'd bought it long before I was born. The lights were low wattage. The garden was dry and unkempt, unlike the small, luscious lawns of our neighbours. Ours was the only house on the street without a car in the driveway; my father couldn't drive anymore, I was too young, and my mother had a car which she left behind, but he got Nate to sell it for him.

Nate came around all the time. He too felt guilty about his sister - my mother; for a long time, my father believed he must know where she was, where she'd gone and with whom, and the only way Nate could convince him he didn't was to come around a lot more than he would otherwise have done or than he used to do before she left. If he stayed away even a week, my father would say he'd heard from my mother, he's hiding something. I used to wonder why Nate bothered, then he told me one day - I was about ten, eleven - it was for me, he didn't want me to lose all my memories of my mother, he didn't want me to feel totally deserted, not just by her but by her family too.

It might have been true.

At school, I excelled at gymnastics. It was the only thing I did well. I was strong. I could lose myself for hours in the gym, on the bars, on the ropes, on the horse. For my confirmation present, when I was thirteen, during one of his intermittent flush phases, Nate bought me a gym-horse and bars which we set up in the garage over my father's protests that he might get better one day, might want a car again, and that we were only doing it to show him we had no faith in his recovery.

Nate winked at me.

'Somewhere to go, Carsie.'

He was the only one who ever called me that.

One day, when I was fourteen, I had been practicing for hours. It was a Sunday afternoon, and my father was asleep in the house, unconscious with drink. I was sweating and hot and my t-shirt and shorts stuck to me like a second skin. I had left the garage doors open. I wasn't wearing a bra. I wore a bra when I ran and at school, where it was compulsory, but I didn't need to the remainder of the time. I was doing bar hoops. I was totally absorbed in them. I was aiming at a whole new personal record. Faster and more, faster and faster; I did it like I was in the school stadium and everyone was watching me; I did it like it was the Olympics, televised world-wide. I was running a fantasy commentary in my mind. I was running fantasy applause in my head.

Nate stood in the doorway applauding. He was leaning against the door-frame. He was not a big man: I had already reached almost my full height; he was perhaps an inch taller than me. He, too, had drunk at lunchtime. He started to applaud afresh, gently and genuinely. I flushed and let myself down, supporting myself between the bars. Now of course, I can recognise the moment and the mood as well as anyone else, but I didn't know what it was about then. We just stood there, staring at each other. I was self-conscious because my nipples were hard. My mouth was dry.

"Lo, Uncle Nate.'

"Lo, Carsie,' he said uneasily.

Normally, I'd have given him a hug and a kiss on the cheek, or somewhere in the air around it. Normally, he'd have given me a kiss and an awkward pat on the back. So we stood there, neither of us moving, and I was tingling with sweat and wishing he was my father instead of my uncle, wishing I was the most important person in the world to him instead of May, or the kids, wishing I was a kid who could curl up in his lap like I used to, wishing if none of this was possible that he wasn't years older but a boy the sort of age I was interested in.

I don't remember him closing the garage doors behind him.

I don't remember him crossing the floor towards me.

I don't remember anything before we were kissing and he was touching me and my hands flailed uselessly behind his back, useless not because they were trapped but because I was too ignorant to know what I was supposed to do with them.

He broke away, backed away, shocked, distraught.

I was confused. Why was he shocked? Why was he upset? I advanced on him, fumbling for words to explain it was alright, it was what I wanted, I might not know how to do it but I knew what it was and I knew who he was and I knew he was who I wanted to be with.

That was the first time.

Nothing happened then. Nothing more than I have described. But it was the first time just the same. That night, I lay in bed, and I couldn't sleep. I lay there, I touched myself thinking about him, thinking he wanted me, fantasising that somehow all the myriad problems would be overcome - relationship, age, May and the kids - and we would find ourselves somewhere, maybe run away like my mother, to live together. I know that there's nothing I can say that would persuade a feminist, a psychologist or a social worker that I knew what I was doing, that Nate was not taking advantage of me, was not abusing me, but I know in myself it wasn't like that at all.

I'm quite clear about this: I wanted it, and after this first time I went out to get it with far more certainty than him, and I succeeded.

* * *

Alan wasn't at the hotel. I got directions to Blyth and drove out there, wondering if the Geordie Queen might have returned to her home port. She hadn't: there wasn't a single ship in the harbour. I returned to Newcastle and parked in the station car park, across the street from the hotel, in the area reserved for people meeting or leaving off railway passengers. I clocked the twenty minute limit and wondered if Mr Hertz could afford the fine or whether he'd chase me for it. Guiltily, having avoided thinking about him for all of the last half hour, I realised it wouldn't be me, but Dave.

There was no Alan Yavitch registered. The receptionist didn't recognise my description of him either. Florence Nightingale on the back of a tenner didn't make her memory a whole lot healthier; I didn't figure even Sir Christopher Wren could make a monument out of it for fifty quid. I didn't bother with twenty: the sort of people I'm likely to be trying to bribe aren't interested in Shakespeare. They can't read, most of them. It's a funny thing about the Poms; none of them ever look at the picture on the back of currency - they're all fixated on the picture of the Queen on the front. It deprives us putative PIs of cracks like: 'Meet Andrew Jackson' or any of the other Presidents who adorn US dollars. Five pounds buys you George Stephenson, whoever he may be. It was frustrating, 'cos I knew Alan was registered.

I asked for a street map of the town and got one, even though I wasn't a resident, mostly, I think, to get rid of me. I looked up Jesmond. That was where Joe Donleavy used to live and where Dave had met his girlfriend Lesley. It wasn't too far from Gosforth, where the offices of Morris and Co were: the Co was illusory.

I had no address in Jesmond to focus on, so I went to Gosforth instead. There was little chance that it had been selected as the meeting-point: ostensibly, Donleavy was in difficulties with his boss, on whom he'd done a runner. On the other hand, there was plenty to suggest Frank Morris was not an innocent employer so he might be willing to forgive his errant trainee. I didn't call ahead but it was already getting close to the end of the working day and if he refused to see me, worst came to worst I would out-wait him. By the time I found the office, it was after five and he was almost alone in the office, personally walking a client to the door, only a secretary still waiting for permission to leave, her coat draped over a chair an unsubtle hint the witching hour had arrived.

Out of his hearing, I tossed my head in his direction.

'Morris?'

'Do you have an appointment?' she asked reluctantly.

'Nope. Name's Carson. I'm a friend of Dave Woolf's, who came...'

From behind me, he said, his voice weary beyond the hour of the day:

'It's alright, Doreen; you can go. I'll take care of this.'

He ushered me ahead of him into his office and didn't speak again - not even to invite me to sit - until he had taken his place behind his desk, the businessman and professional's safety barrier.

I sat anyway.

He said listlessly, like he already knew but also knew to pretend not to:

'What's this about?'

'You don't seem exactly surprised to see me,' I commented.

'I have more strangers coming to see me these days than clients.'

'What sort of people, Mr Morris?'

'Why do you want to know?'

'I said; I work with Dave Woolf.' It wasn't what I had said, but it didn't matter. 'We're working the same case: Joe Donleavy.'

'You and everybody else,' he replied gloomily.

He was an unprepossessing man. The picture on his desk told me there was a Mrs Frank and a couple of Frank-furters, but for the life of me I couldn't imagine anyone loving him or awaiting his return from work with a bound in their hearts. He was balding, but not so badly there wasn't enough hair to generate a liberal fall of dandruff onto the shoulders of his polyester suit; he was bespectacled, but one of the arms of his glasses had been broken and was currently held together with masking tape. There was also the remnant of a bruise below his right ear.

'I was mugged a little while ago. At least, it seemed to be a mugging. It wasn't, of course. Like everything else, it was all about Joe Donleavy. I wish I'd never set eyes on that boy,' he added bitterly.

'Tell me about the mugging,' I suggested.

'I didn't tell the police; I'm not going to tell you. I was expressly - uh - invited not to do so.'

'Male, on his own, small-ish, middle-aged, big fists?'

'That's right. How did you know? If that was something your man Woolf had something to do with...' He half-rose in what was intended to be a threatening gesture but that didn't withstand an airy wave of my hand. He collapsed back into his chair, tired. 'No, I suppose it wouldn't be. But you know who it was?'

'Do you?' I challenged him.

'I know what he said.'

'The boy's father, right?'

'Right. For God's sake,' he expostulated. 'I don't know why he couldn't have come in to see me in a normal manner.'

I did, but I didn't say.

'What happened?'

'I was working late. I was walking to my car. I have a space around the back.' He tossed his head behind him, as if I could see through walls as well as leap through space. 'He seemed to think I'd know where Joe was; he seemed to think I had some responsibility for his disappearance.' His eyes glazed over. 'He didn't seem willing to take no for an answer.'

'How badly hurt were you?'

'Not that badly. Not as bad as it felt at the time. You'd think he was some kind of gangster the way he carried on.'

Again, I didn't enlighten him. All I said was:

'I think you got off lightly.'

He shuddered. 'Who else has been asking about Donleavy?'

'Since Woolf?'

'Yes.'

'The police. One of my other clients has had a bit of, uh, trouble...'

'In Harwich, I know. Bynoe, right?'

'You're well informed; too well informed.'

'Let me tell you what I think, Mr Morris. I don't think you know where Donleavy is, but I think you do know some people who might, like some of your other clients he was a bit too friendly with.' I put the girlfriend's accusation to him much the way it had been recounted to me by Dave.

He neither confirmed nor denied.

'Did you tell Donleavy's father about them?'

He gritted his teeth, tossing up between pretending he could defend privilege under any assault and admitting he was a coward. Glumly, he said:

'Wouldn't you?'

'I'd tell Donleavy's father anything he asked, without waiting for him to force it out of me,' I proffered sympathetically. 'Who did you tell him, Mr Morris?'

'Who is he?'

'A very nasty man; a very dangerous man.'

'Woolf said he was making enquiries on behalf of the family?'

I didn't know if it was true Dave had said it or not, so, in my turn, I kept silent.

'Why would he work for a man like that?'

'Same reason you told him what he wanted to know; same reason I would, any sane person would unless they had him handcuffed arms and legs and covered by a guard with a Uzi.' Most of the allusions went over his head, so I summarised: 'He's a very frightening man, Mr Morris; you don't say no to him lightly - or at all.'

'What's this all about?' he cried.

'Why don't you tell me?' I suggested.

'I don't know,' he said. I recognised the tone. Anyone who's been around lawyers as long as I have would do so. It wasn't the beginning of a denial of all information. It was denial of formal knowledge, denial of any wrongdoing on his own part, because he didn't know for sure. But he had a good idea. In case I missed the point, he added: 'I'm not guilty of anything. Except, perhaps, of turning a blind eye.'

'Isn't that the biggest crime of all, the one most people get away with?'

'Perhaps.' He was too exhausted to argue. He had been so far out of his league for too long even to try. 'I knew Joe was, uh, seeing too much of a client; I had a feeling - just an instinct - he was doing more than just seeing him. I should have asked him, I should have taken responsibility. He was my trainee.'

'But you didn't. Because?'

'It was keeping the client happy, happy to stay here; connected. It's not much,' he waved a hand around him in case I'd mistaken his offices for those of a big, rich city firm. 'We have to hang on to what we can.'

I waited for him to tell me more. He had no more to tell me. I said:

'At least, tell me the name you gave Donleavy's father.'

For a moment, I thought he was going to refuse.

* * *

The name he gave me was that of one Bob Bentley, a local entertainments agent, though not all his shows were publicly advertised on billboards around the North East and that wasn't all he did. He was, according to Morris, who had by then decided that full co-operation would be the quickest way of getting rid of me, a thick-set, muscular man, though definitely and distinctly not fat, in his mid- to late forties, with a full head of straight dark brown or black hair, pug-nosed and with eyes set wide apart, clean shaven: Morris thought he might have tattoos but couldn't remember for sure; just that he had once been in the merchant navy. The place he told me he was most often to be found was a pub called The Cooperage, on the quayside, where small boats and working barges docked, to reach which I would have to go back through the centre of town. The only other piece of information he gave me was that The Animals used to play at The Cooperage but I wouldn't find them there now.

I was driving through the town centre when I saw first Wally, then - maybe forty, fifty yards ahead - Alan, both of them on foot. I took a deep breath and kept my face averted as I passed Tim's oversized assistant, and pulled in beside Alan, the window already lowered.

'Don't argue; you're being followed. Jump in, Alan.'

He hadn't done what I told him so well since he was six years old; it was, I think, at a church-organised barbie, either three or four days before I killed his father.

* * *

We sat in a corner of a bar in a pub I don't know the name of, except it was outside the town centre and wasn't The Cooperage. While I checked the windows to make sure Wally hadn't caught up with us, I sent Alan to fetch us both a drink. He hovered long enough for me to realise he was running out of money. I gave him a tenner, which he took as if it was the poisoned chalice.

In the car, I told him he was being followed by the police, but refused to answer his questions either about how I knew, or about what I was doing there, or why I had picked him up.

Now I told him what I had guessed, in a tone that said I knew:

'You're here to meet Amy, right?'

He nodded, nursing his beer as he listened.

'You met up with Donleavy in Paris. Was the trip planned before he and Amy hooked up on Facebook?'

He hesitated for one last time before deciding to co-operate; he had worked out it was the only way he was going to find out what was happening. He nodded:

'It was something we'd talked about; you know how it is, everyone does it.' A year or two in Europe before settling down was a rite of passage for numerous Australians.

'He's who introduced you to The Accord,' I recited, something else Dave had relayed to me. 'When did I first come up?'

'Amy had told him about you online; I think he looked up a lot about the trial. He was there to meet Amy; he fancied her. He had money. He showed you both a good time then he took her off your hands, and left you with The Accord.'

'If you know it all, why're you telling me?'

'Did you tell him about me and Dave?'

'He already knew.'

Leahy knew about me; Leahy had told his son all about us.

'It was his idea for you to get into The Accord?' Again, he nodded, silently. 'Because he said he had a way of getting back at me?' He flushed at this, as much confirmation as I needed. 'Did you ask him how? Did you ask him to explain?'

'He didn't say. He said he knew them, The Accord. He said they were into some stuff.' He flushed again. 'He said if he could get you to come over, he could make you pay for what you'd done. Amy came up with the idea of Mum involving you, though neither of us thought she'd come over, just that she'd ask you to find us. That's what Donleavy told us, that you'd been asking questions, nothing about our mother.'

'What was his plan? How was he going to get at me?'

'I said, he never told us; anyway, he never told me.' He admitted that Amy could have been more in the know than he was. He stared me in the eyes and said: 'I didn't really care, as long as it got you in trouble.'

'Yes. How did you find out?' We'd moved back home.

For a long time, he didn't speak. Then he said:

'There were some photographs of you, you and him.' He didn't mean pornographic, there were none of those, but I could remember a day we'd snuck out on our own, and the tourists at the harbour who he'd asked to take photos. 'And some letters you wrote.' I cringed to remember the terms I'd written in, and how I'd sneaked the letters into somewhere private that only he'd find them. 'And a notebook he kept.' I tried to hide my surprise at this new insight. 'They were in the attic, hidden, I found them. Later, years later. *I* found them.' His voice rose but it was difficult to tell whether he was talking from pride or anger. 'How *could* you? How could you do that?'

To my embarrassment, he burst into tears, covering his face with his hands. I didn't say anything, or move to comfort him. Just waited for it to subside.

'You never told anyone before now, did you? You never told Amy, or May, or Joe?'

He shook his head, tears still flowing from his eyes.

'I didn't want anyone to know. I didn't want anyone to know about him. What he'd done.'

I said, sadly:

'Nor did I.'

* * *

It had started about a month beforehand. My father began to suspect. He'd been suspicious of me, of what I was up to, from before the abortion and through it, but now, for the first time, he began to suspect Nate. At first, he voiced his suspicions in snide jibes about how nice it was for me to be so close to my uncle, my mother's only brother. Since he never had a good word to say for her, it had to be sarcastic.

Then there were cracks about like brother, like sister, which I only half understood at the time, but later came to realise were part of the pattern: my mother, his wife, had run off, it was generally taken for granted with another man. That put her in the same category as prostitutes, nymphos and other sexual deviants.

Then there were direct questions. What did we do together? One time, we were doing it in the garage when we heard his wheelchair screeching and bouncing in a vain attempt to sneak up on us unawares. We both got the giggles as we struggled back into our clothing. It had been harder for Nate to get into his suit than for me to scramble into my tracksuit. Finally, in the last week, the direct accusations of unnatural conduct - both making it with Nate and of the abortion Nate had organised for me - which led me to call Nate in a panic, first at home then at the office where they said he was working late, tracking him down at his favourite pub where he'd gone to escape us and it all. me as much as his family, and his weak-minded confusion.

He came to the house. The door wasn't locked. I was cowering upstairs where my father couldn't reach me. I was squatting on my bed, hugging myself, crying, mumbling, shutting out the intermittent roars from below that signalled my father's drunken anger and frustration. Nate, too, was well plastered. By the time I timidly, step by step, descended, they were shouting at each other, Nate denying, denying, denying, my father that he knew, he knew. My father had already flung a bottle at Nate, but he was so physically weak, it had fallen short onto the wooden floor without breaking. I screamed:

'Stop it, stop it, both of you.'

It had but a momentary effect. Nate told me to go back upstairs like I was a little child. My father said he was going to call the police, that Nate would be thrown in jail where he belonged, and that I'd be put into a home where any daughter of that slut my father had married belonged.

I ran sobbing into the kitchen. I didn't mean to hurt either of them. I just wanted them to stop. I grabbed the meat cleaver from its hook above the wooden counter. Perhaps I meant to hurt myself instead. At that moment, I felt I deserved it; my father was right, I was like my mother, I was no better than a tramp. As I returned to the front room, where my father ate, slept and sat, I realised the noise had died down. The door was half shut. I had pulled it behind me, to slam it, but - as ineffectual as everything else in that house - it had refused to stay shut and had bounced open instead.

Nate said:

'I never meant it. Can't you understand that, for Christ's sake?'

My father said:

'I understand you're in dead trouble, the age she is. You're her uncle.'

Nate said:

'What do you want, man?'

My father said, a familiar note of craftiness in his voice:

'I don't know. Yet.'

I knew. He wanted power. He wanted control. He wanted the use of his damned legs back and if he couldn't have that he was going to kick arse anyway.

'Money? Is that what this is about?'

I waited for my father to deny it.

After a long pause, he said:

'Maybe.'

That was when I burst into the room, screaming, the meat cleaver poised above my head.

Nate turned, horrified.

Because we never talked about it afterwards - barely talked at all before he died - I never asked my father why there was a look of quiet triumph in his eyes as he watched me, unmoving.

He should have been moving, because he knew it wasn't at Nate that the cleaver was aimed. He was who I wanted to kill.

Nate stepped between us, his forearm up to push the cleaver aside, the other hand ready to grab it away from me.

Like I said, not a big man, not much taller than I, and I was the one who worked out daily, not him.

We struggled for it. He had it firmly in his grasp. I fought him. It slipped, fell, we dove for it at the same moment, I had it, I raised it as I rose, he tripped, I fell on top of him, I no longer knew what was happening, what I was doing. I had as near as dammit blacked out and, for one fatal moment, obsessed by the wish to kill, it didn't matter who, I forgot what it was supposed to be about; he wasn't Nate anymore but my father, my father who I hated more than anything or anyone on earth.

I sobbed and screamed and - far, far later than they should have - neighbours began to bang on the door. My father hissed once:

'He was trying to kill me, he was drunk,' he said. 'You stopped him.'

There wasn't time to check whether this story had sunk in before the neighbours burst in. I didn't listen to any of what happened next, or if I did I didn't hear it. Soon, ambulance men, the police, a social worker, a doctor, half the local community, May, were all crowded into the house, talking at once, and no one was paying me any mind at all.

I heard, then, my father recite and elaborate on the lie he had spontaneously devised. If anyone asked me for my version of events, I don't remember it. I think at the time, they just assumed that what my father said was what I would have said. I was handled with kid gloves, shot full of sedative, taken into immediate care, it wasn't until two days later that the police came to interview me. By that time, I had persuaded myself to believe the account my father had issued. I told myself I was doing it for him, to make amends: he would be in trouble for lying; he would be ashamed - in part because he knew I had been going for him, in much larger part because of what would come out about me and Nate.

At first, they told me there wouldn't even be a trial. That was about the time they allowed me to go back home. Then it was decided there would have to be a trial after all but they let me stay at home just the same. I wished they hadn't. I wished I'd never set eyes on that man again. We lived in an atmosphere of as near total hatred as any parent and child could achieve.

I doubled the hours I spent in my home-gym. I was allowed to go to school, but no one wanted to be seen with me, the few friends I had before shunned me, and of course my extended family - May and the kids - were complete strangers. In the end, I could see my father's condition deteriorating, as the trial drew near. The doctors wanted to take him into his hospital. He forgot things. One of his lungs was near collapse. He barely ate though continued to drink each night, drink himself unconscious. He lost weight. He wouldn't leave the house, he wouldn't leave me, not for love, but to play out to the last moment that extraordinary, intense, desolate contempt we felt for one another.

I was taken temporarily into care between his death and the trial. At the trial, I re-told the same story, now honed as fine and as sharp as the blade of the cleaver - Crown Exhibit A. The one point of evidence that needed explanation was my attempt earlier that evening to find Nate. But Nate was dead and my father was dead and the truth in solitary isolation fit: that my father was drunk, he was abusing me, I was scared, so I called, as always, for my Uncle Nate to come and calm him down. How was I to know he was himself drunk, or how angry he would be with my father, or how it would result?

After, the authorities arranged a family for me to live with while I finished my schooling. I never did so. I left Australia within a year - without permission, with help from newfound friends from the bars and clubs I had begun to frequent, passing easily for much older than I was. I went back to Australia just the once, years later, but it wasn't home. The closest I've ever come to home since was when I was in Baltimore with Dave and said:

'You'll have to be gentle, then, Dave. Can you do that?'
And now my period was late.

I wish I could make sense of it. I wish I could come to terms with it.

* * *

'There's a lot of money around The Accord,' Alan said. 'A lot of the kids come from wealthy families, they've got money of their own - inheritances, family funds: they get it all.'

'And it's never enough?'

'Right. It's incredibly money-conscious: we're all supposed to be out on the street, bestowing - selling magazines, collecting money - as much as we can stand.'

And when they couldn't stand, they found a money-making activity for them lying down?

'What's Donleavy after? Apart from Dave and me,' I added casually, as if it was the least of my concerns.

'I don't know.'

'We're going to have to find out eventually, aren't we?'

'I suppose.'

'Whose side are you on, Alan?'

'My sister's.'

Ah.

'She told you to ring Dave and warn me off; she told you to get onto the Geordie Queen; she told you where you could meet up with her and Joe - at The Cooperage?'

'That was him; he called my mobile directly.'

There was a long pause while he thought about what I'd said. I asked:

'Do you think he killed May, Alan?'

He nodded again, dully.

.   'I've begun to think about it. He had to be using me, us. It's why I've got to find Amy, get her away from him, do you see?'

He read it in my eyes. His eyes widened. He clutched his mouth like he was about to throw up, his eyes were wild, he pulled his hand away from his mouth, gasping for air, shaking his head:

'You're lying, you're lying, you're lying.'

'I wish I was.' I seized his hand across the table and held onto it. 'You think I wanted this, Alan? You think I wanted any of it? For God's sake, Alan, I know you've hated me, I don't blame you, but do you think I hated you back? All I've ever felt is guilty.'

He was crying again. A man came over, the owner maybe, and asked if we were alright. I said I'd given him bad news from home, using my broadest Aussie growl. Without looking up, Alan nodded to confirm my story. The man was kind: he offered us a drink. I shook my head:

'We have to be going.'

* * *

In the car, he asked me:

'Can you explain it all?'

'I don't think so, Alan. I can only make some guesses.' I told him who Donleavy's father was. 'He had a shock, a profound shock, about his father, about what he did for a living, who he was. Dave and I came into that. He found out. Up to then, I don't think he was crook himself, though it seems certain he hung around with some fairly rough types, like a man called Bob Bentley. Bentley and The Accord were connected, though I'm not sure how. After he found out about his father, Donleavy flipped. Threw up his job. In the back of his mind was the idea he had to do something about his father. I'm not sure how that works out. To prove he was like his father? To take revenge on Dave and me for queering his father's pitch - well, we can be sure of that. He didn't realise that nothing we did had made that much difference - his father was already a much-hated, much-feared, much-wanted man. Maybe he thought his father had lost his bottle and he had to retaliate on his behalf, a matter of family honour, maybe. He used the internet to look into my background and found you and Amy and saw his chance to reach us. That was the key, the coincidence that unlocked it all. It led him to May and me.'

It wasn't really coincidence; opportunity is a better word. There's always an opportunity; it's just a question of whether someone uses it or not. I paused for thought.

'I'm wondering how he got May to leave the hotel.'

'Do you think Amy helped him?' It was the same general direction I had been implying a few minutes earlier but in truth I doubted it: Amy was quite immature but she wasn't stupid and she wasn't evil. Or maybe I didn't want to believe it any more than Alan.

'I think he found May and told her he could bring her to you and Amy, took her somewhere, a hotel or an apartment, kept her there with the promise of finding you again, probably after a bit against her will 'cos she was a feisty woman and not easily fooled.'

'What was he after?'

'I was over there with her on my own, without Dave. I'm wondering if he wanted her to disappear so that I would have to send for Dave to come help look for you guys. It was fairly obvious that's what I'd do once I'd lost May. And it's what I would have done, too; it's what I was planning to do if things hadn't started to move at the other end - when his father contacted us to find him and Dave told me to come home. Once Dave came over, though, it wasn't May he was looking for so much as Donleavy himself. I think that's where it went wrong for him; it wasn't what he had planned. Then, he had the problem of what to do with May.'

'He killed her,' Alan repeated flatly.

'I guess so.' I didn't know as much as I was later to find out Dave knew; at that time, though, I thought it was all Donleavy.

'I don't understand what he was doing with The Accord.'

'I'm not sure either,' I admitted. 'Using them because they were there? He didn't have many other tools.'

'Seems a stretch,' he commented. 'It might've come to nothing. We might not have been interested. You might not have looked for us.'

'Sure, absolutely. That's always the case, with any plan.' I could think of a scam or two Dave had run in the course of a case that were no less of a long-shot. 'You get an idea, you try it; if it doesn't work out, you try something else, is all'.

'He would've just dumped us,' he said bitterly.

'Probably. Well, he dumped you anyway. Amy was win-win; few blokes would mind being stuck with her.'

'But he killed her too,' he pointed out. It was also a guess, but, as with May, at that stage it was what I thought too. 'It's crazy; he's crazy.'

'That's the only certainty, Alan.'

I saw The Cooperage and drew up on the street behind it, clocking the rear exit for a quick getaway. Neither of us got out immediately.

'And Amy? Another loose end?' he asked, his eyes hollow with horror.

'Ah, Alan.' I admitted defeat. 'I can't hang it all together for you. That's part of growing up, I suppose, finding out that it won't all fit however hard you try. I don't know. I think people get mixed up in all sorts of things; things connect - much more than we realise, more than we want and more than we can control. Sometimes, something happens somewhere - perhaps something relatively small - that causes a reaction - a disproportionate reaction - somewhere else, leaving most of the people affected by it stunned, confused, ignorant. Sometimes I think the best thing to do is to stay as far away from everything and everyone else as possible.'

We were about to get out of the car when we saw two men emerge from the pub, walking in our direction.

Alan said:

'That's him.'

I didn't need to be told who. I said:

'The other one's Bentley.'

Oh, shit, Morris was right: he was muscular.

'Let's wait and see what happens.'

Alan wasn't listening.

He leapt out of the car and ran straight at Donleavy.

'Donleavy you bastard, you killed my sister, you killed my mother, I'll kill you fucker, fucker, fuck, fuck, fuck.'

I dove out the driver's side and screamed after him:

'Wait, Alan, for God's sake.'

Donleavy took one look at the charging boy and drew something from his jacket pocket. I assumed it was a gun. I caught Bentley's look of shock. I grabbed my own gun and raised it:

'Don't do it, Joe.'

As Alan flung himself on Joe, I saw Joe was wielding not a gun but a knife. I hardly had time to register my surprise, let alone to remember what his father had said about only defending himself. Bentley knocked Joe's arm upwards, and the knife drove straight into Alan's throat, so fast he did not even scream, blood bursting out of the gaping wound like a fountain, spraying the two men and the street alike as he fell backwards from the sheer impact, leaving the knife in Joe's hand. He was dead before he hit the ground. My own reaction was automatic. I fired, and Donleavy, already turning on me, stopped short, a shocked look on his face, before crumpling slowly to the ground.

Bentley and I stared at one another. He reached down and picked up Joe's knife as if to go for me next despite my superior weapon. Suddenly, simultaneously, we heard a siren. Bentley turned and ran up the street, into the darkness, still holding the knife. I jumped into the car and followed in the same direction, not to catch him but because he would know the best way out.

* * *

I slept in the car in a layby and washed up in the toilet of a petrol station on the A1 motorway going south.

I still wasn't sure where I was headed, just that I ought to keep moving and that railways and airports were not a great idea. In the morning, I hit off west, driving right into Britain's most anonymous metropolis: Birmingham.

I lost my gun in a canal and ate breakfast at a cheap cafe on the Coventry Road. I was hungry as hell and - if the expression may be excused - would have killed for a plate piled high with bacon and eggs and sausages and fried bread. The moment it was served, I couldn't stand the smell and pushed it away without touching any of it.

I paid and left and bought newspapers and chocolate which I gobbled as I scoured the news standing up in the street. There was a short paragraph in one of the papers reciting that there had been a fight outside a Newcastle pub, that shots had been fired, two were dead, and police were looking for a local man. There was no mention of a woman.

I was still undecided where to go next. A chemist's shop attracted my attention. I thought, why not? It was time to confront reality.

I checked the instructions. Yeah, more than four hours had gone by since I last took a leak. I read, too, what I already knew: if it shows up negative, there's a fair chance it's wrong, but if it shows up positive, it's nearly certain to be right.

I asked the assistant if I could use their lavatory and she said sure.

CHAPTER TWELVE

The war itself had started a while ago; the battle was about to begin.

I felt like saying 'Sorry, guv'nor, didn't mean it', and I probably would have done so if we knew exactly who the governor was, more particularly than some po-faced gangster from across the Atlantic who resented our intrusion into his affairs and the threefold loss it implied for him: of The Accord as a porn-manufacturing, trafficking, income-generator; of The Accord as a laundry facility; and, of the edges of his north-eastern network in the person of Bob Bentley.

* * *

Carson got home about midday.

I was waiting for her, hoping she'd come back, believing she'd come back, sitting in the living room listening to Plácido Domingo (or Placebo Dominica as Carson called him): a taste for opera was one of the two legacies my friend Lewis had left me, of which the other was the club.

I had promised Tim I would bring Carson down to the Yard as soon as she arrived: by that time, Wally had caught up with the events outside The Cooperage and knew, along with every other copper in Newcastle, that a gun had killed Joe Donleavy while a knife had ended the life of Alan Yavitch.

'So,' I snapped down the line. 'So the Bentley character had two weapons. So what? Or he had one, Donleavy had one, they both got used.'

'Yeah.' How could anyone make one word - really, no more than a grunt - sound so sarcastic?

Wally had not - yet, Tim added darkly - disclosed to the Newcastle police Carson's presence in their crummy city, and thus far she was entirely off their guest-list.

'Hi,' she said defiantly, dumping her small suitcase on the floor as she slumped onto the sofa without kissing me.

I pointed to it accusingly.

'You want me to list what's in there?'

'Not 'specially. I'm back, aren't I?'

'For how long?'

'Nine months, anyway.'

'Ah.'

I was too tired for any of the reactions that might have been expected or - perhaps - required: I had been up all night waiting to hear from her; I knew the gun was gone - I knew where she had gone - and I had plenty of other reasons to worry whether I'd ever see her again.

'Yeah, "ah",' she scowled. 'Is that all you got to say?'

'How do you feel about Alan? That was Joe, or was it Bentley?'

'Not sure - Joe was holding the knife but Bentley gave it the final shove.'

'No weapons found?'

'Nope.'

'And, uh, you don't have a gun on you, do you?'

'Who, me? Nope. We got any white spirit?'

'Sure. In the cupboard.'

'Good shot,' I grunted as she went to fetch it.

That was all we said about who killed Joe Donleavy. There were just too many issues to cope with. He was clearly responsible for a lot of what had gone down, but it was less clear how much of it he intended: to the contrary, my theory - yet to be fully explored with Carson - was that we were the only people he wanted dead and the only ones he wasn't getting dead. Even Alan was not clearly his fault, according to her; while he had, perhaps instinctively, drawn out a knife when Alan came at him, it was consistent with someone acting defensively, which Carson reminded me was what Joe Leahy had said. At this stage, it seemed that she had killed if not an innocent man then someone who was guilty of less than murder himself. His father was not going to be pleased.

Carson scrubbed her hands with white spirit, washed them with soap, then she took a bath and I scrubbed her back wondering if I'd ever know her as well as our intimacy suggested I ought and we drove down to the Yard, spending longer finding somewhere to park than the journey itself.

On the way, I said:

'Pregnant, huh?'

'Yup.'

Not bad for a bum with a low sperm count, I thought. I didn't ask if it was mine; because of that count. I'd asked

Sandy; but I wouldn't've asked Carson even if there was nothing there at all.

'You gonna keep it this time?'

Out of the corner of my eye, I saw her gawp.

'This time?'

'Right. That's right, isn't it? That's why it always made you so antsy, right, when you didn't come on? I can work things out, too, you know.'

'Right. What else you work out?'

'None of my business,' I declared, not entirely honestly. What I figured was, she'd gone to Newcastle to try and find - save - Alan, but she had taken her belongings because, like when Sandy had asked me to stay away one night, before she told me she was pregnant, she wanted to work out whether she really wanted to have it.

'Right.'

And that was all we said about the fact that she was pregnant.

I don't mean that's all either of us felt about it, but it's all we said at the time.

* * *

Neither Tim nor Wally was in a particularly pleasant frame of mind, especially the latter. Before we had shut the door, he snarled:

'I ought to do you for interfering with a police investigation.'

'Sweet,' Carson said, patting him on the cheek. 'Who's your main witness, Alan Yavitch?'

'Sorry about the kid,' Tim said from behind his desk.

'He might be alive now,' Wally said, not needing to complete the thought.

I came gallantly to my lady's rescue:

'You don't behave yourself I'll make you pay to come into the club to see Joannie, Wally.'

'What makes you think I want to come there anymore?' he sulked, adding, lest I misconstrued his point, 'or that she does either, for that matter.'

This was getting heavy. Wally's custom I could do without; but no way did I want to lose Joannie: Natalie would never forgive me nor, maybe, stay on without her.

Tim held up a hand.

'Order, order, order.'

Wally and I sat and waited for his command.

'This is a bit of a mess. It wasn't supposed to go down like this.'

'You can say that again,' I contributed helpfully. 'I've got a client I've yet to tell the news to.' I wasn't looking forward to doing so.

Wally looked confused. Neither Tim nor I had confided in him Donleavy's true identity, or the identity of my client. Tim coughed discreetly, to warn me to keep quiet. I studied his expression non-committedly and said:

'Seems like we've all got a bit of egg on our faces, then, haven't we?' I looked around our motley crew and recited: 'Wally, you lost Yavitch; Cars, you cost us Donleavy; Tim, you should've levelled with me about the background. We had a right to know what kind of scene we were fucking around in, right? As for me, I was a dumb fuck to trust any of you.' I glanced around me darkly; it wasn't fair to include Wally, but I had cause to call both Tim and Carson to account.

Carson asked:

'What background?'

I filled her in, as I had not yet had time to do, what with her disappearing act, her pregnant re-appearance and the small matter of her fast-dissolving family.

'Your pal Bob Bentley was mob-linked, distributing porn from and moving money, drugs and people through The Accord. About it, Tim?'

'Something like that,' he mumbled, embarrassed.

'So what were you trying to pull?'

'I have orders too, Dave.' This, I confess, was news. 'And, uh, one of those orders was to, uh, co-operate, in order to make amends.' I didn't ask what for: he was talking about the way his escape from Joe Leahy's clutches had been cluttered with bodies - in particular, dead ones of the American persuasion.

'So why not tell me, Tim?'

'I didn't think you'd feel like making amends yourself. If you knew who was pulling the strings. If you see what I mean.' He knew I wouldn't piss in Bob'n'Dick's mouths if they were dying of dehydration.

'In the past, you know, you've jerked me around, but I could always see some sense in it - maybe it took me a while.' There was a year or so at one point when we didn't exchange a civil word - or any other. 'But in the end, I felt you'd probably been right to leave me in the dark, let me go my own way. But this is lame. This is police politics. International, maybe, but police politics just the same. This isn't something to fuck your friends up for, you know, to leave us out on a limb.'

'You've got this rosy image of me. You're a cowboy. You think I'm a cowboy too, that I can just go my own way regardless.'

'You can't?'

'Some of the time, maybe; but the rest of the time, it's a freedom I have to pay for.' He had his eye on the formal squad he was seeking to establish before the Commissioner went off to pastures new.

Wally snorted: he wasn't impressed with Tim's reasons either.

Carson said disgustedly:

'We're your best friends, for Christ's sake.'

'Who says it didn't work out alright anyway? Joe Donleavy was bad news. He's dead.'

'So's my aunt and my cousins,' Carson said grimly.

'So's Colin Wrighton,' Wally contributed. 'And his girlfriend.'

Tim looked around us: his friends; almost family; his closest and most - if not only - trusted colleague. We were all telling him the same thing: he stank.

I loved it: it was usually me on the receiving end of so much consensual stick.

Then I put the boot right in.

'Besides which, Tim: you want to be the one tells the boy's father he was bad news? Joe Leahy, I'm referring to, in case you forgot.'

I got up to leave, accompanied by Carson, while it sunk in on Wally just how much more Tim had withheld.

* * *

Against my advice, Rupert and Mercury flew to London. Against my advice, they filed suit to freeze the assets of The Accord in this country and in Europe. They also instructed American lawyers to take similar steps over there. It was about the worst move they could have made, but they were adamant they wanted what was theirs - which included a lot of what had been other people's.

To do all of this required legal assistance, in particular talented legal assistance. I didn't offer mine, or even that of my firm. Instead, I turned the matter over to my old friend Martin Mather. Martin had recently re-asserted majority control over the family firm his father had founded, and of which his sister had assumed temporary command in circumstances that are too complex to explain but which involved jerking me around about as extensively as Tim had done now, if admittedly more enjoyably.

Ali had newly married an American TV magnate and departed to live and bring up brats in Boston, Massachusetts. Next time I visited the States, I could drop in and discuss old times with her. Or I could drop into the polluted harbour and die less painfully.

Tim took Rupert and Mercury in for formal questioning, but the only charges on which they might have been held were for the film and the very way it had been spliced together was the strongest evidence of their non-involvement. On Martin Mather's advice, they refused to co-operate further by disclosing all of the accounts on which they had been able to lay hands, which were for the time being mostly those in the London offices of the cult. As Martin said, they didn't want to help the police prove that the money was, as suspected, dirty; what they wanted was to get their hands on it and do whatever good works with it they felt most inclined towards, like buying a house to live in and relaxing after the arduous years with Felice Hayat or, as I suggested might be more appropriate, plastic surgery and new identities.

As for Felice, an appearance in the American litigation was filed on her behalf, but she personally took off for Antigua with a half-dozen of her closest allies, presumably to guard as well as to pay tribute to her body. It might be too hot for some, but Felice could go back; her connections and influence were still sufficient.

For ourselves, there were no effective precautions we could take, except to be careful walking down a dark alley at night. There were too many directions from which an attack could come. I tried to talk with Carson about relocating, temporarily or even permanently. She wouldn't listen. She knew the risk, but as she said, nowhere was safe and she wasn't going to spend whatever time she had - long or short - hiding.

She was as pregnant as she believed and started spending more days at the Royal Free Hospital - ironically where Sandy had died, and where Alton had been born - under the care of the dour professor in charge of the Department of Obstetrics and Gynaecology than she did at the office.

I caught up with Alton: I couldn't believe how he seemed to have grown, in body and mind, in the few weeks that had passed since I last spent regular time with him. He was talking the whole time now, and I mean the whole time, even when I was trying to sleep. He'd taken to calling me Dave because that was what everyone else called me, and there was no Mum to refer to in daily counterpoint.

I also caught up on my paltry work in progress, my partners and employees, Jada and Frankie and the club, in that order. I was - as I don't think I'd ever felt so markedly after any earlier case - tired, just plain damned tired. I was getting too old for all of this rushing around and, looking back on the case, I hadn't been that great at it either. I had personally neither killed nor saved anyone and solved nothing. Maybe I should give it up: I was losing my touch.

During the next couple of months, Tim maintained a discreet distance. I saw Wally often at the club: despite what he'd said at the Yard that day, he and Joannie were a developing item; they were talking about buying a flat together and, reluctantly, I assented to Nat's proposal to jack up Joannie's pay to give them a chance to find something larger than a shoe-box to live in, persuaded by the double-sided threat that it would otherwise prove impossible for them to find anywhere near enough to allow Joannie to keep her job and that Nat herself would find it impossible to carry on without her.

I didn't care. I hadn't been intended to inherit the club; I could never view it as truly mine; I neither looked to it for income nor felt comfortable with so much of it as accrued to me. I was minding the club as trustee until either Lewis came back from the dead or Alton came of age and could do whatever he wanted with it. Wally and I talked as friends, but we didn't talk about our friend.

I had a postcard from Dolly, in Switzerland. It said:
'The skiing's better here. But that's all. Love from Dolly.'
There was no more news of Felice Hayat or her associates.
There was no news at all of Bob Bentley or his.
There was no news of Joe Leahy.
We watched a lot of television.

* * *

Martin Mather rang me at the office. He invited me to lunch. We met, as we usually did, at the gym club where he worked out most days, and ate in its restaurant. The last time he'd done me a favour, he'd ended up in the Charing Cross Hospital in Fulham.

'Why do I think this could turn nasty, too?'

'It's just a case,' I protested. 'I'll pay for lunch.'

'Too right,' he muttered, selecting the most expensive wine on their list. To add insult to injury, he chose a red wine, knowing it tended to disagree with me.

After we'd ordered, he asked for a full briefing.

'And I mean the truth,' he warned me, pointing at my throat with his fork.

Considering how strong he was, I shuddered at the thought of being skewered in the middle of my *mange-touts*.

'How much do you know so far?'

'Your man's been fairly straight with me. I like him,' he admitted. 'I mean, he's a naïve berk in some ways, and a monstrous egoist in others, but he's got a sense of humour about this whole Accord thing and, as he says, it was as good a way to pass a decade or so as any. He says there's hard evidence on the pornography but no one to pin down as responsible for it. None on trafficking people either, though he thinks that was part of what they were doing. He says the police suspect The Accord was a channel for naughty money.' Not dissimilar to the sort that had got his brother killed. 'He had the wit to stay silent about drugs, so I should think he's not averse to using them himself.'

I picked up his association.

'Ever think about him?' I asked about his older brother.

'No,' he said bluntly. 'If it comes close, I think about what it all did to my father.'

'How's Andrew?' His other, younger brother, not left untainted by the affair but, on balance, on the salvageable side of the line.

'Divorced, remarried, on the verge of divorce. He does his job, though.'

'Do you have any contact with Ali?' Once, I thought I'd loved her; once, I thought I might even love her more than I loved Sandy. One way and another, Ali almost cost me my life. I could forgive her that. Ali also nearly cost me Sandy: that I never forgave.

'Yes, a lot.' They always had a special closeness, even if Martin no less than the other boys had been a target in the frame of her ambitions. 'She rings two, three times a week. I think she's lonely. She's pregnant,' he added, unsure how I'd take the news.

'So am I,' I told him proudly. 'Well, Carson.'

'Congratulations. I'm pleased. I'd like to meet her again one day.' By common accord, we didn't socialise in couples: the only time he'd seen her was during the case he'd helped me out on, when Carson and I had only recently met and were still trying to decide which impulse was going to be stronger - Sandy's love for the two of us or our initial mutual antipathy. 'It'll be good for Alton.' Who he had also never met.

'Yeah. Make him less of a spoiled brat. You seeing anyone?'

'Maybe.' Meaning he wasn't about to elaborate. 'Had another call from the States recently.'

He had finally drifted around to his point.

'Yeah? It's amazing, modern technology.'

'An old client called up. An old client who doesn't come to this country much anymore.'

I whistled through my teeth.

'Sterling Latimer?' The everything magnate. Too big, and too legally so, to touch, but Martin and I both knew where he'd come from and where he owed his allegiance.

'You're not as stupid as you look.'

'It'd be difficult,' I said before he could. 'What'd he want?'

'Just a friendly call. How was I, how were you, sort of thing.'

'Asked after me, huh?'

'Yeah, most specifically. Then he asked if I had any interesting new cases. Then he asked if I'd like some of his work. Like, maybe, a lot of his work, like it used to be. Then he said that if I took it, I'd probably be a bit too busy for some of my current cases. Like, maybe, The Accord.'

'And you're asking me why you think it could turn nasty, already?'

'I didn't say already, did I already?'

He wasn't Jewish but from him I could take it.

Besides, he still had his fork.

'Interesting,' I admitted. 'You think it's his own business, or he's fronting for someone else?'

'I'd say that was a difference without a distinction; he doesn't do anything for free. Either way, he was delivering a message.'

'You told your client about this yet?'

'No names, but yes, I told him I'd had a warning call. I also tried to speak to the American attorney we're working with over there. I couldn't get hold of him; seems to have difficulty finding time to call me back. My guess, sometime next week we'll get a letter explaining why they can't continue, with a fat bill enclosed.'

'No problems elsewhere in Europe?' I wouldn't insult him by asking how he had responded to Latimer's offer of a bribe.

'Too much at stake. We're part of a network. It's my case.' Many firms of lawyers in England had formal links with firms on the Continent, to handle cross-boundary work. I was unsurprised that Martin Mather should have done so. The famous name of his firm might well have gone into deep decline after I'd played around with it for a while, but I could think of other firms one would at some point or another also have written off for good which, within a few years, were nonetheless basking afresh in their former glory. Name counts for a lot in the legal profession.

'What'd your client say?'

'Laughed it off. Wouldn't take it seriously.'

'Which is why we're having lunch? So I can talk to him?'

He reached across and patted me on the cheek.

'Like I said. Not as stupid as he looks.'

* * *

It explained a lot more. It told me why I and Carson had been left alone; I knew too much about Latimer and his enterprises, his affiliates and subsidiaries, and he would have suspected that I would have left an account of them to surface should anything foul up my life, as indeed I had. Even if he was only peripherally involved with the people behind The Accord, he would not want the risk to be taken.

It confirmed what I had guessed, that whoever was behind The Accord had the connections to establish Colin's identity. I also knew that the people with whom he associated never left any loose ends they could afford to clean up: as I had already concluded, May and Amy would be down to them, and, at a guess, Felice had put Joe up to bringing Alan to Newcastle for Bentley to finish off the pair of them. For sure, by then, they would have put Donleavy high up on their list of favourite hits.

It was anti-climactic; there was no mystery left. Exactly as I had speculated, Donleavy had tried to use The Accord and, in doing so, had triggered a reaction he could not control, not even to achieve his initial intention.

It didn't mean, however, that there were no loose ends left.

* * *

Rupert said:
'Felice called me. She wants to meet me.'
'Where? When?'
'Soon. She asked me to come to Antigua.'

'Don't be daft.' The last time he went anywhere against my advice, upstairs with Hiram, it had cost him - and me - a few bruises. This time, it could cost him his life.

'No, I'm not going. I invited her to come here.'

'Which she refused, of course.'

'No, that's what's odd. She said she'd think about it.'

'What do you think?' I asked Mercury.

'I think he should see her, here.'

'Set a trap. Let me tell Dowell. Why would she come? She knows she's at risk of arrest.'

'She asked if I'd promise she'd be safe, that I wouldn't tell.'

'How'd she get in?' I cried. 'For Christ's sake,' I added, disgusted he should even contemplate a meet.

'I'm sure she wouldn't find it difficult.'

Nor would she: The Accord had access to numerous passports of its members - maybe some, too, of its former members; it was the way they moved people for money. Amongst them somewhere would be a name and a sufficient resemblance.

'What did you say?'

'I agreed.'

'So? You don't owe her anything. Lie.'

As soon as I said it, I knew he wouldn't do it: it wasn't part of his make-up.

'Let me know, though,' I said. 'I'll treat it as privileged, there's no warrant out for her, but I want to keep you covered.'

'I'll think about it. She won't hurt me, Dave. All I need to do is talk to her.'

Where had I heard those words before?

* * *

They never found Bentley. Not alive. Just his body. It had bullet holes in it. Frank Morris suffered another mugging, this time terminally: I was more worried by his death than any other - they didn't even care about the fuss the killing of a lawyer would cause. Tim called around to see us with this news and - wonder of wonders - to apologise. I figured Sheila made him do it: she's the source of most good things he ever does. I accepted the apology. There was little choice: I had few enough friends.

I didn't tell him about Felice's call to Rupert, but I did tell him about Latimer's call to Martin Mather.

'Figures. They're not going to give up what they own without a fight.'

'You think it goes that deep?' I knew he was right but I wished he wasn't.

'Figure it for yourself. She's sucking in their money, cooking the books of The Accord, money flowing outwards too. Who's going to be able to draw a line between what's theirs and what belongs to the group? It's not how these people operate, you know that. You take any of their money, they own you and everything you've got that they aren't willing to let you keep, which is only just enough to keep you functional.'

'Crazy,' I mused. 'They're about to start a war for the ownership of a weirdo cult?'

'Not so crazy,' Carson chipped in. 'What about the Vatican Bank, Calvi?'

'They never wanted to own the freaking Catholic church.'

'No,' she said snidely. 'Just its assets.'

Which is all Tim was saying, scaled down by a billion or ten.

'It's the way they are. You touch anything of theirs, they're going to touch you – it doesn't matter how little harm you did.'

'Or who did it,' I responded. *I* had done nothing to The Accord.

'They'll go after de Villiers, maybe his woman too. They should be careful. You think they'd accept some protection?'

'No.' I knew for sure they wouldn't. 'I saw them. I didn't get more out of them than Mather did: they wouldn't take it seriously.'

'What about you, Dave? You and Carson and Alton?'

'What are you doing for yourself?'

'Not much. Being careful. They're not the major problem,' he added, meaning whoever was gunning to get back control of The Accord. 'And my instinct says he'll be more interested in you than me.' Leahy. 'After all,' he waved apologetically in Carson's direction: another thought that didn't need elaboration.

I exchanged a look with her. She said:

'We'll take care of ourselves.'

But she didn't have a gun left, so what she meant was me. Touching faith and loyalty. Blind.

I stayed up late, on my own, drinking, brooding about what Tim had said. That was why I was still awake when the phone went at two thirty in the morning. I picked it up, expecting a wrong number.

'We've some unfinished business, you and I.'

'I've been waiting for you to call.'

'I'm calling.'

'I'd like to see you.'

This wasn't true. He was the last person on earth I wanted to see, with the possible exception of the reincarnation of Russell Orbach. But I needed to see him: until I did so, unless I could come to terms with him, this thing wouldn't be over.

He laughed.

Then he hung up.

I was still pleading into the phone:

'Look, Leahy, I've got a lot to tell you.' Stupidly, though I could hear the dial tone, I finished my futile sentence: 'There's a lot you don't know; it wasn't her fault; there's other people involved.'

* * *

I rang Rupert to find out what he was doing. Neither he nor Mercury was at home. I called Martin Mather to see if he had any knowledge of their whereabouts. He did not. There were only a million places they might be in London; who knew if they were in the country at all. Nonetheless, I was beset by the notion that the planned meet with Felice was already going down and that unless I did something, Rupert and Mercury would not be walking away from it.

Perhaps what I meant was, because I had achieved so very little in the course of the case, I was desperate to try to find a role, something concrete I could claim for myself. Which is why, without thinking too hard about it, I pocketed the remaining gun in the house.

There was only one place I could think of to look that made any sense. I didn't ring first, just went straight there. The Accord's offices, re-occupied by Rupert under the terms of the court order, were - in common with their tradition of headquartering themselves in the best parts of the cities without regard to cost - in Mayfair.

I found the building easily enough: they only occupied a small portion of it. The part they occupied was in the basement. There was a brass plate identifying a number of companies with office-space above ground. One of the names was familiar, but I didn't place it immediately.

The insignia of the cult was still posted on the cast-iron railings beside the swing-gate, and an arrow pointed down the well-maintained, daily-swept, outer steps to a smart, polished door with an iron grille over a small opening, like a speakeasy in prohibition America, with a voice-box by the buzzer as an alternative means of controlling entry. I braced myself and pushed the button, and was relieved when Rupert himself answered:

'Yes?'

'Rupert. It's Dave.'

There was a long pause. The hiss of the speaker died out. He had switched off the microphone at his end, probably to confer, presumably with Mercury. Then:

'Go away, Dave. I don't want you here, not just now.'

'Don't be an idiot, Rupert; let me in.'

Another electronic silence, voices exchanged but not directed at me, Rupert and Mercury arguing, seeming to struggle. The moment the speaker barked again, I heard the door unlock and kicked it in before he could change his mind.

Rupert looked up with an exasperated sigh and let go of Mercury's wrist. She grinned triumphantly.

'Too late now.'

I shoved the door shut behind me and looked around. It was just the two of them in the reception area but the door to what I presumed was the main office was fully open, which presumably was where they had been waiting when I arrived. There were two more doors off the reception, both of them shut. I glanced pointedly at them. Mercury gestured:

'Lavatory. You want to use it? The other office is also empty.'

'What gives?'

I followed them into the main office and settled myself behind the desk as if it were my own. Unconsciously, I stuck my hand into my pocket, letting it rest on the gun butt, flicking the safety on and off but keeping well clear of the trigger.

Rupert sighed.

'This is going to muck everything up, Dave. Felice rang me. She said she would meet me here. She implied it was already under observation; she'd know if I notified the police. She'll have seen you arrive.'

'Well,' I replied humourlessly. 'At least she knows I'm not the police.'

Mercury grimaced.

'I still think it's a trap.'

Rupert shook his head.

'Why would she take the risk of coming here herself, if she doesn't really want to settle the whole thing? If anything happens to me, it won't be difficult to prove she was in the country, if she even gets out of it again; she's got too much motive to risk it.'

'Fucking amateurs,' I said, even though I wasn't feeling too professional myself. 'Who said she was in the country at all? She could have been calling from anywhere.'

This was a thought that must have occurred to them but that I guessed he had brushed aside because he wanted to meet with Felice so badly, he wanted it all over.

'Tell me the layout of this place.'

Mercury did so.

'There's only the front door, which you've seen.'

'Out back?'

'Just the well of the building. Safety grilles on the window.' I swung around in my seat for confirmation. 'They can only be removed from inside; it's an alternate fire safety route. You can see the steps from the door, or from the other office. That's also got grilles on the window. There's no window to the lavatory. It's under the stairwell. No one gets in here without us knowing.'

I only had time for two thoughts before it came down: literally. The first was 'famous last words'; the second was that I remembered why the name of the company on the ground floor was familiar: it either was, or at some time had been, a Latimer affiliate, which was hardly surprising in view of what I by then knew about Latimer's involvement.

What came down was the ceiling: in the main office and in the reception simultaneously. They came down in two, neat sections which told me the holes had been well-prepared with small explosive charges to finish off the job. A moment later, I heard a further blast from the front door. It was the mob and they were mob-handed.

Mercury was knocked to the ground by the falling plaster. I ducked below the level of the desk. Rupert swung around maniacally, to confront an armed man entering the office from the reception. He screamed as the man shot him, no more than a second before I shot the man. They both fell in a huddle on top of Mercury.

The man had dropped through the hole in the ceiling into the reception area. No one, as yet, had entered through the hole in the office ceiling. I saw the barrel of a shotgun poking through and sent a bullet up in its general direction. I mustn't have hit anyone, because it replied as clear and as timely as a country-and-western duet.

I wasn't about to play fairground target and darted for the door to reception as two more things happened at once. A third armed man burst through the door and - as he did so - he took a bullet in the back and toppled wide-eyed into the lobby. I backed up against the door of the lavatory, banking on Mercury's assertion that it was empty and under the stairwell. I heard a thump and caught a glimpse of someone - a man - in black slacks and black sweater landing in the main office. I was trying to look in both directions at once: the door to the main office and the front door itself.

Joe Leahy half-entered, cautious and crouched, unconcernedly stepping on the leg of the man he'd shot. Panicked, I almost didn't recognise him. My gun wavered between the two doorways. The command in his eyes signalled me which way to turn. We shot the man emerging from the office at the same moment. All was suddenly silent except for Mercury's cries from where she was trapped beneath the bodies of her boyfriend and his killer.

Leahy explained casually:

'They had a lot to do with my boy's death; they had it coming.'

'Thanks anyway.'

'And I thought you could find him for me,' he added sarcastically. 'Even your girl got further than you.'

'Look, Leahy, I've got a lot to tell you...'

The sirens told us that the police could not be far away. For a moment, I thought that was it, that my time had come. Then he grinned malevolently and said:

'I'd rather you lived.'

* * *

I was still trying to work it out the next day, while Tim - forewarned there would be one bullet too many to account for - and the uniforms were cleaning up behind us. I understood why he wanted to kill the Americans but why had he bothered to save my life? He'd threatened it often enough.

Carson was due another scan at the Royal Free. She said she'd pick up Alton from pre-school afterwards. We hadn't talked enough yet: I knew there were things she'd never told me, and I was beginning to think that minding my own business might not be the best approach - for me, for our unborn child or, above all, for her. She needed to learn that whatever she'd done was alright by me; maybe that way someday it'd come to be alright by her.

So I decided - not entirely without precedent - to quit work early and to surprise them both, to join her outside the gate and await my son with her. I almost made it on time. A few minutes earlier, and I would have left the car at home and walked around to the kindergarten. Instead, I drove straight there. Who knew, maybe for a treat we'd all drive off somewhere: Ealing, maybe - Sheila hadn't seen Alton for a while. For a year, after Sandy's death, he'd more or less lived with her; they were his other family.

I drew up a little way down the road, unable to park right outside because a VW van was inconsiderately double parked, facing the other way. As I did so, Alton came running out, to my eye as distinctive within his class as if he was standing on stilts and waving a bottle of Southern Comfort, crying some gleeful news to Carson that I was too far away to make out. I could have picked her out, too, from a crowd of a thousand without a second's hesitation.

Alton was only a few feet from Carson when the van started up, a single shot rang out and she crumpled silently at his feet. I reversed maniacally up the street, after the van, shouting and hooting, past the gate until I lost it at the corner, catching only a quick glimpse of Leahy as he turned and sped away. I tried to corner but backed into a concrete post on the pavement; the next I knew, the car had stalled.

I fell sobbing against the wheel for a moment until I saw other parents approaching slowly, scared of me until they recognised me as one of their own, and for the first time could hear the sounds from the playground - howls, screams, tears, roars of anguish. I got slowly out of the car and, brushing the others aside, went back to where Carson had fallen. In a corner of the yard, I saw a school-teacher clutching Alton to her, turning his face away from the horror.

I knelt briefly beside her. She was dead. It was a clean hit.

I shouldn't've expected anything else.

* * *

I took my son's tiny hand in mine. We walked down the street. Together. Alone.

I thought: *people get mixed up in all sorts of things; things connect - much more than we realise, more than we want and more than we can control. Sometimes, something happens somewhere - perhaps something relatively small - that causes a reaction - a disproportionate reaction - somewhere else, leaving most of the people affected by it stunned, confused, ignorant. Sometimes I think the best thing to do is to stay as far away from everything and everyone else as possible.'*

* * *

We arrived home. I let us in. I shut the door behind us, double-locked it, put on the chain.

Alton asked:

'Is Carson with Mummy now, Dave?'

I knew I was supposed to comfort him; I think I might maybe have been able to do so if he hadn't used my name. It broke me.

We wept in each other's arms until forever.

www.ingramcontent.com/pod-product-compliance
Lightning Source LLC
Chambersburg PA
CBHW051644180726
48284CB00006B/1864